I0611905

Restoring
Destiny

E J Ouston

Published by

Morris Publishing Australia

http://morrispublishingaustralia.com

Restoring Destiny

E J Ouston

ISBN: 9780645238891

Published by

Morris Publishing Australia

http://morrispublishingaustralia.com

CHAPTER ONE

A Flight into the Unknown

His hands deep in suds, Rais stared out the window. The sun's rays illuminated the farm's grain fields as it rose higher into the sky, claiming back the right to light the land from the waning moon. He scrubbed the porridge pot furiously. Frustration boiled in him like a fever. His mind swirled with a thought that, lately, ran continuously. *I am sick of never being able to leave the farm or see anyone… it's like living in a prison.*

His restless, wandering eyes surveyed the farm that had been his home for more than a decade. From the elevated position of the homestead, nestled contentedly in the lower slopes of the Mountain of Dread, the coast of East Nevaah stretched before him enticingly. The faint glimmer of the sea in the distance beckoned him like a temptress. He had never been there. His only knowledge came from books and his guardians' stories. As much as he loved Nona and Pap, as he got older, the need to explore the world outside the farm got stronger. With a huge sigh, he rinsed the pot and put it in the draining rack.

Sensing his mood, his twin sister, Kanda, sidled up beside him and picked up the pot to wipe it. She put it down again and rested her hands on the edge of the metal sink, staring at the far horizon. The same frustration and longing he felt simmered in her. She sighed wistfully. "Sometimes I think we should just run away. Maybe then we would find out why we were kept prisoner here."

"Don't think I haven't thought that too. My only concern is the fate of our guardians. They are getting old and need us to help them on the farm."

"Yeah, I know. They have been kind to us. They did say they would tell us where we come from and who we are when we were older. We are nearly sixteen. Maybe they will tell us soon." She sighed and picked up the pot, then with a determined expression she said, "If they don't by the time our birth celebration comes around, I'm leaving."

"Where would we go? We don't know how to get to anywhere except the town down river. If we went there, we would soon be found. We have to stick it out a bit longer. I'm sure they will tell us soon."

Kanda slammed the pot down on the bench. "You can stay if you like but I'm going – with or without you!"

Rais sighed and pumped water into the sink to rinse away the suds. *She's right, it is time. Anyway, I would have to go with her, to make sure she was safe.*

He lifted his head to brush his chin-length blonde hair out of his eyes with the back of his wet hand and glanced out the window. A movement on the edge of the road to the left caught his attention. He stared into the dimness of the overhanging trees. He was just able to make out the shape of a man coming towards the house, hugging the shadows as he walked.

Frowning, he hurried out the back door to find Nona who was watering the vegetable garden. "There's a man on the road coming this way. It looks like he doesn't want to be seen."

"Now who could that be?" Nona turned off the tap, came in and shuffled inside towards the sink. Rais went back to the window and pointed to where he had seen the stranger. She pushed in beside him and peered out into the trees' shadows.

Kanda, still drying the dish in her hand, squeezed in beside them.

Catching sight of the man, Nona patted Rais and Kanda on their shoulders and said, "You two stay out of sight." The old woman hurried to the door as fast as her arthritic legs could carry her.

Kanda shook her head in exasperation. "Yeah, stay out of sight… that's what she always says. You would think we were lepers the way no one can see or meet us."

Rais nodded, a frown creased his forehead as his eyes narrowed in frustration. They watched the man until he disappeared around the front of the house, then went back to their chores, glancing curiously and anxiously towards the entry. After a short while, Rais tapped the side of the sink impatiently with a spoon. "I wish she would let me go with her. I didn't like the way that man was hiding in the shadows." Kanda nodded, biting her lip anxiously.

Worry about his ageing guardian's safety intensified. Rais paced the room, running his hands through his hair as he fought the desire to disobey the order to stay. Finally, he stopped and said, "Maybe we should make sure Nona is okay."

Hanging up her drying cloth and wiping her hands on the sides of her brown, knee-length trousers, Kanda followed him.

They crept into the front room. Seeing the door open a crack, they tiptoed to it and peered through the gap, listening to the conversation taking place on the front porch.

The frail old woman stood clinging to the railing. Her long grey hair swayed as she shook her head, her expression showing her confusion. Rais went to go to her, but Kanda held him back.

Nona's quivering voice just reached their ears. "How can they be the only ones? What if they haven't inherited their parent's powers? If they had, they should be showing signs now that they are almost sixteen, but there has been nothing."

Rais and Kanda looked at each other, eyebrows raised. "Is she talking about us?" Rais said. They stared at the short man standing beside her. He wore a ragged light grey uniform of the deposed King's guards, but he was holding his battered and chipped helmet in his hands as a sign of respect.

The stranger, his expression grim, replied strongly, "Yaholo must be defeated. The King is ailing too and I'm not sure how long he can last. The twins are our last hope. They only have until the full moon to save her."

Nona wrung her hands anxiously. "You must fetch Briador. Someone in Adaya will know where he is. He's the only one who can find out if they have powers and take them there before the full moon. It's time they knew their destiny, but I didn't expect it to happen this way. God help them if they can't defeat the evil ruler and save her life."

4

The man murmured a reply and went on his way. Nona stood leaning on the rails, staring after him as if his success depended on her watchful gaze.

The twins' sapphire blue eyes locked; their faces mirrored the bewilderment they felt.

Kanda whispered, "What's she talking about? Powers? What is that about? Only a few people have powers. And who do we have to save and how?"

Rais shrugged. "And who's Briador?"

Kanda shook her head. "Beats me."

The stranger melted into the distant landscape, and with a weary sigh, Nona turned to enter the house. The twins scurried away, returning to their chores as Nona entered the meals area.

"Who was that?" Kanda asked innocently.

"No one you need to know about just now," she mumbled, wiping tears from her wrinkled cheeks.

Kanda hurried to her side, putting her arms around her guardian. "Nona, are you okay? What did he want?"

"Yes, yes, I'm alright. Unfortunately, you'll know what he wanted soon enough," Nona said as she pulled herself away and shuffled out the door into the yard.

Kanda stomped her feet. "Rais, we should go after her and demand to know what that was about. How can she not tell us? Someone's life is at stake."

Rais shook his head as he watched her leave. "She's too upset, and we can't let her know we were listening. Wait until they come in from their chores. I'll question them about our origin again at the moontime meal."

Kanda smiled ruefully. "I suppose it's worth a try."

"I wish I did have magic powers, then I could read their minds. But if we offer to help get the meal, maybe we can get them in a good mood," Rais said.

They headed out to the pastures to begin their work of feeding the animals and tending the fields of grain. Searching for their guardians, they saw the old couple huddled together, their heads close as they talked.

"Obviously, she is telling him about our visitor," Rais muttered. Kanda nodded.

Pap's eyes fixed on the twins as they approached. His look of shock and anxiety sent a shiver of fear and foreboding through both.

***

When they came in at sundown, Rais and Kanda followed Nona into the kitchen. Kanda pulled her long blonde hair into a tail at the back of her head and tied it with a ribbon. "Do you need help to prepare the meal?" she asked, reaching for her apron.

"That would be lovely, thanks," Nona said, beaming.

Kanda's heart filled with love as she watched the side of the old woman's eyes crinkle and the skin on her face fold as she smiled. Guilt painted her neck and face a dull red. *How could I even think of leaving them? They need us more than ever.* She reached out an arm and hugged her.

Rais grabbed an apron and tied it over his brown work clothes. He went to the bag sitting on the wooden bench and picked up a tuber. "I'll rinse these for you."

Nona patted his arm and smiled. Kanda took them from him as he cleaned them and started peeling.

When he had washed enough for the meal, Rais said, "Hand me a knife and I'll help peel them too."

Later, sitting at the large, worn, wooden table, the delicious scent of roast meat and vegetables wafting from his plate, Rais eyed his guardians. His mind swirled as he tried to find the right way to approach the subject of their origin.

Impatient, Kanda kicked him under the table to prompt him. When he glanced at her, she glared at him, eyes wide, and spread her hands questioningly.

Rais took a deep breath. "Nona, Pap, you have always said that when we were older you would tell us where we came from. We'll be sixteen soon, would you tell us now, please?"

Nona and Pap exchanged weary glances.

Pap stared at the twins; his eyes troubled. He pushed his thin grey hair from his brow and slumped his frail, bony shoulders as he exhaled loudly. "You will soon have the answers to your questions. They are not ours to tell."

Kanda's frustration rose and she turned to Nona. "But... Nona..."

The old woman dabbed her moist cheeks and gazed at the girl. "Hush, child, I just wish I could protect you from the truth forever. Be patient a little longer. It may be as soon as next sun."

The twins lapsed into a brooding silence for the rest of the meal. As they cleared the dishes, Kanda's eyes lit up. "Next sun, Rais – we may know next sun."

Her brother nodded but didn't say a word. During the meal he had studied their guardians. If knowing the answer to the puzzle meant they would have to leave the old couple to fend for themselves, he now wasn't sure he wanted to know. He glanced at where they now sat by the fire, their grey heads nodding, their tired, frail bodies hunched towards the fire for warmth and comfort. Their expressions of sadness caused his heart to twist in his chest.

Kanda's eyes followed his gaze, her face reflected his feelings. "They'll never survive without us. The farm is too much for them now. What will they do if we have to go away?" she said softly.

Rais nodded, his face grim. "Not sure." As he washed the dishes, he stared through the window at a half-moon. "But wherever we have to be, we only have around 14 suns to get there."

Kanda moved to his side and gazed up at the moon. She clenched her fist and pounded it gently on the bench. "If nothing happens tomorrow, I'm going to tell them we heard and make them tell us what it is about. All this secrecy is doing my head in."

"Okay, I'm with you on that. If a life is at stake we should be told."

When they finished their chores, the twins kissed their guardians and trudged to the washroom. They went to bed with their hearts torn. They rose at dawn and, still troubled, hurried to their tasks.

During their work, they searched the horizon for signs of a visitor. No one appeared.

After his hard toil in the fields, Rais sat on the front verandah to witness the sun take its last spectacular bow to the rising moon and surrender the sky to her keeping. The fiery glow of the retreating sun was mirrored on the surface of Lake Adaya. The reflected sunset was often a blending of blue and pink or apricot, but now the lake's surface was a still deep red, as if it were a pool of blood. He shivered with foreboding. His eyes wandered around his surroundings.

The position of the farm homestead on the side of the mountain meant that by sunlight no one could draw near the house from any direction without being seen. To one side, the river, gouged deep from the waterfall at the base of the mountain and hidden from view by the trees, formed a part of the farm's southern boundary. The sheer rocky cliff face behind the house protected them from approach from the mountain. *The perfect place to hide us,* he thought, *but from what ... or who... and why?*

A herd of chinows played in the dam, rolling their large, heavy muscular bodies in its muddy water. The horns on their long snouts dug up the reeds and grasses that grew near the bank and they fed hungrily on the tender roots. A couple of the tame ones hung their heads over the fence, looking for the tubers Rais sometimes fed them. "Not now," he called.

The turquoise temptress on the far horizon gleamed enticingly. His heart swelled with longing to feel the lapping water of the sea goddess fold his feet in her embrace. Rais sighed at the memory of their last secret trip downriver; they were so close. He then pondered last sun's event. The tickling sensation of a large furry head wriggling under his arm and a long snout nuzzling into his chest brought him from his reverie.

"Nobosi, you startled me," he said, fondling the liogon's ears and ruffling the thick fur of his mane.

A scarf of white dropped from the sky and the rustle of feathers signalled the arrival of another favourite creature. Owl landed on the rails. Rais reached up to pet the bird. As far back as he could remember, Owl had been there. It followed them everywhere they went. *I'm amazed you are so tame,* Rais thought again as he stroked its snow-white head. His other hand strayed to the gold locket he wore – Kanda had one too. An engraving of an owl, the mirror image of the bird before him, adorned the face.

Kanda appeared at the door. Her eyes surveyed the scene before her. The glistening water of the lake and the sea tantalised her. With a determined expression she thought, *So close but so far away. Soon I will get to explore the world outside the farm. Soon, we learn the truth. I will make them tell us tonight.*

"Time to eat," she said, smiling at Rais and stroking Nobosi's fur. She placed a dish of meat on the floor at his feet and both Nobosi and Owl fed from the plate. Kanda gazed fondly at their pets. Such a stark contrast – Nobosi was the size of a chinow calf, his strong, powerful, feline body, crouched to eat, seemed menacing, but he had welcomed Owl and happily shared food with her daily.

She patted Nobosi's head. "In the wild, a liogon would hunt birds for food, but Nobosi allows Owl to share his meal. He's truly tame now."

"Mmm … Pap says they're never truly tame," Rais muttered as he rose, and stretched his slim, muscular body.

As he approached the door, Kanda put a hand on his arm to stop him. "Rais, if they don't say anything, I'm going to demand answers. You still with me on this?"

Rais stiffened and took a deep breath. "Okay but leave it until we have eaten and cleaned up. They will be more relaxed by then."

The meal was eaten in silence as the twins rehearsed what they would say later. Their guardians' faces wore anxious expressions and they kept sighing and glancing at each other. Afterwards, the twins were in the kitchen with Nona, helping clean up, when Nobosi suddenly rose from his position by the fire and bounded to the front door. A growl low in his throat warned them of an approaching stranger. Rais turned from pumping water into the sink and looked at Kanda expectantly. Maybe this was the news they had been waiting for.

Suddenly, a huge fist pounded the front door. Paintings rattled on the wall as if in an earthquake. Nobosi scratched at the door, barking, and growling menacingly. Startled by the noise and Nobosi's anger, Rais headed towards him, but Pap rose stiffly from his seat by the fire and signalled him to wait. The old man hobbled to the door to see who disturbed their peace. The twins wanted to follow, but Nona held them back. She ushered them into the hall that led to the back of the house and put a finger over her mouth to silence them as they listened to the conversation. The twins glanced at each other, frowning, not sure what was happening.

"The twins – I know they are here. Bring them to me," an unfamiliar voice thundered.

"I … don't know who you mean," Pap said, glancing over his shoulder and putting his hand on Nobosi's head for reassurance. The throaty growl coming from the liogon was all that stopped the visitor from pushing past the old man and entering the house.

"Don't play games with me. The King's messenger is dead, but before he died, he told us what we wanted to know. If you don't call off that animal and let us in to search the house, you and your wife will die."

"If the children were found here, we would all die anyway," Pap said loudly.

Nona pulled them back further into the hall. Through the window of the nearest room, in the soft light of the rising moon, they saw another man in a dark blue uniform looking around the other side of the house. "Who are they? What do they want with us?" Kanda asked.

Her face pale and tears streaming down her cheeks, Nona cried, "There's no time for explanation. Go! Go now, out the side window. I was afraid this might happen. I have packed some of your things. Go to Adaya. Find a man called Briador." Nona's hands shook as she pulled two leather packs from the hall cupboard and pushed them into their hands.

Rais hesitated. "But Nona … what will happen to you if we go?"

"If you go, we will be fine. If you are found here, we will all die." She brushed away her tears impatiently.

The twins hesitated for a second, glancing towards the front door then at their frail guardian. Nona pushed them towards the window. "Go!!"

After a quick hug, the twins sprinted for the opening, struggling into the backpacks as they ran. Outside, their hearts racing, they sped for their concealed tunnel that led to the river. Once inside, they replaced the bush that hid the entrance and peered through the branches to see if they were being followed. The other soldier stood looking around the side of the house. Rais stared at him for a moment in the soft light. Like their evil ruler, he was obviously from their neighbouring country, Gantis, the land of the giants, as he was much taller than their race. He wore the dark blue uniform of the troops of the ruler. They held their breath until he disappeared.

"Are you sure Nona and Pap will be okay?" Kanda whispered.

His expression grim, Rais shrugged sadly. "I hope so. We can send back help as soon as we find this Briador person. At least they have Nobosi to protect them." He took her hand, urging her to hurry. They scampered as quietly as possible for the concealed tunnel they had made between the two rows of bushes that formed the boundary between the house and the animal enclosure. At the other end, hidden in the bushes at the top of the riverbank, lay the hollowed, split-log canoe they used to go fishing and take secret trips on the river. They reefed it out of its hiding place and dragged it down the slope to the edge of the water. All was quiet.

Suddenly, they heard Nobosi barking. Rais climbed the riverbank and peered over the top. The soldier who had been behind the house was racing towards them, Nobosi on his heels.

Rais' heart rate increased with dread. "Quick, get in the canoe," he shouted as he slid down the bank. They waded through the dense reeds at the edge of the water, pushed the canoe into the stream, and scrambled on board. Behind them, the soldier slid down the bank and shouted at them to stop. Nobosi growled menacingly as he gave chase.

As they paddled frantically away from the bank, the soldier plunged into the water and swam towards them, with Nobosi close behind. Heart beating rapidly, Rais rowed harder towards the other side of the river where the current from the waterfall was strongest. Kanda huddled in the bottom of the canoe willing it to go faster. She shivered with fear, as she watched the soldier get closer. Just as they got to the fast-flowing water, he reached for the canoe.

Kanda screamed when his hand grabbed the side and pounded his knuckles with her fist. The stream plucked the vessel into its clutches like a playful water sprite, but the weight of the soldier made the canoe turn side-on and it rocked violently. Kanda lost her balance and tumbled into the bottom. Rais frantically paddled to try to steady it.

Nobosi appeared beside the man and bit into his arm. Their combined weight made the boat tip sideways as they struggled. Rais and Kanda threw themselves over to the other side to try to balance the craft. Nobosi tugged harder and the man screamed and lost his grip. The canoe rocked again. Kanda shrieked as she plunged backwards into the river.

Rais fought to steady the vessel and turn it downstream. He thrust a paddle towards his sister. "Kanda, grab the paddle."

Heart racing, Kanda battled the flow of the stream as she tried to swim towards the canoe, but the playful water sprite changed character. Like a predator, it caught her in its clutches and tugged her away.

Nobosi lost his hold, and the soldier was swept away by the current. The man battled the flow trying to reach the canoe again. Kanda whirled by him, and he flung himself at her. She screeched as his hand closed around her hair. "Rais, help!" she shouted. Gasping for breath, she clawed at her assailant as she was pushed under.

Terror screamed through Rais as the water covered her head. He jumped into the river and swam. Like a saviour, the flow of the stream soon helped bring him to them. He clutched the shirt of the soldier as he swirled by them.

Moving behind him, his arm locked around his neck in a strangle hold. The water bubbled and churned as the man wrestled to get away. Nobosi appeared and sank his teeth into the arm that held Kanda. Fighting for breath, the soldier let go of Kanda, shook off the animal, and clawed at Rais' arm.

Rais' heart beat rapidly and his mind swirled as he watched for Kanda to surface. He was torn between securing the soldier and saving Kanda. Deciding that he had to overpower the man first, his strength increased by fear and anger, Rais tightened his hold. His leather backpack helped to hold him afloat, but the extra weight of the soldier threatened to pull him under. The water roiled around them as if joining in the fight.

With the force of the water dragging on her backpack, Kanda fought her way to the surface, gasping for breath. Nobosi swam to her. She grabbed his collar, laid her head on his back, and treaded water until she recovered her breath.

Turning to Rais, she went to move towards him but saw the man had stopped struggling and had gone limp. Rais let go and swam to Kanda. "Are you okay?" he asked wrapping his arms around her and taking her weight off Nobosi. Kanda nodded. Her eyes followed the guard's body as the water sprite gleefully closed on it and swept it down stream. Her eyes troubled, she asked, "Did you kill him?"

Taking hold of her hand, Rais said, "No, I don't think so. He just passed out from lack of air. Lie on your back and float. The water will take us around the corner, and we can swim out of the stream's grasp." Clinging to each other's hand so they wouldn't be separated, they turned over. The playful river sprite returned, cradled their bodies, and carried them safely down the river. Rais stared at the moon as he floated. He could already see the movement in the moon's shadow. Two suns gone and they still didn't know what this was all about. He frowned and clutched Kanda's hand tighter.

As they rounded a bend, they rolled over and swam closer to the bank where the water was calmer. They struck out for the grassy river's edge, Nobosi close behind.

They looked back to where the soldier floated. He was conscious again and fighting for breath. Knowing they were still in danger, they struggled out of the water and raced down-stream towards Adaya. The trees' black shadows hid them from the moon's usually welcome glow. The haunting cries of moontime birds and the chatter of insects filled the air. The cold of the early spring evening had settled on the water and spread to the bank. Kanda shivered and huddled into her wet clothes as she ran.

Although they moved swiftly, they didn't seem to be making much progress. What had looked like a short distance, seemed to be taking forever.

"Why is it taking so long to get there?" Kanda muttered, "It's like the river is made of elastic and someone is stretching it to its max." Then suddenly it snapped back, and they were there.

A faint breeze disturbed the dark surface of the lake and it shimmered and sparkled like diamonds on black velvet in the light of a rising moon. They crept along the grassy shore towards the town. The murmur of voices grew louder.

The shadows of the stone buildings swallowed their bodies as they made their way to the town centre. Kanda peered into the windows of the shops they passed. Her heart raced with excitement. She had dreamed of this moment her whole life. It was like a magical world to her. She longed to reach out and touch the objects to make them real. But the shops were all closed now and the streets almost deserted. In the clothing shop, a soft light shone on a blonde mannequin in a dark blue suit. As Kanda gazed at it, it triggered a memory of a woman with long blonde hair and sapphire blue eyes. The same warm feeling of love she felt when she looked at her twin brother washed over her. She frowned as she tried to remember the woman's identity.

Rais interrupted her concentration, pulling her after him impatiently. He scanned their surrounds for signs of danger.

The streets were quiet. Only a few people made their way along them. The aroma of cooking food wafting from the windows they passed signalled that the residents were preparing for the moontime ahead. As they reached the town centre, they saw a group of teenagers gathered in an open outdoor stadium.

Rais and Kanda hid behind a hedge and crept closer. Kanda held Nobosi's collar urging him to be quiet as a low growl began in his throat.

Rais stopped abruptly. *She was there.* His heart leapt in his chest as he saw the auburn hair of the girl he had seen on the shore the last time they followed the river to the lake. That time, as they always did, they stayed in the shadows so they wouldn't be seen. But he had longed to join the group of teens fishing on the dock and meet this girl.

Now, the twins cowered in the shadow of the bushes, not sure who to trust. Nobosi sat in front of them, his mane standing on end and his ears pointed forward. The vibration of a suppressed growl shook his body. Kanda placed her hand on him to quieten him.

Rais gazed at the girl in awe. Up close, she was even more beautiful than he remembered. Her hair fell softly around her lightly freckled face. Her slender body, leaned casually against an iron lamp pole, bathed in the light. Except for Kanda, Rais had never interacted with females his age and a red glow like the one he often saw on the lake settled over his features. He longed to speak to her but was not sure how to make the approach.

Kanda stared at her too, but for a different reason. Her clothing fascinated Kanda. She and Rais wore the dull brown costume of farm workers or peasants, but this girl was dressed in a soft, sky-blue suit. Kanda had studied the clothing of their race. While each of them wore the same costume of loose, knee-length trousers and long, loose tops with flared sleeves, the colour signified their position in the hierarchy of the land. Businesspeople or court officials wore sky blue. Over her shirt, the girl wore, unfastened, the soft, liogon fur wrap of her station. Fur boots covered her legs, to keep out the cold of the spring evening.

Kanda studied the ornate decoration on the shirt's bodice. Tiny pearls, sewn into delicate flower patterns and lace trim were something she had only seen in sketches in books. Envy stole through her as she glanced down at her own shirt. She grimaced at Nona's attempt to decorate it. Large flowers in the material of the suit, adorned her bodice. When Nona had sewn them on, she had thought them lovely, but compared to this girl's costume they were dull. The teenagers, who surrounded the girl like devoted disciples, wore the same colour as her, but the decoration on the other girls' shirts was not as ornate or as delicate.

Soon a voice called to the group, and they melted into the darkness as they made their way home. Kanda and Rais crept into a shadowed area under the seats in the stadium and huddled together for warmth.

"There's no use searching. We don't know our way around or who to trust. We'll sleep here and search for Briador in suntime," Rais said.

They opened their packs to pull out their wraps and boots. The things in the top of Kanda's leather pack were damp, but the leather had kept out the moisture lower down and everything was dry. She reefed out dry clothes and reached for her wrap. "I'm glad my wrap was at the bottom," she said as she tugged it. As it came free, a book fell to the ground. "What's this?" she said picking it up. Peering at it in the dim light she could just make out a symbol of two open hands facing down on the front cover. She opened it, but it was too dark to read. She put it carefully back in her pack. They crept through the deep shadows to the stadium's washroom block and struggled out of their wet clothes and into the dry ones.

Nona had included a food pack and when they got back, they tucked into a meal of biscuits and dried meat – sharing it with Nobosi. They crawled further under the wooden stadium seats to where they couldn't be seen and tried to sleep, using their packs as pillows and their wraps as blankets. The heat from Nobosi's body lying between them helped to warm them at first, but, as the moontime progressed, cold seeped into their limbs, numbing them. The scuttle of rodents and the call and movement of insects surrounded them and disturbed their sleep. Twice Rais grabbed Nobosi's collar to stop him from chasing them and creating a disturbance that the occupants of the nearest buildings would hear.

Kanda lay there, her mind in a whirl. *I wanted to leave the farm, but not like this. I hope Nona and Pap are okay,* she thought as she drifted off.

Dawn's rosy glow finally appeared as the sun rose to claim back the sky. Neither had slept well. They stretched the stiffness from their limbs and hurried to the washroom block before the town awoke. Huddled again under the seats, they watched as people emerged from the houses and started their sun-time ritual. While Kanda and Rais snacked on their meagre provisions, Nobosi crept silently under the seats, hunting for a breakfast of the rodents that had disturbed their sleep.

The sun crept higher on its victory lap through the sky and the streets became crowded with people. No one came near the stadium. The twins were just about to leave its shelter when they saw two men in familiar dark blue uniforms leave the group on the footpath and stride towards the stadium. Rais and Kanda clutched each other's hand and slunk back to their hiding place under the seats. Many of the crowd followed the men. Nobosi, hackles up, started for the exit. It took the strength of Kanda and Rais to restrain and quieten him.

The twins held their breaths and listened as one of the men mounted the stage and called to the assembled crowd. "Good people of Adaya, in the name of our esteemed ruler, Yaholo, we come seeking the whereabouts of three people. A boy of fifteen named Rais and his twin sister Kanda. These youths are blonde and blue-eyed and wear the suit of farm workers. The other is a man named Briador, who we believe is a member of your community."

At the mention of Yaholo, the faces of the crowd closed and, whispering to each other, the townsfolk drifted away.

The soldier scowled at their retreating backs and shouted, "I assure you that no harm will come to these people. Our esteemed ruler has offered a reward of fifty gold pieces for information that leads to the capture of the trio."

***

The girl with auburn hair stood at the back of the crowd. Her eyes lit up at the mention of the reward. *With that sort of money, I could go back to the city and live like a queen*, she thought. She was sick of this small town where she had been for more than a decade and longed to travel back to The Walled City in West Nevaah. She knew she had lived there until she was almost four. Her mother's wistful stories of their life in the palace before the King was deposed had fuelled this desire, and now, with her mother passed on, she felt a stronger tie than ever with the city. While she didn't remember much about her life before she came to Adaya, her dreams were filled with her time in the palace and shadowy images of the other people who lived there. Without knowing who they were, she felt a longing to see them again. But her concern that the evil ruler would not allow her to return had stopped her from going.

Her eyes searched the crowd for strange faces that might be the twins mentioned. She caught a glimpse of a fair head and brown costume and wandered over to the other side of the stadium. The person she had seen turned out to be a farm boy from her school. Disappointed, she headed for the seats to listen to what else the strangers had to say. As she sat, she glanced down, and through the crack between the seat and the back, she saw two pair of terrified blue eyes. A low snarl alerted her to the presence of Nobosi and she hesitated.

Moving further along, she was just about to call out when she heard the man say, "The esteemed Yaholo would even be prepared to welcome his loyal subject into the palace as a part of the reward if they found them and turned them in at the palace after we have gone."

The girl slumped in the seat her mind racing with possibilities. *If that's true, then I'm better off taking them there. All I have to do is get the twins to Briador and convince them all to travel with me to The Walled City.*

When no response came to their offer of reward, the man shouted, "You have had your chance. If they are found hidden in your town, the person hiding them will be executed." They stalked from the stage and proceeded to roughly search every building.

The girl stayed where she was while the fearful crowd deserted the streets. When the streets were quiet and the troops out of sight, she slipped under the seat to where the twins were hiding.

"Thank you for not turning us in," Kanda said, relief obvious in her voice.

"Why does Yaholo want you?"

Kanda shrugged. "We have no idea, but if we could just find this Briador, he might be able to tell us."

The girl looked down her nose at Kanda, huddled at her feet. *What would Yaholo want with this weakling?*

Rais stared at her. He was trying to speak, but he had to untangle his tongue first. He had been hoping for a chance to meet her and now she had come to their rescue. He could not believe his luck.

"I'm R... Rais," he stammered at last.

"Palesa," the girl replied.

"I'm Kanda. You don't happen to know where Briador is, I suppose?"

Palesa smiled smugly. "I don't, but I know someone who does."

"Would you take us to him?"

"I would love to, but we had better wait until late afternoon when the guardsmen have completed their search and moved on."

Rais bit his lip anxiously. "What if someone turns Briador in before then?"

The girl tossed her copper head importantly. "Only Markos knows where he is now, and they won't find Markos. Besides, everyone hates Yaholo since he imprisoned the king and took his place, so no one will turn Briador in. You, on the other hand are strangers, so, you stay well-hidden and do as I say."

Kanda raised an eyebrow at the order but they both nodded.

"I'll be back at sunset. Go further back under the seats and stay hidden until then. Oh, and keep that mangy mutt quiet." Palesa wriggled out and disappeared.

"Mangy mutt? I should have set Nobosi onto her. Bossy, isn't she?" Kanda snapped.

Rais gazed after her, his eyes glazed. "She's beautiful."

Kanda looked at his dreamy face and shook her head. "What a fool. Fancy falling for a girl the first time you see her."

"I didn't *just* see her. We saw her when we came down to the lake last time, remember, and again last moontime?"

"Oh sorry... my mistake, the third time you see her then. I don't remember her from the lake."

"Anyway, I haven't 'fallen for her', I just think she's beautiful, that's all."

Kanda shook her head. "Right!"

***

For the rest of the suntime they were not game to speak as people walked through the stadium and gathered in small groups to talk about the situation. But their minds were busy trying to work out why they were being sought and wondering about the safety of their guardians.

As the sun sank behind the mountain, handing the moon the duty of lighting their way, Palesa called softly to them, "Okay, let's go. There should be enough light from the moon and there are no clouds. Slip the hood of your capes over your heads to hide your hair."

Rais and Kanda crawled from their hiding place, glad to stand up straight and stretch their aching, stiff bodies.

Palesa studied Rais as he stretched his taut body, built from the hard work of the farm. *Nice ... real nice, shame he's just a peasant.*

Rais glanced up at the moon and grimaced. *I hope we make it wherever we need to be before it is full.* He turned his attention to their rescuer, still not believing his luck that she was there.

She grinned as she saw the look of adoration he gave her. *Can't hurt to foster that feeling,* she thought as she slipped her arm through his and said, "Follow us, Kanda."

Kanda glared at her back. *Snotty, bossy cow; how can he be so smitten?*

They soon left the town behind and skirted the lake. Following a faint path worn in the grass, they reached the reeds that signalled the start of the marshland. The stiff stalks parted with a whispered swoosh as they pushed through and then closed behind them, as if they had never passed. Thick with the roots of the grasses and reeds, the ground was damp and springy under their feet. Water squelched with every step. The dampness increased the deeper into the marsh they walked.

Rais dropped back to check on Kanda.

"Where the hell is she taking us? There's only swamp and marshland up ahead. What if she's leading us into a trap?" Kanda whispered in his ear.

"Shhh ... she'll hear you. Just follow her; I'm sure she knows where she's going. We sure don't, so we have to trust her. If she wanted to turn us in, she could have done it back there."

Pulling a face at his back, Kanda muttered, "Yeah sure, little Miss Perfect can't be wrong." She shrugged resignedly.

Finally, the springy roots gave way to thick clingy mud and the water level reached their calves, soaking the legging wraps of their boots and chilling their legs to the bone. Nobosi whimpered in discomfort as cold water lapped his belly, but he continued to follow. Kanda's nose twitched as the rank, musty smell of the mud assaulted her. Now they had to walk single file, with Palesa leading the way. Above them, a white shadow followed their every move.

They trudged on until the moon was high in the sky. The only sounds were the swishing of reeds as they closed behind them, the scurrying of moontime creatures, and the call of the birds and insects. The sludge became sticky like molasses and the thickness of the soles of their boots tripled with caked on mud. Each step took twice as much effort. The twins were starting to wonder if they would survive this trek, when Palesa stopped suddenly. "Quiet. Stay still. I heard something. It might be a croragon."

Nobosi, ears alert, growled loudly. The white shadow streaked ahead.

Kanda dropped her hand on Nobosi. "What! They live here? Are you out of your mind bringing us here with nothing to protect ourselves?"

"Yes, they live here. It *is* a swamp, isn't it? Is it my fault Markos chooses to live in this filth?" Palesa snapped.

An image of strong jaws full of sharp teeth and large bulging eyes formed in the twins' minds and they glanced around apprehensively. They trudged on, eyes darting in every direction and ears tuned to pick up every sound. Nobosi walked closer to Kanda now, his body alert, a soft warning rumble constant in his throat.

The desire for the reward began to fade a little and Palesa was wondering if it was worth it, when the reeds beside her split. It was her worst horror: a croragon. Fire spewed from its huge mouth as it charged for her, its four short legs trampling the strong reeds as if they were straw.

Its long reptilian body and tail thrashed the mud and created a filthy shower. Palesa yelped and jumped aside just in time. Nobosi leapt forward and planted himself between the croragon and the twins. He barked ferociously.

"What do we do?" Kanda cried to Rais, backing away as the creature turned towards them.

The croragon hesitated as Nobosi moved forward slowly, his growl menacing. A warning blast of fire shot from the creature's mouth just missing their pet.

Rais grabbed Nobosi by the mane to halt his progress. "I'm not sure. I think we're done for," he cried.

CHAPTER TWO

Markos

Just as Rais spoke, a spear flew through the air and pierced the croragon's eye. With a loud plop, it slumped into the water.

As if mesmerised, Rais and Kanda stared at the creature lying at their feet. Its green, scaly body, longer than they were tall, so powerful a few moments ago, was now limp. They had never seen a croragon in the flesh. As they stared at the strong tail, capable of breaking their legs in one swipe, they shuddered and made a wish never to see one again.

Palesa turned to the man who had appeared before them. "Wow, good shot!" she cried clutching his hand. Then she sighed and said, "Markos... am I glad to see you."

His face livid with rage he shouted, "What in the name of insanity are you doing here in the dark, and without a spear for protection?"

Palesa shrugged. "These two want to find Briador and you are the only one who knows where he is. So naturally, I brought them to you. The troops are after them and Briador, so we had to come during the moontime. I thought about bringing a spear, but I have no idea how to use it, so I didn't bother."

"Just the kind of irresponsible behaviour I would expect from you, Palesa," Markos snapped, "Who are your friends and what do they want with Briador?" He turned to them. He frowned as he looked into their faces, then his eyes moved down to their lockets that glimmered in the moonlight. He moved forward to inspect them. Eyes wide with shock, he bowed from the waist. "Master Rais, Miss Kanda. What are you doing here?"

The twins had been staring at the sight of this man before them. Grey hair hung to the shoulders of his small thin body. His faced was lined with the signs of age. Kanda blinked in surprise. "You know us?"

Markos bowed again. "I would know you anywhere, at any age, even without the lockets. You both have the look of your mother. Why are you here? Has something happened to your guardians?"

Rais opened his mouth to speak, but Markos held his hand up to stop him. "On second thought… save it for later. Let's get out of this swamp before the mate of the croragon I killed comes looking for him."

Watching this exchange with great interest, Palesa's mind swirled with excitement. "So, who are these two?" she asked. Walking forward and peering at their lockets, she shrugged.

Markos turned to leave. "Follow me and stay on your guard."

Rais and Kanda looked down at their lockets. "Obviously they mean something," Rais muttered as they exchanged a puzzled glance. They hurried to keep up with the strides of their saviour.

Palesa stayed close beside him, eyeing him curiously. "How did you know we were here?"

Markos glanced skyward. "A bird told me." Following his gaze, they saw Owl soaring above them.

"But how?"

"Later," Markos grunted and ploughed on.

The path wound through the swamp a little further, and then began to rise. As the ground became dryer, they scraped the mud from their boots on the reeds' coarse roots.

Kanda took a deep breath. "Arrr... fresh air. I am so sick of that stench." She looked around. They were on an island at the outer edge of the marsh. A large tepee, constructed of woven reeds and grasses, and plastered with mud, sat in the centre. Smoke wafted skywards from a hole at the structure's apex.

Owl drifted down to land on Markos' shoulder. Reaching up to stroke the bird, he murmured, "Well done, boy."

Kanda watched this exchange with wonder. "You seem to know Owl; do you know where he came from? He has shadowed us as long as we can remember."

Markos nodded. "He belongs to your father. I have no doubt that he reports to him daily."

"Our father? Where is he? And how can Owl do that?"

"It is not my place to tell you that. When you reach Briador, he will fill you in." Pulling aside the tepee flaps he said, "Welcome to my home; humble as it may be."

His guard duty over, Owl flew off in search of food.

Frowning in frustration at having to wait for knowledge, Kanda and Rais slipped off their wet boots and entered first. Warmth cloaked them like the breath of summer, and they paused to allow it to soak into their freezing limbs. A low fire burnt in the very centre of the structure, the smoke drifting in curls to where the poles that held the walls aloft met. The scent of burning wood was welcome after the stench of mud in the swamp. A delicious aroma wafting from a pot suspended over the flames on a steel tripod, mixed with the scent of the fire and tantalised their taste buds.

"Bring the boots with you and put them by the fire to dry," Markos told them, and then he turned to Palesa, "Thank you for bringing the twins to me. I am most grateful. I will escort you home through the swamp now, or at sunrise; it is up to you. Does your father know where you are?"

Thinking quickly Palesa answered, "He doesn't expect me home. I said I was sleeping over at a friend's place. I'll wait until suntime if you don't mind." She ducked past him into the tepee. Her mind was set on the reward. *No way am I going to lose contact with these two.*

The interior of the tepee was more spacious than it appeared from outside. The inside of the walls was caked with mud, baked on by many preceding fires, giving the illusion of a solid structure. Chinow hides covered the dirt floor. A long, leather-covered, straw sleeping mat was off to one side. A crude wooden cupboard with two drawers and a large fabric-covered compartment was the only furnishing.

Nobosi immediately curled up close to the fire, but he kept a watchful eye on the twins and the stranger who had saved them. Moving close to the fire to warm their freezing legs and dry their soaked trousers, the twins rubbed stomachs that growled in hunger. Palesa joined them.

31

Markos let them settle, then, concern obvious in his tone of voice, asked, "How do you come to be here? Where are Nona and Pap? Are they okay?"

Rais shook his head, his face grim. "We don't know." Then he and Kanda told the story of Yaholo's guardsmen and their escape.

Kanda's eyes misted. "We can't go back to see if they're okay. The guardsmen may be watching the farm."

With a reassuring glance, Markos reached into a covered cage that hung beside him. "I'll send a message. We will soon know." When he extracted his hand, a small blue bird was sitting in it. The three teenagers watched in wonder as he slipped a ring onto its leg. Writing a message on a piece of paper from the drawer in the cupboard, he tucked it under the ring. The bird flew out of the tepee and disappeared into the moontime sky.

Rais was fascinated. "Who are you sending that to?"

"I have a friend who lives near the farm. I have asked him to check on Nona and Pap. I have also asked him to inform your father of your whereabouts, Palesa. Now let us get you settled with dry clothes and a warm meal."

"First, can you please tell us what this is all about, where we come from, and why Yaholo is so desperate to find us?" Rais begged.

Palesa, eyebrows raised, stated, "Yes, and I'm very interested to know why our illustrious leader wants them so badly that he'll pay to get them."

Rais and Kanda frowned. "Will you *please* tell *us*? Nona said we only had until the full moon to get somewhere and save someone's life? What is that about?" Kanda said her voice edged with desperation.

Markos nodded; his face grim. He put a hand on her shoulder comfortingly. "The messenger came to me, and I told him where Briador was living. He had set off to fetch him. Obviously, he didn't make it. Only Briador knows the full story, so he has to be the one to tell you. Try to be patient. Change into dry clothes and I'll dish you a meal."

The twins dug into their backpacks for dry trousers. One by one, they removed the wet ones behind a blanket that Markos had hung. Palesa grimaced as she was forced to replace hers with a pair of their saviour's.

Warmer already, they wolfed down the bowl of fish stew offered and turned to Markos expectantly.

"So, where do we find Briador?" Rais said impatiently.

CHAPTER THREE

Finding Briador

Markos turned to Palesa. "I'm sorry, Palesa, but only the twins are allowed to know his whereabouts. Please wait outside for a minute."

"What… you want me to go out into the cold. I won't tell anyone. Anyway, I'm going to take them there. Someone has to. They don't know the area like I do."

"I think your father will have something to say about that. Besides, that is my job now. Please wait outside," he said firmly.

Grumbling, Palesa walked to the tepee's entrance.

Kanda's eyes followed her exit. "I wish she would go home now."

Rais glared at his sister. Markos raised an eyebrow but said nothing in reply. When he was sure she was outside, he turned to the twins. "Before I tell you, you must swear not to share this knowledge with anyone. The troops have been hunting him for years." They nodded. "He is over the other side of the Mountain of Dread, in a cave that is hidden behind a waterfall. The only way to get there, unfortunately, is over the mountain." He drew a map of where it was and handed it to Rais. "Of course, I will come with you, but keep this map on you in case something happens to me, or we become separated. With the troops hunting for you, it will be a very dangerous journey. Are you sure you want to do that?"

"We don't have a lot of choice, do we? It appears we have a life to save – how and who, I wish I knew," Rais muttered looking at Kanda. She nodded, her expression showing she too was sure she wanted to take the journey.

Rais put the map carefully in the bottom of his pack. Markos turned to Kanda. "Come with me. Let's see if the bird is on its way back."

Grabbing her wrap, Kanda followed him into the cold air. As they left the tepee, Palesa rushed back in. They heard her say in a honeyed voice, "I'm so cold now. Would you please warm me up?"

Kanda glanced back to see Rais, his face the colour of the fire, walk to her and start to rub her arms. Palesa grabbed his arms and wrapped them around her back snuggling her head into his shoulder. Her twin's face glowed and a blissful smile curved his mouth.

"Eww!" Kanda cried. "How can he be so smitten? She's a bossy witch. Can't he see that she looks down on us? She's just pretending to like him, for some dumb reason; one I can't figure out yet," Kanda said as she stomped away from the entrance.

Markos frowned. "I wanted to talk to you about your earlier comment. Why don't you trust her?"

"For all the reasons I just said," Kanda snapped.

"Are you sure it's not just jealousy? After all, you have never had to share your twin with anyone before."

"No… I don't think so. She just rubs me up the wrong way somehow, with her superior ways… and her sky-blue costume… with the lovely decoration."

"Mmm … more jealousy perhaps? Her parents fled from the palace when Yaholo imprisoned the king. Her father owns the clothing store in Adaya; hence, the ornate costume. While she is a bit spoilt and stubborn, Palesa has always been a good girl. She recently lost her mother. The woman had never settled to her new life and missed the king's court where she was one of the few women allowed. Until she died, she acted as if she was too good to live amongst the people of Adaya. She, unfortunately, passed her pretentiousness on to Palesa."

Kanda sighed. "Poor thing. Well, if you think she is okay, I'll try to like her," she muttered.

They searched the sky for the blue bird, but the only bird they saw was Owl. He was circling above as if he was back on guard. They hurried back to the fire to get warm.

Markos found bedrolls for all, and they settled down to sleep. Comfortably warm and exhausted from their previous sleepless time under the seats, the twins slept soundly.

Which is just as well, as this was to be the last good sleep they would have for some time.

CHAPTER FOUR

The Rescue

Rais woke at first light and looked around. Markos and Nobosi were missing. He wandered out to greet the sunlight and look for the old man and their pet. From the elevated position of the island, he looked towards the ocean, a couple of hundred strides away. Entranced, Rais watched the sun rising out of the water. The ocean's surface rippled as if the globe shook large drops of water from its moontime cloak. A golden glow touched the top of the ripples and created a shimmering staircase leading to the sky. The moon retreated, as if turning its back on the sun's blinding light.

A movement from his left roused Rais from his trance and he turned to see Markos and Nobosi emerging from a track that led towards the seashore. Markos held a brace of fish high for him to see and called, "Breakfast!"

Rais waved a hand in greeting. "You should have woken me. I would have come with you. I have always wanted to go to the seashore."

"You can all do that after breakfast."

As they turned towards the tepee, a flash of blue passed between them. The small messenger bird landed on Markos' shoulder. He reached up and took the bird on his hand, stroked it gently and removed the note. Frowning, he read the message and then lifted troubled eyes to Rais. "The guards who were in Adaya told one of the traders that Nona and Pap are being held prisoner at the farm while they search for you two and Briador."

Rais punched his fist into his hand in frustration. "I knew I shouldn't have left."

"It's not your fault, Rais. If you hadn't, they, and you, would be dead."

Rais nodded, his face showing the misery he felt. "We have to do something. What can we do?"

"I'll rally the king's sympathisers from the town, and we will free Nona and Pap this evening. They have only left one guard. I'm sure you know some way we can get close without him seeing us; don't you?"

"Yes, we have a secret passage to the river. We used it to sneak away and play on the water."

"Good. Just give me the details and we can use that. You will have to wait here as it is not safe for you to travel at the moment. When we have freed your guardians, I will come back to get you and we will travel to Briador."

"No way! I can't stay here while Nona and Pap are in danger. It's our fault, so I'm coming with you."

"Me too," Kanda said from the tepee doorway.

"No, Kanda, you and Palesa stay here where it's safe," Rais instructed. Markos nodded his support for Rais' order.

Kanda shook her head. "Not happening. I want to make sure they are okay."

Palesa sauntered over to Rais. Looking into his eyes she smiled coyly and said, "I'm coming too."

Shaking his head, Rais told her, "We'll take you home on the way, Palesa."

The girl slipped her arm through Rais'. "Oh no, I wouldn't miss this rescue for the world. And if you intend to travel to find Briador I'm up for that as well. I'm not letting you out of my sight."

A scarlet flush swept from Rais' neck to his hairline, and he stammered, "B… b… but… it's too dangerous, you might get hurt."

Gazing adoringly into his eyes, Palesa said, "I'm sure you will protect me."

"Oh please! I'll puke if you don't stop," Kanda muttered, then added, "Will you get serious for a minute? This will be very dangerous and as you seem to have no sense of danger – leading us through the croragon-infested swamp without protection – we would all be safer if you stayed behind."

Markos frowned at Kanda, and she hung her head. Turning to Palesa, he said, "Palesa, your father will be worried about you if you don't go home soon."

"Not if you send that message bird to him," she replied. Then she glanced sideways at Rais. "And if you leave me behind, I'll follow, and then who'll protect me?"

Kanda sighed and bit back the retort that was bursting to escape.

Markos shook his head in frustration. "Okay, we'll let your father know, but don't be surprised if he insists on you returning home."

Palesa slipped her arm around Rais' waist and smiled smugly at Kanda. Kanda glared at her, wishing that her eyes could spit out daggers and pin Palesa's feet to the ground.

Markos sighed resignedly. "I'll contact my friend, ask him to speak to your father and rally a rescue party to meet us by the lake just after sunset." He strode into the tepee, and they followed him. He scribbled a new note, slipped it into the ring and the bird vanished out the door and into the sky.

After a breakfast of fresh, grilled fish, they wandered down to the seashore. Rais and Kanda hurried to the water's edge and stood transfixed, staring at the vast ocean as the sea goddess massaged their feet with her cool calming water.

Markos threw in his fishing rod and proceeded to catch their lunch while Nobosi wandered along the water's edge.

Palesa sat on a rock brooding, impatiently brushing sand from her feet, and shielding her face from the sun's rays, as she watched the twins enjoying the experience. Finally, she called to Markos, "Can't we go back now. The sun is too hot."

The twins reluctantly returned to the island when Markos called. The rest of suntime was spent watching him create spears out of driftwood and listening to him tell tales of life at the palace, where he had been the King's guard. The girls and Rais were set the task of fashioning pouches for the weapons out of leather scraps.

Vague images flashed in Kanda's mind as Markos described life at court. Her frustration rose as she tried to remember her previous life there. The ghostly form of the blonde woman she had imagined in the store window taunted her as Markos mentioned her mother. She could see by the faraway look on Rais' and Palesa's faces that they were feeling the same way.

Heavy clouds scudded in from the sea as the sunlight began to fade. Looking to the sky to gauge the time, Markos told them that they should prepare to leave. "As we are all going, we had better take our packs and prepare for our journey over the mountain. Once Nona and Pap are rescued, the troops will increase their search," he said. He packed supplies of dried meat and fish and biscuits into their leather packs and filled soft leather bladders with fresh water.

As the sun took its last bow and slowly slipped behind the Mountain of Dread, Markos hung a long leather pouch with a spear inside over his shoulders. It hung down his back and he strapped it to his shoulder and waist. He handed a spear to Rais to place in the spear holder he had made. Kanda and Palesa received a shorter version to go in their pouches. He helped them strap the weapons in place.

"It doesn't pay to be unarmed in this swamp, as you saw, besides, we may need them later. Do you know how to use a spear?" he asked. Rais and Kanda nodded. They learnt to hunt with spears at an early age. Palesa shook her head, took hers out of its cover, and twirled it merrily. Kanda and Rais had to duck to avoid a blow.

"Will you get serious!" Kanda snapped.

"Of course," Palesa said. A mock serious expression appeared on her face, and she stood with her spear held in a defensive position.

Kanda sighed in exasperation. *I hope her father does call her home*. She shivered as she peered in the direction they had to travel, remembering the croragon, the cold water, and the thick mud they ploughed through to get to the island.

The moon shirked its responsibility, playing hide and seek behind the thick black clouds that threatened to spread the dampness to the top half of their bodies as well. A heavy fog shrouded the swamp and swirled eerily in the half-light of dusk.

Markos led, his long strides setting a swift, steady pace. He brushed aside the strong reeds as if they were pampas grass. The three teenagers had trouble keeping up as they sank into the sludge under-foot. Many times, they lost sight of him in the haze, and followed him using nothing but the sound of the reeds parting and swishing back into place, and the call of disturbed insects and birds as a guide.

Nobosi followed the twins closely. A low growl, designed to keep all creatures at bay, came from his throat the whole journey. Senses alert for any sign of a croragon or other danger, the twins stayed close together. Owl soared above keeping a watchful eye on the surrounding water.

Behind them, Palesa struggled to keep up the pace, mumbling, "This isn't a race you know."

Every few steps, Rais turned back to ensure she was still behind them and to reassure her that he was near.

Finally, they staggered out onto the banks of the lake, glad to be out of the cold water. Shaking off the mud and moisture, they wrung out the bottom of their trousers and leggings as much as possible.

Looking skywards, Markos said, "The lack of moonlight will be a bonus. It will mask our travels on the river and our final approach."

Palesa moaned. "I hope it doesn't rain. I'm wet enough now."

"Quiet now," Markos warned.

They paused in the eerie silence. The mist swirled around them like a veil of silk blocking out anything more than a stride away. The call of a moontime bird close to them split the silence. The melodious sound was repeated three times in quick succession. Markos put two fingers into his mouth and echoed the call.

Nobosi growled ferociously as three figures appeared out of the veil. Kanda and Rais held the animal to quieten him.

A lanky man with short black hair greeted Markos. "Evening, Markos, good to see you."

Markos nodded a greeting. "Evening, Quinto. Thanks for coming."

Beside Quinto stood a short man with long brown hair and a goatee beard. He folded his arms as he nodded to Markos. His eyes narrowed as he surveyed the teenagers. "They're not coming with us, are they?"

Markos shrugged. "Afraid so, Wabster. You try to stop them; I can't."

A stooped, older man with a grey beard and short grey hair hovered behind them, gazing anxiously at Palesa. "Evening, Harrie," Markos said.

Palesa flinched at the sight of the third man and rushed to him. "Father, are you coming too?" She waited nervously for the answer.

"No, I have come to take you home," he said taking her hand.

Her eyes wide and pleading, Palesa shook her head. "No, I want to go with my new friends. After they rescue the old couple, they are going to find Briador. I know he is in the mountains somewhere and I know the mountains better than any of them. They will need me to show them the way."

"You certainly know the mountains well; I'll give you that. I have been hard pressed to stop you playing on them, despite the dangers."

"Then I can go?"

"It's not safe there. I beg you to come home with me."

Pouting and pulling her hand free, the girl backed towards the twins. "Please, Father! Markos is going. Besides, you know I'll go anyway … and if I'm on my own it will be even more dangerous."

Kanda shook her head. *She even pulls her pouting stunts with her father. No wonder she is so good at it.*

The old man sighed and looked to Markos. He shrugged. "You and I both know we would have no way of stopping her, Harrie. I would rather have her with us than worry that she was behind us and in danger."

Harrie sighed. "Very well, then I will come with you on this mission to save Nona and Pap. At least I can keep an eye on her for that long."

Markos turned to the other men. "Did you arrange the canoes and weapons?"

Quinto nodded. "Follow me and go quietly. Yaholo's men were spotted searching the lower slopes by the bay. Who knows where they are now."

"No more talking," Wabster whispered.

He led them to two canoes hidden in the reeds. They pushed them as silently as possible onto the calm water side of the river and prepared to climb aboard. "You take those kids with you and keep them quiet," Quinto hissed to Markos.

The fog on the water was thicker than on land and settled over the canoe and its occupants like the fine mist from a waterfall, dampening their clothes and hair. The twins and Palesa crouched down in the vessel beside the warm body of Nobosi. They pulled up their hoods and huddled together for warmth.

The canoes glided through the ghostly fog. Many times, the twins had been grateful for the river's calm side where the water spread to the bank nearest the farm and allowed them to return easily. The oars in the hands of Markos sliced the water without a sound. Even the moontime creatures were silent.

It's as if the whole world is holding its breath, Kanda thought.

Then the sound of the rush of water reached their ears. Rais could picture the waterfall where the water flowed from the mountain's underground stream and created the fast-flowing stream on the other side of the river. He knew they were close to the farm.

The canoe turned to the right, nudged the bank gently, and came to a halt. The ghostly shape of an overhanging branch and a ferny bank loomed out of the mist. Markos reached out and took Kanda's hand, urging the others to follow him. They alighted from the canoe as silently as possible, climbed the bank, and followed Markos a few strides into the bushes. The veil thinned as they walked away from the water. Rais paused to get his bearings.

Markos had brought them directly to the bank behind the farm.

The old man put his hand on Rais' arm. "Where is your secret tunnel?"

Silently, Rais led the way. "Do we have a plan for what we will do when we arrive at the farmhouse, Markos?" he asked as they reached the entrance to the hollow bushes.

"Yes, you children, Harrie and I will stay hidden while Wabster and Quinto deal with the guard."

Rais bristled at being called a child. He knew he was as strong as both men. Eyes flashing, he snapped, "I know the layout of the farm better than anyone."

Markos firmly clutched Rais' shoulder. "The men have intimate knowledge of the farm too. We can't risk you being hurt or captured. You have an important mission to complete. This time you *will* stay with me."

Rais bowed his head, fuming. *Yes, an important mission no one will tell us about.* Then his thoughts turned to the task at hand. Worry about the safety of Nona and Pap was all that occupied his mind.

At the other end of the tunnel, he paused to listen before he removed the bush that hid the exit. No sound reached Rais' ears. He lifted the bush and peered out. Except for the swishing of the tails of the chinows just ahead of him, there was no sign of life. Total darkness engulfed the house and Rais' heart missed a beat. "There should be lights. It's only early evening."

Kanda peered over his shoulder anxiously. "There isn't even the glow of a fire."

Markos gripped their shoulders reassuringly. "The guard will make sure they have no comfort at all. But I'm sure they are still okay. They will keep them alive to give you a reason to come back. Let the men through and they will soon find out."

Reluctantly, the twins stepped aside. The two men patted Rais' shoulder on their way past. "We'll get them out," Quinto assured him.

Nobosi went to follow, but Rais restrained him. The twins clung to each other for comfort as they waited to hear the fate of their beloved guardians. Behind them, Harrie sat with Palesa and Markos. All were praying for a favourable outcome.

The time passed slowly, and they shuffled impatiently. Then a resounding crack broke the silence and shouts echoed. Then silence again. A flickering light appeared at the kitchen window and Rais could contain himself no more. He rushed from the tunnel, followed closely by the rest of the party.

They halted at the kitchen's broken door and peered in. The flicker of light came from the hall and lit the sitting room with a faint glow. Stretched out on the floor of the room was a still, human form. Holding his breath, Rais hurried to the body. His sigh of relief was audible when he saw that it wore the uniform of Yaholo's guard. The rest of the group caught up and stood peering down at the body, shivering. The room was as cold as the air outside.

The light became brighter and into the living room came Quinto, carrying the lamp and half carrying the frail form of Pap. Rais and Kanda hugged the old man, relief creasing their faces into a strained smile. They helped him into the nearest easy chair. Behind Markos, Wabster appeared carrying Nona. He gently laid the old woman on the sofa and stepped back as Rais and Kanda hurried to her side.

"Nona, are you alright?" they asked as one.

"A little cold and weary, but I'll be fine. Why are you still here? You should be on your way. Time is running out," she replied in a shaky whisper.

"We wanted to make sure you were safe first, to put the twin's minds at rest," Markos said as he moved to the fireplace. He soon had a roaring fire warming the room. The twins hugged the old couple as if they would never let go. "What do you mean, Nona? No one will tell us anything. Please tell us what we have to do and where we have to go?" Kanda pleaded.

"Briador is the only one that can tell you that. Please don't pester Nona about it," Markos said as he fetched blankets, and handed them to the twins. The twins sighed in frustration, as they tucked them around the old couple.

"Once we get them warm again, we'll get them out of here," Markos said.

Concern creased Rais's brow. "Where will they be taken? Will they be alone?"

"We have a safe house already assigned, and there they will have someone to care for them," Markos assured them.

Rais and Kanda hovered over the old couple warming soup and feeding it to them. They frowned in concern at how weak they were but were not surprised when informed they had no fire since the twins left and only meagre food. Anger surged through Rais as he tended them. He would somehow have his revenge.

While they tended the couple, Wabster and Quinto took the body of the guard to the river and dumped it in, weighed down with rocks. When Nona and Pap were feeling stronger, they wrapped them in the heavy blankets and Quinto and Wabster carried them to the waiting canoes. The twins stood on the bank and watched them being loaded.

Once their guardians were settled in the bottom of the craft Markos turned to the twins. "As we are planning a trip over the mountains, I think we had better get started before Yaholo's men find the house empty and the guard missing. More troops will be brought in then to find us."

Harrie hesitated and looked at Palesa. "You're sure you want to go with them?"

Palesa looked around her at the ghostly mist and thought about the uncertain fate that awaited her on The Mountain of Dread. Fear crept in for a moment. Its icy fingers stroked the back of her neck and she shivered. But her desire for the reward and her need to return to the palace and the shadow people from her dreams, soon overcame her fear. Hugging Harrie, she replied, "I'm sure, Father. I'll be fine. Rais will look after me."

Harrie stared doubtfully at Rais then turned to Markos. "I guess I have no choice but to turn her care over to you. Are you sure you want to accept the responsibility?"

"I really don't think I have an option," Markos told him chuckling. "Perhaps there will be, as the old saying goes, safety in numbers. She will be another pair of eyes and if she is as familiar with the mountain as she says, she will be a big help."

With a loud sigh, Harrie climbed into the canoe and handed them their backpacks. The twins said a tearful goodbye to Nona and Pap and stood back as the canoes silently pulled away. The mist soon swallowed them. They vanished from sight as if they had never been there.

Kanda scrubbed at her cheeks to dry them and looked imploringly at Markos. "You're sure they will be safe?"

"Yes, I'm sure. Now let's find a place to sleep. We'll set off at first light." Overhead, the heavy, black clouds closed in ominously. Markos looked skyward. "I think it will have to be close by. The heavens will open soon. We don't need to get drenched in this cold air."

Rais pointed upriver. "There's a cave there, behind the waterfall. We've been there many times. I think I can find it, even in this fog."

"Yeah, we just need to follow the riverbank," Kanda confirmed hurrying off.

Stumbling along in the dark, Palesa and Markos finally arrived at the waterfall. Kanda, Rais, and Nobosi had bounded over the familiar rocks and disappeared into the gloom behind the falling water. Markos and Palesa scrambled over the unknown territory as quickly as possible. Soon they caught up with Kanda and Nobosi who were waiting at the mouth of the cave.

Peering into the darkness, Palesa moved forward and moaned. "Where is the cave? I can barely see a thing past my hand."

Kanda placed a hand on her arm to restrain her. "We are in the mouth of it now. Just wait a minute. Rais has gone to start a fire and light a torch. We always have dry wood and fire stones for when we come here to explore."

From up ahead, they heard the faint rustle of cautious footsteps in the loose gravel of the cave floor. Rais suddenly appeared before them, his hand to his lips to silence them. "There's a fire burning in the cave up ahead. You can't see its glow until you go around that corner. I didn't get far enough to see who is there."

Markos frowned. "It may be Yaholo's guards. We should get out of here now."

Rais shook his head. "There was no noise or chatter. If it was the guards, they wouldn't feel the need to be quiet. I can't think of any other place to sleep that is nearby. That storm is coming in fast now and we'd get drenched before we found shelter."

"Palesa, do you know of anywhere else close by?" Markos asked.

"No, I usually climb further over towards the bay."

Rais began walking. "I'll sneak up to the next bend and see who is by the fire. Lots of travellers shelter here."

"Take Nobosi with you," Kanda cautioned.

Drawing his spear from its leather holder, Markos followed. "We'll all go. We shouldn't be split up, and besides the more of us the better if we have to fight."

Rais drew his spear and the girls followed suit. They crept towards the first bend with Rais leading and Markos behind him.

When they reached it, they saw the faint glow of the fire behind a low wall. Cautiously they approached. Rais peeped over the wall. Markos was close behind and felt the youth's body relax. Breathing a sigh of relief Rais whispered, "It's just travellers – a youth and a man."

"Let me see," Markos muttered and pushed in front of Rais. "It's Leopold and Varn," he exclaimed and set off around the corner.

As soon as he appeared, the youth jumped to his feet grabbing his spear and holding it in a defensive position. Reaching for his weapon, the man tried to stand, but collapsed to the ground with a loud moan.

Markos held up his hands. "Varn, it's okay. It's me, Markos."

The man sighed and relaxed. "Markos – am I glad to see you."

Their escort introduced Leopold and Varn to his companions. Varn's eyes narrowed when he heard their names and looked at Markos questioningly.

"The twins' sanctuary has been compromised and I'm taking them to Briador." He explained what had happened at the farm. "Palesa has decided to travel with us – much to her father's displeasure."

Palesa, Kanda, and Rais stood staring at Leopold. He had not spoken when introduced. He was not much older than they were, but taller than Rais, and well-muscled. He wore a crumpled, dirty, sky-blue costume and a liogon fur wrap. Slumping to the ground with his spear close by, he stared back. Filled with contempt and disinterest, his dark eyes travelled from Palesa to Rais then to Kanda. His eyes rested a moment on Kanda and inspected her from head to toe. Finally, he ran his hand through his thick black hair and turned to throw another log on the fire, stirring it with his spear.

Kanda blushed as his eyes swept her.

"What's wrong, Varn, are you injured?" Markos asked.

The short, well-muscled man, his coarse brown hair in total disarray and his weathered face covered with grey stubble, shifted wearily. "I've copped a spear in the leg. The troops came to the cabin. We just got out before they barged in. They chased us and I was injured. We managed to give them the slip. Leopold had to practically carry me to safety." He indicated his right leg, the trousers ripped and covered with blood. Markos moved to inspect the wound.

The twins and Palesa crouched down by the warmth of the fire. Nobosi lay between them and Leopold, eyeing the surly stranger suspiciously.

Varn continued, "Leopold has filled my wound with healing herbs, but it will be some time before I can walk far."

Markos shook his head. "The troops are looking for the twins and Briador. They will check this cave when they find their guard and the old couple missing. It is not safe for you to stay here."

Varn grunted and looked at Leopold. "They'll be looking for us too. The boy knew a hiding place at the base of the mountains, and we hid there until they passed, then came here. I'll have to take my chances here until I can walk again."

"There's a small opening into another cave back there," Rais said pointing to the back of the cave. "No one knows about it but us. The opening is narrow, but I'm sure you could squeeze in."

Varn nodded. "Thanks. I'll get you to take me there at dawning. I might be stronger then. Markos, will you take Leopold with you? He is not safe here."

Markos looked around the group before him. "I would prefer not to. I have my hands full already. Besides if we are all captured …" he left the last part of the sentence unsaid and Varn nodded to indicate he understood.

"I know, Markos, but there's no-one else to care for him. I will follow as soon as I am able."

Markos nodded reluctantly.

Leopold had been listening to this exchange with interest. Now he laughed, and taunted, "What makes you think this old man can care for me? I have no doubt that I will end up caring for him."

Varn bristled. "Watch your tongue, boy. You are in the presence of one of the King's head guards. He could floor you before you could blink."

Eyebrows raised, Leopold looked at Markos with more interest. "Really, I'd like to see that," he scoffed.

Varn glared at him. "Just hope you never have to, you spoilt brat."

"Show us your stuff, Markos," Leopold challenged.

"That's enough, Leopold," Markos snapped. "Now I think it's time to get some sleep. We'll have to move out at first light, so we are deep into the lower part of the mountain before the guards start their search."

They settled down, but no-one got much sleep. Kanda and Rais tossed and turned as they pictured their guardians being captured again.

Palesa could not get the image of Leopold out of her head. She had a vague feeling of having known him before. *I wonder if he used to live in the palace.*

Markos lay there trying to plan the trip over the mountain. The worry that the twins would be captured under his watch kept him awake. After some time of tossing and turning, he walked to the mouth of the cave and sat staring at the rain. Humming softly, he relaxed into a deep meditative state. A rustle of feathers from above startled him. Owl dropped from the trees and landed reassuringly at his side.

Markos stroked the bird. "Been to report to the boss, have we?" Finally, he closed his eyes and allowed himself to drift into a light sleep.

When he opened them again, the rain had stopped, and dawn bathed the trees in its welcome glow. He hurried to wake the sleeping group and prepare them for the journey ahead.

Rais and Leopold made a fast trip to the farmhouse to get supplies for Varn and Leopold and top up Rais's pack. When they came back, they helped Varn to his feet and showed him the smaller cave. They took his supplies in and made sure he could get in without help.

Markos checked Varn's wound and reassured him that it was healing well. "It is only a flesh wound so it won't take long to heal. You should be able to join us within a couple of suns. We will wait with Briador in the cave at the mouth of The River of Safe Passage."

Varn shuddered at the thought of travelling on the mountain. "Good luck and God speed, Markos. You will need both on that dreadful mountain. I am familiar with the many dangers that lurk there and I'm not looking forward to facing them again."

Markos nodded. "I am well aware of the dangers. Although I have never faced them personally, I have nursed to health many messengers from the palace that have."

Varn limped to the cave entrance with them, and Rais pointed out their secret tunnel. "There's a store of dried meat and vegetables at the farm. Enough to keep you well-fed and give you strength to travel when it is time. We brought back enough for a couple of suns. The troops will have no interest in the place when they find it empty."

Varn patted his shoulder reassuringly, "Good luck, my boy. I only hope you make it over that evil mountain. Stay safe."

CHAPTER FIVE

The Mountain of Dread

Leopold surveyed the scenery around him. "I've spent a lot of time climbing on this mountain and know it like the back of my hand. A passage in the back of a cave closer to the bay leads through the mountain to the top on the other side. If we use that, we could avoid being seen."

"Have you ever used the passage?" Markos asked.

"No, just heard about it. I went to the entrance to the tunnel, but the sign there put me off, and I didn't want to chance it alone. But with a small party it should be safe enough."

"What did the sign say?" Kanda inquired.

Leopold started to climb. "I'll let you see for yourself. It's an easy climb. Best to stay off the path. Follow me."

Palesa watched him climb with ease over the rough terrain and turned to see Kanda watching him too. "Sure, an 'easy climb' if you're as tall and as fit as he is. A bit snooty, but kind of cute don't you think?"

A crimson glow appeared on Kanda's face when she realised she had been caught in the act of admiring

Leopold. She turned on Palesa. "Coming from *you*, that snooty comment is a bit rich, don't you think?"

Palesa bristled. "What? Are you saying I'm stuck-up?"

"Enough, girls," Markos snapped. The girls glared at each other then turned to follow Leopold.

"Something tells me this trip will be very eventful," Markos muttered to Rais.

Rais smiled ruefully as he watched the girls hurry after Leopold. "It certainly won't be dull, that's for sure."

With Leopold leading, they scrambled along the lower slopes of the mountain through the dawning light, gaining a little height as they went. A couple of times they lost sight of Leopold as he forged ahead. He set such a swift pace that even Rais had trouble keeping up. He would just start to worry they had lost him, then turn a corner and find him waiting impatiently for them. The sun was high in the sky when Rais finally called a halt. He could see that Markos was tiring and said to Leopold, "Let's stop and rest for a moment."

Leopold scowled. "What's the problem, farm boy? Having trouble keeping up?"

Rais nodded towards Markos who had gratefully sunk to the ground behind the shelter of a large boulder. Leopold frowned and muttered so only Rais could hear, "I knew he would be a burden." Sulkily, he slumped to the ground and pulled his water skin and food sack from his backpack. The rest of the group followed suit.

Kanda settled near-by, fishing in her backpack for food and water. "How far is it to the cave now?"

Palesa sat next to her, rubbing her aching feet. "I know this section of the slopes; there's no cave here."

Leopold arched an eyebrow haughtily. "You obviously haven't spent as much time here as I have, Palesa. As a matter of fact, it is just over there behind those boulders." He indicated a group of boulders a couple of hundred strides away.

Rais had been lying on a rocky platform scanning the area below them. He dropped to the ground, raised his hand for silence, and pointed.

Leopold and Markos peered out from their shelter. On the path on the lower slopes of the mountain, a troop of guardsmen marched, searching the area as they went. The advance scouts were inspecting the muddy ground for signs that someone had used the path recently.

The group held their breath as they crouched behind the cluster of boulders and watched the search party's progress. Finding no signs of travellers, the guardsmen soon disappeared.

"They will be heading to the farm to change the guard. We had better reach the cave's shelter before they find the house empty," Markos said, rising stiffly.

Leopold bounded to his feet, bumping into Kanda who had also moved to rise. He reached down and helped her up. "Sorry about that. You okay?" His usually superior expression softened as he gazed into her eyes. His hand held hers for just a fraction longer than necessary. A tingling sensation ran through Kanda, and she felt her face burning. Confused, she pulled her hand away with a gruff, "Watch what you're doing."

Leopold's face turned to stone, and he turned and loped off in the direction of the boulders he had indicated. Kanda stared after him, her heart beating faster than normal. She rubbed the hand that he had held as if trying to remove the tingling feeling that his grip had evoked.

Rais came to her side. "You okay?"

"Sure, I'm fine," Kanda replied stalking ahead. Her mind was in turmoil; the sensations she had felt when she looked into Leopold's eyes and felt his hand holding hers, were new to her, and she didn't know how to handle them. "I don't even like the stuck-up jerk," she muttered to herself.

Palesa had watched the exchange with interest. She raised her eyebrows. *How can a guy like Leopold be interested in that mouse?* She hurried past the rest of the group and caught up with Leopold. He squeezed between a huge boulder and the rock face of the cliff. Palesa pressed in after him. She peered into the cave's dark entrance. "You're so clever finding this cave. How far in have you been?"

"A few hundred strides; I came to a huge pool of water and the strange sign. I wasn't sure what it meant so I didn't go any further. I tried to get Varn to come and explore it with me. But, at that time my nanny was still around, and he said she would skin him alive if I got hurt."

"Nanny? Where are your parents?"

"I don't remember my father, but my mother died just after we moved here. My nanny and her husband, Baris raised me. Then last year, when Baris died of the fever, Varn came to help. Nanny died recently so it's been just him and me since then."

"Did you live in the palace before… you know… the invasion?"

"Yes, I still have hazy memories of my life there. It would be good to go back. But not while Yaholo is the ruler. I guess we fled from him. Anyway, I'm not sure I'd be welcome now that my mother is gone. And, as I don't know who my father is..."

Palesa saw tears close to the surface as he told his story and placed her hand on his arm in comfort.

Kanda had paused outside the boulders to listen to the story. She pushed through the gap just as Palesa reached out. Leopold looked up and saw Kanda staring at Palesa's hand on his arm. He shrugged it off and turned away.

Palesa frowned at the other girl. "What are you gawking at?" she snapped and followed Leopold into the mouth of the cave.

Unfamiliar feelings of jealousy washed over Kanda. She lashed out. "Oh sure, you really like Rais, huh. Give you two seconds alone with someone else and you're all over them," she shouted after her.

Taking a deep calming breath, Kanda stared into the cave entrance as both Leopold and Palesa dissolved into the inky darkness. The mouth of the cave had jagged, broken stones hanging down. Raised in the centre, the floor was well-worn and smooth. Gravel spread around it. The sun illuminated just the first couple of strides into the cavern, beyond that was like a black veil had been dropped. Kanda shivered as the elevated path took on the form of a tongue and the jagged rocks, teeth. "It's like looking into the mouth of a dragon," she said to Rais as he joined her.

He smiled reassuringly. "I'm sure it's not as dangerous as walking into a dragon's mouth."

He would soon change his mind about that.

Markos joined them and they stepped through the opening. He produced three bundles of grass and sticks that he had gathered and two flint stones. He struck the stones together and Rais and Kanda jumped back as the first bundle burst into flame. From that torch, he lit two more and handed one to Rais and Kanda.

Leopold came back. "It's pitch black in there. We need…" He stopped as he saw the torches. "Where did you get them? We were coming back to look for something to burn."

"I brought them in with me," Markos responded. "Three should be enough. Now let's get started before we attract the attention of the troops."

Kanda thrust her torch at Leopold. "If you like, you can carry mine."

Leopold leapt back as the flame touched his arm. "Wow, watch what you're doing," he said. He took the torch, brushed past her without a word and proceeded to lead the way. Kanda stumbled behind, biting her lip anxiously. *I just keep making him mad. Not that I care, of course,* she thought tossing her head.

The terrain became rugged as the passageway narrowed. Rocks jutted from the floor and walls. Kanda watched uneasily as the shadows of the obstacles became dancing monsters in the flickering light of Leopold's flame. She slowed her pace and Palesa passed her, carrying Markos' flame. The light of their torches disappeared around a bend. Kanda shivered as the cold darkness wrapped its icy cloak around her. She paused and glanced back. She could just see the flicker of Rais's torch as he walked slowly with Markos.

She peered around fretfully. The walls were close now and were closing on her like a huge monster's hand. She glanced up; the ceiling pressed down. Her heart raced in panic as she felt the giant squeeze the breath from her body. Her head spun. She groaned as her body folded like a wet dishcloth and slumped to the floor. Nobosi loped up beside her, whimpered softly and nudged her to rise.

Leopold came around the corner as she fell. He raced to her side. "Kanda, are you okay," he cried. Laying his torch on the floor, he knelt beside her, took her hand, and patted it anxiously. He cradled her in his arms and looked around for help. The flicker of Rais' torch as he and Markos rushed towards them made him sigh with relief.

They too had seen her fall and hurried to her side. "Kanda," Rais cried kneeling down beside them.

Leopold looked imploringly at them. "I saw her fall. What happened? What's wrong with her?"

Markos sank down and felt for Kanda's pulse. He sighed with relief when he found it beating strongly. "I think she has just fainted." Reaching into his backpack, he pulled out a small pouch of herbs, took out the stopper, and waved it under her nose.

She stirred, opened her eyes, and looked up into Leopold's. "Quick the walls are closing in. We have to get out of here," she exclaimed.

Leopold and Rais looked around urgently. All was as it should be. "Kanda, the walls are fine," Leopold assured her.

"Well, they *were* closing in," Kanda murmured and looked at them again. Her heart raced as they started to move. She clutched his hand and buried her face in his chest. He pulled her closer to him for comfort and looked at Markos, frowning.

The old man took her hands. "Kanda, don't look at the walls, just look straight ahead. You are suffering an illusion brought on by the confined space. Many people feel this way their first time in a dark, restricted place. You'll be fine if you only look ahead."

Kanda nodded and tried to stand. Leopold helped her to her feet. She glanced ahead, then snuck a peek at the walls. She quickly turned back to the path ahead.

"I came back to give you your torch. Palesa's got one so I don't need it," Leopold said offering her the torch.

"Oh thanks. That would have helped, I think," she said blushing.

"The cavern isn't too far ahead now," Leopold said. Palesa was waiting impatiently so Leopold set off with her. Kanda hung back with Rais and Markos. They started walking slowly. As they rounded a bend, Kanda locked her gaze on the flickering light of Palesa's torch, which had again become visible.

Rais too focused on their light. "They seem to have stopped."

They hurried to the cave entrance. The passage opened into a small cavern. Leopold and Palesa were staring at the wall near a pool of water. Rais looked around with interest. A trickle of water that fell down the rocks from a crack in the roof above created the pool. Ferns cascaded down the damp walls beside it like a green waterfall. The torch glow caused tiny lights to sparkle in the black rock. It had the appearance of the moontime sky.

Kanda stood beside him taking in the beautiful sight. "Oh, Rais, isn't it lovely," she exclaimed. Rais nodded, smiling.

As he joined Leopold and Palesa, Markos asked, "Is that the sign you mentioned?"

Leopold nodded. Rais and Kanda came to join them, and they gazed at the sign. Kanda read it aloud, her voice rising in amazement as she read.

"Follow the Passage of Death if you dare.
You could be the one the gods will spare.
Beware the lure of liquid death
And think before every breath.
Brave the fire and the fangs
And furry fiends in their gangs.
Every turn will test your mettle
Before your bones begin to settle
For the sleep that begins
A new adventure without earthly sins."

"What could it mean? It sounds scary," she asked.

Leopold smiled at her. "I'm sure it's not too scary. Probably meant to stop people going through the passage."

Markos stroked his chin thoughtfully. "I don't know, Leopold. It could be meant to stop people using the passage, or it could be a genuine warning."

Kanda's eyes widened as she stared at Markos. "Do you think it's safe?"

"It has to be safer than climbing in plain view of the troops who are looking for us," Leopold commented.

Markos stared into the dark tunnel ahead. "Mmm ... I wish I had your confidence on that point. However, we will have to take a chance. Stay sharp and keep an eye out for danger."

Rais nodded, his face grim. A feeling of foreboding settled on his shoulders, and he shivered.

He would wish later that he had taken more notice of that emotion.

CHAPTER SIX

Into the Passage of Death

Kanda stared at the narrow passage ahead. The chilly darkness hung like a heavy blanket, masking the possible dangers. Silence pressed in on her as her companions contemplated the journey. Nobosi rubbed up against her leg and she absentmindedly stroked his head, unsure if she sought reassurance or gave it. She longed for the home she had known, the warm fireplace and the comforting care of Nona and Pap. Finally, she shook herself free of the yearning. *That's all gone now, we have to reach Briador.* Taking a deep breath to quieten her pounding heart she turned to her brother. "Rais, do *you* think it's safe?"

Rais jumped as she spoke. He had been running the words of the strange sign through his mind, searching for a meaning. Smiling grimly, he said, "Don't know, but I suppose there's only one way to find out."

Leopold shouldered his backpack. "What, scared, farm boy?" he sneered.

Rais ignored his taunt and asked, "How long will it take to get through? We are on a time limit."

"Not sure. What's the hurry?"

Rais grimaced and looked at Markos. "I wish I knew. But we only have about 10 suns to get there... wherever there is."

Leopold raised an eyebrow and grinned. "So, you don't know where you're going, but you're in a hurry to get there. Sounds about right, farm boy."

Kanda frowned at Leopold's taunting tone. "They won't tell us. That's why we don't know. We have to get to Briador as quickly as we can. He knows," she snapped and strode away.

Leopold followed her. He placed a hand on her shoulder. "Sorry. You want to tell me what is going on? I know the troops are chasing you, but I don't know why."

"We don't either. All we know is that someone came to the farm with a message. We didn't hear the whole conversation, all we heard was that we had to be somewhere by the full moon to save someone's life. Nona told the messenger to find Briador, but the man was captured and killed before he found him."

Leopold's face softened and he stroked her arm in sympathy. "Oh, that's tough."

Kanda nodded. "Then the troops came, and we had to leave suddenly." She told him about meeting Palesa and what had happened afterwards.

"Wow. Well, we must get you to Briador quickly. It's a couple of suns to the top, I suppose."

"I hope that's all it is," Markos said.

"I'll go ahead and make sure it is safe. You take your time and take the torch," Leopold said to Kanda.

Palesa had watched the exchange with jealousy raging through her. "Yeah, I'll come with you. I can keep up. You obviously can't, Kanda." She strode ahead.

Leopold gave Kanda a rueful smile. "You okay?" he muttered. Kanda nodded and he set off after Palesa. The light of Palesa's torch bounced off the glittering rock walls like dancing sprites.

Kanda pulled a face at her back, but she was thankful for the torch Leopold had returned. In the torch's light, the walls appeared more stable. A warm glow coursed through her from the concern he showed. She and Nobosi set off after them, with Rais and Markos behind.

The black walls pressed in on Kanda as she walked, and the dampness increased. She shivered and focussed on the passage ahead. The only sounds were the trickle of water, and the echo of their footsteps on the hard rock path. The musty aroma of moist earth filled the air.

As they walked, the passage narrowed and the walls turned rust red, with patches of green and bright yellow. Occasionally, they had to duck to pass under the low ceiling. The water flow increased, trickling down crevices in the rock and running along the edge of the path. The stream got wider and deeper as they progressed.

Kanda, her boots damp, shivered in the cold. She hoped that they would soon come to a wider passage, or a cavern of some kind. Even with the light, the close walls and ceiling created a feeling of panic that climbed from the pit of her stomach to her mind and threatened to consume her.

Palesa's light grew dimmer as she and Leopold charged through the darkness. Then they rounded a corner and the glow disappeared. Kanda's torch light jumped off the uneven walls creating shadow monsters all around her. She shivered and increased her pace. She was grateful to have Nobosi close by.

When she reached the corner, their torch had disappeared. She hesitated. Unknown dangers pressed in on her from the eerie darkness outside her flame's glow. Her palms suddenly moist with sweat, she cringed against the wall. Finally, behind her, she saw the faint glow of Rais' torch and fixed her eyes on it, willing them to hurry.

Nobosi lifted his head and sniffed, then suddenly bounded forward into the darkness. He disappeared around the next bend and silence closed in on Kanda. All alone now, she stood nervously waiting for Rais and Markos to catch up.

As he approached, Rais peered into the gloom ahead. "Where's Nobosi?"

"I don't know. He raced off." Just as she spoke, they heard Nobosi bark. They knew that sound; it was his warning bark and meant someone was in danger.

"Go find out what is wrong. The other two may be in trouble," Markos said.

Rais and Kanda didn't need any further urging and set off at a run. Around the next bend, they saw the light of Palesa's torch and rushed towards it and the sound of Nobosi's frantic barking.

The twins skidded to a stop and took in the sight before them. The animal sat in front of Palesa and Leopold, his hackles alert, teeth bared in his long snout, his large feline body quivering with the force of the low growl that had replaced the barking when they came into view. Leopold swatted Nobosi and shouted at him, but the liogon sat as if made of stone. Behind him, the stream of water that trickled down the passage had created a pool in the centre of the cavern.

"What the hell is wrong with that mutt?" Leopold shouted.

Kanda grabbed him by the collar. "Sorry, I don't know what the problem is, but he only carries on like this if there's danger."

Palesa and Leopold brushed past her. "Well, if there's danger here, I don't know where. All we wanted to do was have a drink and fill our water sacks," Palesa said. She and Leopold knelt by the pool. Nobosi began barking again and strained against Kanda's hold.

Rais had been surveying the scene and suddenly shouted, "No, don't drink the water!" Palesa stopped to look at Rais, but Leopold, hands full of water, brought them to his mouth. Rais launched himself forward in a full tackle and knocked Leopold sideways. The youth struggled to his feet, swinging his fists at his assailant. Rais ducked back. "Poison," he gasped.

Leopold froze. "What! How do you know that?"

Still winded, Rais pointed to the edge of the pool. Animal bones surrounded the pond like a border decoration on a plate. Kanda's hand flew to her mouth, and she rushed to Leopold's side. "Did you swallow any?"

"No," Leopold grunted.

"*Beware the lure of liquid death,*" Markos quoted as he joined them.

"That's right! That was the first part of the verse. So, the verse *is* a warning. What came next?" Kanda asked.

Palesa frowned in concentration. "Something about breath, I think."

71

Rais nodded. "Yeah, '*think before every breath*'. Maybe we should stop to try to work out what it means before we set off again."

Palesa moved to Rais' side. "You saved my life," she said kissing him on the cheek.

Rais' face turned crimson. "At least I didn't have to tackle you to do it," he said glaring at Leopold. Palesa snuggled up to Rais as he perched on a rock. He squirmed and moved away a little. *Wish she would make up her mind. One minute she is following Leopold like a devoted puppy, the next she is all over me. Maybe she is not as wonderful as I thought.*

Kanda shook her head. *Boy is she two-faced.* "What do you think poisoned the water?" she asked, looking at her soaked shoes and leggings nervously.

Markos had been studying the pool. "I think it is something in the pool. Maybe some sort of rock that leaches poison. The base of the pool glows green in the torchlight. That could be copper."

Leopold paced impatiently. "Shouldn't we just get on our way? We can think about the verse as we walk."

"Yeah, I just want to get out of this tunnel as quickly as possible," Kanda said. She shivered as she regarded the narrow passage before them.

Rais rose grudgingly to his feet. "Okay, but this time we'll all stay together."

Leopold threw his head back in scorn. "What, walk like a geriatric? Maybe we should leave the old man behind. He's just slowing us down."

Rais' eyes flashed. "Maybe we should leave you behind. Then I wouldn't have to save you from your own stupidity."

Leopold turned and stalked off into the passage. Palesa hesitated; she glanced from his retreating back, to Rais.

"Rais, you and Palesa go after him; Markos and I will catch up," Kanda said.

Rais looked to Markos for confirmation, and when the old man nodded his consent, he and Palesa hurried after Leopold.

Markos sighed. "He's probably right, Kanda, you would get there faster without me, but you might never find Briador alone."

Kanda hugged him reassuringly. "We couldn't do it without you. You are the only one who can help us."

Nobosi hung back with Kanda until, with a rueful grimace, she told him to go to Rais. "You may be needed to save Leopold again." Nobosi obeyed, his long loping stride covering the ground swiftly. His black coat soon merged with the darkness of the tunnel. Kanda anxiously bit her lip as she followed at Markos' side. She had a strong feeling that something bad was going to happen.

And she was right.

CHAPTER SEVEN

The Cave Dwellers

Even though they set off at a swift pace, Rais and Palesa had trouble catching up to Leopold. Rais' temper rose with every step. "He must have jogged to get this far ahead."

Then, Nobosi growled and streaked forward. Rais and Palesa raced after him. They could now hear him barking ferociously, and when he came into view, they could see why. Leopold was prone on the floor and leaning over him were two strangers. Rais came to an abrupt halt as the figures turned and raised their hands in a gesture to stop. Palesa hid behind him, peeping out at the strange sight before them.

A youth of the twin's age and a younger girl stared back. The strangers' skins were so white that the light gave them a luminescent glow. Their hair was long and blonde, but their eyes were black and looked like raisins in their pale faces. They wore garments of animal skins.

Fear making his voice squeak, Rais called, "What have you done to him?"

"We have done nothing. We found him lying in there and brought him to safety," the youth remarked indicating the passage ahead.

Rais peered at them, not sure what to believe. "In where? What is ahead?"

"A small cave; the air is not pure."

"It's the breath warning," Palesa gasped as she and Rais rushed to Leopold's side. The strangers stepped away and let them examine their friend.

Palesa sighed with relief. "He's still breathing."

"Run back and get Markos. He'll know what to do," Rais told her.

The youth shook his head. "There's no time for that. We will take him to a healer – our mother – she is closer."

Rais scanned the area around him. No more passages showed. "Where? The only way ahead is through that cave."

"That's not true. Follow us," the young girl said walking to the right-hand wall of the passage.

The youth pushed at a small rock set in the wall, and a boulder, almost as tall as Rais, rolled to one side. Behind it was another passage lit by torches high on the walls. The aroma of burning animal fat, and cooking food, wafted out to greet them. Rais and Palesa exchanged puzzled glances. The two strangers picked up Leopold effortlessly and carried him through the gap. Rais marvelled at their strength.

He glanced behind them. No sign of Markos' torch showed. "I'll go with them. You wait for Kanda and Markos."

Palesa shook her head decisively. "No way! I'm not staying here on my own. We'll come back for them once Leopold is healed."

Rais put his hands on his hips and looked at the girl anxiously, his anger rising. "But what if it's a trap? What if they're not friendly? Someone has to let Markos know where we are and warn him about the cave. You have to stay."

A scraping noise startled them. The rock had begun to slowly fall back into place. With an anxious, "No! Leopold!" Palesa jumped through the closing gap.

Rais clenched his fist in anger at Palesa's refusal to stay. *Thoughtless cow. All she thinks about is herself ... and Leopold. I was so wrong about her.* He stood indecisive for a moment, but finally decided he could not let them go alone. He took a nearby rock and wrote, 'Danger ahead! Wait here!' in the loose gravel on the path, then followed Palesa. Nobosi hesitated and looked back for Kanda, but finally jumped through the gap as it closed.

The strangers had carried Leopold into a small cave off to the left side of the passage. He lay on a bed of animal skins, and a statuesque woman tended him. Her hair was grey with streaks of black, and her skin was pale, but not the luminescent white of their rescuers. Her dark brown eyes regarded them briefly, then turned to her children.

"We found him in the Cave of Doom," the young girl said.

The woman fetched a small animal skin pouch from the shelf nearby, placed it under Leopold's nose and squeezed. A fine powder rose from the pouch. Leopold didn't respond. "He is not breathing deeply enough to take the cure," she said urgently.

Palesa rushed forward and cradled Leopold's head in her arms. "Do something!" she screamed at Rais.

Rais looked appealingly at the woman. "What can we do?"

"Both of you can stand back," she snapped.

The healer compressed Leopold's chest to make him breathe deeper, then sprayed again. Still no result.

"Why isn't it working?" Rais asked the healer.

"I'm not sure. He must have been in there too long. His heart rate is better, and his breathing is still strong. We will wait," she replied.

The young girl placed her hand on Rais' arm comfortingly. "I am Caria. Come, I will make you a drink and some food while we wait."

Rais studied Caria. An attractive, if strange, young girl stared back at him, her eyes mirroring Rais' curiosity. Mesmerised by the darkness of her eyes, Rais felt drawn into their depths and dropped his gaze first. Flustered, he stammered. "I'm Rais and this is Palesa. Our friend on the bed is Leopold."

The young girl introduced the healer as Andoli and the youth as Yanis.

Rais' stomach growled in hunger as the aroma of cooking food tantalised him, but his concern for Leopold made him decline the offer. "Thank you for rescuing our friend, but we won't leave his side for now, if you don't mind."

Yanis nodded and he and Caria left the room, leaving them with the healer. Caria returned a few moments later with bowls of a thick meaty stew. Grateful they didn't have to leave Leopold, Rais and Palesa tucked in hungrily.

Their hunger satisfied, they paced the floor, every few steps checking to make sure that Leopold still breathed. Rais' mind was in a whirl, worry about Leopold, Kanda, and Markos; Palesa's obsession with Leopold; and the strange feeling he had experienced when he stared into Caria's eyes had him in total confusion. Finally, he turned to Palesa. "You'll have to go back for Markos and Kanda. They will be in the passage by now and may go into the cave."

Palesa walked to Leopold's side protectively. Her auburn hair danced as she shook her head. "We'll send Nobosi."

Rais bristled. "I can't believe you, Palesa. All you think about is yourself." *And Leopold.* He turned to Nobosi. The liogon guarded the door. Rais sighed and checked Leopold again. Even though he was worried about leaving his two companions with these strangers, he decided that if Leopold didn't wake shortly, he would go himself.

CHAPTER EIGHT

A Magic Connection

Kanda and Markos had heard Nobosi barking and hurried towards the sound, Markos in the lead. The girl's heart raced in panic as she followed the old man. As they approached the entrance to the cave, he raised his hand to stop her progress. "There are many footprints in the loose dirt here and drag marks leading back from the cave ahead." He and Kanda surveyed the area.

"Look, over here; there's writing on the ground," Kanda exclaimed. Markos moved closer with the torch and the girl read the message aloud. "Danger ahead! Wait here!" Dread dropped its weight. "Where are the others and what could that mean?"

Markos studied the ground. "It's strange, but there seems to be four sets of prints, plus Nobosi's, and they lead to this wall and then stop."

They examined the right wall carefully, pounding it, looking for a way through. Finally, Kanda slumped to the floor in frustration. "I guess all we can do is wait." Her skin crawled as anxiety crept up her arms like a giant spider, making each hair stand on end. Her panicked mind imagined Rais lying injured somewhere behind that wall. But, as she pictured Rais, the image of Leopold also invaded her mind.

She clutched her pendant, rubbing it absently as she worried where Rais could be. The pendant suddenly felt much warmer. She jumped as she saw a bright white light appear before her. It sped towards the wall and disappeared. She stared at the light in amazement. Within seconds, the thoughts of her twin were clear to her, and, to her shock, she appeared to be looking through his eyes. "How…?" She looked away from the light and everything was as before. Her eyes were drawn back to the glow and the image appeared again. In front of Rais, she could see someone lying on a bed. The image was blurred. She focused harder. Then she yelped with fear. "Leopold is hurt. He's lying on a bed with his eyes closed. Palesa and a strange woman are there, hovering over him."

As she spoke, she picked up a startled thought in Rais' mind as he felt her connection. *Kanda! Where are you?*

Her mind swirling with amazement, Kanda focused on sending back a message. *At the entrance to the cave.*

Rais started towards her. *Stay there; I'm coming to get you.*

To Kanda and Markos' astonishment, the wall in front of them opened and Rais and a stranger stood there. Her brother rushed forward and hugged her. "Kanda, how did you do that mind connection thing?"

"I'm not sure. I was just clutching the owl pendant and worrying about you, and it happened. It must be something to do with the pendant."

Rais shook his head in confusion. "Maybe this is part of the magic powers we are supposed to have… maybe it's true…?"

Kanda stared at him her face reflecting the awe he felt.

Markos had watched the connection with interest. "It will all be explained when we reach Briador," he reassured them. The twins shook their head in frustration.

"What's up with Leopold?" Kanda asked.

"I'll tell you on the way." As they hurried back to Leopold, Rais explained what had happened.

Kanda eyed the girl who had come with Rais. She had never seen anyone with such white skin before. But her worry about Leopold soon overcame her curiosity and she rushed to his side. Rais introduced the healer and Caria. Markos asked Andoli about Leopold's condition.

Concerned, the healer confessed, "I have never had this happen before. Usually, the herbs quickly clear the lungs of the poison from the gas in that cave."

After finding out the herbs used, Markos scrabbled through his backpack. "I have a potion here that may help." He drew out a vial and asked for a small amount of water. Stirring in a few drops of the potion, he held it to Leopold's lips and forced him to drink.

They held their breaths, willing him to open his eyes. He didn't move. Fear gripped Kanda's heart. She knew now that she really did care what happened to him and moved to his side. Laying her head on his chest and gazing into his face, she whispered, "Leopold, please wake up. I couldn't bear it if something happened to you."

She felt Leopold's heart rate quicken and called his name. His eyes fluttered open. "Kanda, do you mean that?" he whispered.

A crimson glow crept from Kanda's neck to her face, and she nodded. "You okay?" she asked breathlessly.

Reaching up to stroke her cheek he said, "I am now."

Jealousy consumed Palesa and she rushed to his side, shoving Kanda away. "Leopold, I'm glad you are finally awake."

Leopold's eyes never left Kanda's as he replied, "Me too."

Rais scowled. *One minute she's sucking up to me; then she's fussing over Leopold. She is driving me crazy.*

The healer came forward and checked Leopold, then helped him sit. "I too am glad you are back with us."

Introduced to his rescuers, Leopold took the healer's hand and said, 'Thank you for saving me."

She shook her head. "I didn't do it. My cure didn't work. I was at a loss to know what to do next, until Markos came with his potion."

It was Leopold's turn to look uncomfortable as he mumbled, "Thank you, Markos."

Rais bristled. "Still think he is useless, and we don't need him with us?"

Kanda glared at her brother and moved protectively to Leopold's side.

Leopold shook his head. "No, I'm sorry I said all that. I knew that we needed you. I guess I just didn't want to admit it."

Markos dismissed his apology with a wave of his hand and turned to Andoli. "We have met before – in the palace."

Andoli considered Markos for a moment. "Yes, I was – oh, now I remember – you were one of the King's guards," she exclaimed. She indicated the twins. "I recognise the pendants. These are…" Markos shook his head. Andoli frowned but said nothing more.

Kanda had heard her remark and seethed with frustration. *It seems everyone knows who we are except us.*

Andoli regarded Leopold. She looked at Markos and raised an eyebrow. He nodded. "You sure have your hands full," she said.

"I'm taking them to Briador. After that they will be his problem."

Andoli smiled. "Poor Briador."

"It's been so long. How did you come to be living here – underground?" Markos asked, changing the subject.

"When we fled the city, pursued by a battalion of Yaholo's troops, my husband, Wason, and I, and the children, hid out in a cave at the top of the mountain. When the troops were getting close, we moved to the back of the cave and found a passage. We hid in there, rolling a boulder over the entrance, waiting for them to leave. But the troops moved into the cave to camp, so we followed the passage to see if it would lead us back out onto the mountain at some other spot. It led us in deeper. We found a pool of clear water and decided to stay for a while. We have been here ever since."

Kanda regarded the youth and his sister. Blushing, she asked, "Why are the skins of Caria and Yanis so white?"

Andoli explained that they came here as small children and they had not been in the sun much before they came; and have not been in the sun since. "Without sunlight to give their skin colour, it has whitened."

"Where is your husband?" Rais asked.

"Wason went to the surface for food. Some animals do venture into the passages that lead here in winter, but right now there are none, so he has gone to hunt and get news from the city. I'm getting a little worried; he has been gone for a long time now."

"Maybe we'll see him as we travel to the surface. If you feel up to it, Leopold, we must be on our way." The youth nodded and Markos continued, "Yanis, can you show us the passage around the deadly cave?"

Yanis smiled. "I'll do better than that; I'll take you all the way to the surface. I want to check on Father." He looked to his mother for consent, and she nodded.

"I'll come too," Caria said, glancing sideways at Rais for a reaction.

She received the response she wanted; Rais smiled and nodded. Palesa watched. Scowling, she moved possessively to Rais' side.

Kanda shook her head in amazement. *Wish she would make up her mind.* Then, to Kanda's delight, Rais took Palesa's hand off his arm and walked away.

Palesa stood still in complete shock, biting her lip in anxiety. She realised she had upset Rais by spending so much time with Leopold. She glared at Kanda, who talked quietly with him. Her scheming mind got busy formulating a treacherous plan.

CHAPTER NINE

Brave the Fire and The Fangs

Rais set off on the next stage of their journey, his mind busy running through the warning verse. He had asked Yanis and Andoli if they had any idea what the next clue, '*Brave the fire and the fangs*' meant, but they were as puzzled as Rais. He had told Leopold again that they had to stay together and suggested that he and Yanis lead this time. Leopold bristled, but before he could reply, Kanda placed her hand on his arm, and he conceded defeat.

Rais, Caria, and Yanis led the way, walking at a steady pace so Markos could keep up. Palesa fell in beside Markos, glaring daggers at Kanda's back. The old man didn't miss the look of jealous hatred on Palesa's face and quietly said, "Let that one go, Palesa – Leopold is not the one for you."

She turned on him. "What would you know about it, old man?" She stalked forward and pushed in between Leopold and Kanda.

Kanda slowed her step, uncertain of how to react to Palesa's intrusion. Scowling, Leopold dropped back to Kanda's side, taking her hand so that it couldn't happen again. Kanda's hand tingled at his touch. A warm rosy glow rose from her throat to her cheeks, as she held tightly to Leopold's hand. Hurt and humiliated, Palesa strode ahead until she walked behind Rais. Yanis had glanced back and seen what happened. Feeling sorry for her, he dropped back to walk beside her. She smiled gratefully.

Finally, they reached a cavern with a large pool of clear water. Caria told them, "This is where we get our water supply. In the next cave is a smaller pond that we bathe in."

They filled their water skins and walked on to the next cave. The walls had a strange, bubbled appearance and the air was warmer there. A faint pungent odour made their noses twitch.

"We should camp here. I could do with a bath," Kanda said.

Peering into the dark passage that led from the cave Markos asked, "What's up ahead?"

"A series of small caves; the next is dryer than this one. It will be a better place to camp. Besides, then we can come back here to bathe in private," Yanis replied.

They moved on to the next cave and rolled out their bedrolls. "Are you sure it is safe?" Rais asked Yanis.

Yanis nodded. "Look around; there's nowhere for anything to hide in this cave. And because it is small, the entrance can be guarded by one person." Rais scanned the area and decided that he was right; the walls were solid red rock, with no deep crevices at all.

Kanda headed back to the deep pool to bathe. She had just removed her clothing and sunk into the water when Palesa appeared. The water flowed over Kanda, and she relished the comforting warmth. She turned to Palesa, "I expected the water to be cold, but it is surprisingly warm. I wonder why?"

Palesa tossed her head scornfully. "It's a thermal spring. Can't you smell the sulphur? Don't you know anything? This mountain was once a volcano you know."

Kanda ducked under the water, smarting at the reply. *Know-all!*

When she surfaced, she could hear Nobosi barking furiously. She hurried from the water and dressed, totally ignoring Palesa.

The whole group, spears in hand, hurried towards Nobosi. They found him staring into a deep crevice in the wall of the small cave that came after their camping spot – hackles standing on end as he voiced his warning. Kanda put her hand on his back to quieten him, but his warning just dropped to a fierce growl. Leopold, Yanis, and Rais inspected the crevice, but it was too dark for them to see in far. Finding no sign of danger, Leopold, Yanis and the girls returned to their campsite. Nobosi went reluctantly, glancing over his shoulder to growl as he went.

Not convinced no danger existed, Rais stayed back for a closer look. He poked his spear into the depth of the crevice but touched nothing. Weary after the trek, he sank onto a rocky ledge to rest. Placing the torch and spear at his feet, he leaned back and closed his eyes.

A sudden blast of hot air hit his face. His eyes flew open. There on the ledge beside him sat a young croragon. Teeth bared, it breathed fire, and started to skulk towards him, its reptilian body and squat legs moving in a slow and deliberately menacing manner. Stark terror coursed through Rais, trampling his exhaustion. He took a flying leap off the ledge, shouting a warning as he landed. He charged for the entrance but skidded to a halt when he saw that a fully-grown croragon blocked his way. His heart raced as he faced the beast. He turned back for his spear. The young creature blasted flames his way. He had nowhere to go. He screamed for help.

Nobosi reached the entrance before his companions and charged at the closest croragon, barking fiercely, leaving the reptile in no doubt of his intention. It turned and sent a blast of flame his way, but Nobosi didn't stop his charge. The smell of charred fur reached Kanda's nose as she rushed to stop his attack. "No, Nobosi, come back!" she screamed.

He ignored her and barking furiously rushed at the croragon again. His barking angered the creatures and they hurtled towards Nobosi and Kanda.

Rais tore back for his spear. He and Leopold shouted for Kanda to run, but she shook her head, and tried to drag Nobosi to safety. The youths threw their spears. Their target fell, but, unfortunately, they had both aimed for the adult croragon. With its parent dead, the young one went into a frenzy and continued towards Kanda and Nobosi, fire blasting from its mouth. Rais dived onto its back, his only thought to save Kanda. He wrestled it to the ground.

However, he had not counted on the strength of the beast. Rais hung on with a vice-like grip as the reptile flayed about, his powerful tail thrashing through the air. The rest of the group watched in horror, shouting for him to let go. Leopold tried to get close enough to the dead croragon to retrieve his spear, but the battle blocked his way. He knew that one blow from that thrashing tail would break his legs. He rushed back to the camp to look for another weapon.

Kanda let go of Nobosi and grabbed her spear. She and her pet charged towards the struggling pair. "Rais, let go so I can spear him."

"No, get back," her brother shouted breathlessly.

Nobosi attacked, trying to catch hold of the flaying tail of the creature. But he was no match for the croragon, and it tossed him aside with a flick of its powerful body.

Caria and Yanis grabbed Kanda and pulled her to safety. She struggled against their grip, but they were too strong for her. Leopold appeared with Palesa's spear and joined Markos in trying to get a shot at the croragon.

"Let go now and roll away," Markos commanded.

Exhausted, Rais gratefully obeyed. However, they hadn't counted on the croragon's reaction. As soon as it was free, the creature turned on Rais and attacked him with a furious blast of fire. Leopold and Markos threw their spears. The croragon slumped to the floor, dead.

Kanda rushed to Rais' side. "Are you okay," she asked. There was no reply or movement. Then she saw the burns on the side of his arm and face and screamed, "He's hurt. Quick, help him!"

Markos and Yanis rushed to his side. Holding her breath, Kanda whispered, "He's not moving. Is he dead?" She closed her eyes trying to fight the wave of despair that swept over her.

Leopold put an arm around her and gently pulled her out of the way so Markos could examine her twin.

"He's just unconscious. He would have passed out from the pain of the burns. Let's get him back to the other cave," Markos said.

They lifted him carefully, carried him back, and placed him on his bedroll.

"What can we do?" Kanda cried. Caria and Palesa fell to their knees beside his prone form, tears streaming down their faces.

All eyes turned to Markos as he sorted through the contents of his pack. "I can give him a potion to ease the pain – but I have nothing that will heal burns as severe as that." Taking out a vial, he held it to Rais' mouth, forcing him to swallow.

The group held their breath as they waited for a reaction. None came and they turned to Markos in despair.

Panic showed in Palesa's face. She wasn't sure now if she was worried about Rais or the reward. She shouted, "Will someone do something?"

"It didn't work. What else can we do?" Kanda asked.

Markos patted her arm reassuringly. "It will take some time for the potion to work. Yanis, do you have anything that will heal the burns?"

Yanis shook his head. "Mother could heal him, but he would never make it back to her."

"Yes, you're right. We'll just have to do our best. The first thing we must do is bathe his wounds, so they don't become infected."

"The bathing pool – Mother uses sulphur to help heal our wounds," Caria said.

Markos sighed with relief, "Yes, that's perfect. Place him in the pool, boys."

Rais stirred as they lifted him and lowered him into the water, but his eyes remained closed. Kanda dug in her bag to find something soft to put under his head. As she pulled out her wrap, the book she had seen under the seats fell out. She glanced at it curiously, but her mind was on Rais. She folded the wrap on her lap and placed his head on it. She sat holding his head above the water, sponging his face with the end of her wrap, and quietly begging him to wake. Her mind swirled, searching for a way to help him. Her heart was heavy with worry that he would die in her arms.

The old man had been pacing anxiously searching his mind for a way to aid Rais. He saw the book lying on the ground and picked it up. He flicked through the pages. A letter dropped out. He picked it up and read it, his eyes lighting up with hope. "Kanda, there may be a way to help Rais. Palesa or Caria, take her place please."

The two girls rushed to obey, and a small tussle ensued. Finally, Caria backed down and Kanda reluctantly turned the task over to Palesa. Caria slumped down beside her, staring at Rais as if her intense gaze could cure and waken him.

His face lit with optimism, Markos held up the book and placed his hand on Kanda's shoulders. "Kanda, have you looked at this book?"

Kanda shrugged. "No. It fell out of my pack when we were under the stadium seats. I have never seen it before that. Nona must have put it in there. What is it?"

"It's a book on healing. Your mother is a healer. Have you ever tried healing?"

Kanda shook her head, but her expression changed to hopeful. "No… my mother is a healer?"

"One of the best. She sent this book with you when you left the palace. Read the letter." Markos solemnly handed it to her.

Kanda read, her eyes swimming with tears.

My dear Kanda.

Healing powers are possessed by the women of our family line. I'm sure you will have them too. If I am not there to help you learn when you become old enough for the powers to show, what is in this book will be all you need.

Love

Mother.

"She says I should have her healing power. What do I have to do; tell me quick?" she begged.

Markos spread his hands in a gesture of helplessness. "I don't know. I am not a healer."

"Maybe I'm not either," Kanda said biting her lip and staring at Rais.

Markos held out the book. "I guess there couldn't be a better time to try than now."

Kanda took the book reverently. A stamped image of two open hands, palms down, adorned the book's leather cover. Inside were spells and potions for healing. Searching quickly through them, she soon found the healing spell for injuries.

The instructions read:

Hold the healer's pendant in your hand
Over the patient you must stand.
Fill a bowl with dawning dew
Picture the skin become as new.
Sprinkle the dew as you chant these words:
"The healing light I call to me
Heal these wounds that all can see

Make the skin as it was before
And take the pain so there is no more."

Kanda lifted troubled eyes to Markos. "It says I need a healer's pendant, and dawning dew. Where am I supposed to get dew in these caves, and what pendant?"

Markos frowned and reached into his pack. "I have a vial of dawning dew with me. It is good for mixing potions, but I don't know what pendant it refers to."

In frustration, Kanda flung the book to the ground. "So, this is no help at all," she cried. The sound of metal striking rock echoed around the cave as it hit the floor. Curious, Kanda recovered the tome. A pendant on a chain hung out of a pocket in the back-cover lining.

Her skin crawled with excitement. The pendant sparkled in the torch light. The book's front cover symbol appeared on its golden face. Eyes alight with exhilaration, Markos took the pendant and placed it around Kanda's neck. A shiver passed through her body and a faint white glow surrounded her for a moment. Kanda took the vial of dew and a small wooden bowl from Markos. "Oh, Markos, do you really think I can do this? she said hopefully.

"It can't hurt to try. You have nothing to lose."

Kanda turned to stare at Rais. *But if I don't try, I could lose Rais.* She read the instructions again and, taking a deep breath, she practiced the chant.

Her body tingled from head to toe, and a feeling of great energy coursed through her as she said the words. Confidence she had never experienced before settled over her. She walked slowly and sedately to Rais. Leopold and Yanis stood beside him. She smiled at them and said,

"Please take him out of the water and place him on the floor." She filled the bowl with the dew.

Rais' eyes flew open when they lifted him from the water. His scream of pain echoed around the cave, as the cool air hit his burns. He clutched his burnt arm and a searing pain, more severe than he had ever experienced before, attacked his senses. Groaning, he slumped back into unconsciousness.

Her confidence shaken for a moment by the pain in Rais' eyes, Kanda hesitated. However, while she practised the healing chant in her mind, the confident feeling returned. She stood over his still body, clutching the pendant so hard that the edges almost broke the skin of her palm. She pictured Rais' body as it was before. A tear came to her eye as she saw him whole and strong. As she sprinkled the dew and chanted the healing words, the white glow that she had seen when Markos placed the pendant on her neck spread around her. It soon encompassed Rais' body until he glowed like a lighted torch.

When the spell was complete, the glow disappeared. Kanda's strength and confidence went with it. Weakness and fatigue claimed her, and her body folded like wet newspaper onto the floor. Leopold rushed to her side, cradling her head in his lap, and stroking her face gently.

She woke just as Rais sat up and rushed to his side. "Rais are you okay?" she cried.

Her brother looked down at his arm in wonder. The new skin was pink and healthy. "What happened? How did the burn heal so quickly?"

Markos checked where the burns had been, and smiling, declared, "Your sister healed you. Thankfully, she has inherited your mother's healing powers."

"I did, didn't I?" Kanda whispered.

The twins hugged each other tightly. Rais pushed her back and stared into her face. "Healing powers? What do you mean?"

Kanda handed him the letter and held up the book. Tears ran down his cheeks as he read the letter.

He shook his head in wonder. He reached out and hugged his sister again. "A healer... wow! You're just awesome... thank you," he whispered hoarsely. He rose to his feet, and staggered when Caria and Palesa both tried to hug him at the same time. He hugged Palesa briefly, then warmly took Caria into his arms.

Tears of frustration and anger came to Palesa's eyes. She ran off to the next cave, and threw herself down on her bedroll, sobbing. Yanis hesitated long enough to shake Rais' hand and hug Kanda, then went to Palesa's side. "Are you okay?"

"I didn't mean to upset Rais. But now he hates me," Palesa sobbed.

Yanis took her hand. "We will not be with you for long, and when Caria is out of the picture, you will have a chance to make it up to him."

Palesa's pride took over and scrubbing her damp cheeks dry she snapped, "I may not want to then." Startled by the venom in her voice, Yanis moved away. Palesa's thoughts returned to the plan she had made earlier, and her eyes narrowed maliciously. *I just have to get Leopold alone.*

CHAPTER TEN

Treachery

Leopold took the first watch at the entrance to the cave while his companions slept. Palesa feigned sleep until the others had settled, then crept to his side. "I can't sleep, so I thought I would keep you company. Is that all right?" she said smiling sweetly.

Leopold shrugged. "If you like. I'm having trouble staying awake. I think that incident with the gas has taken more out of me than I thought."

"I'll keep you awake," Palesa assured him. Then, taking a deep breath to give her courage she blurted, "Do you know that Yaholo has offered a reward and the freedom of the city to whoever brings him the twins?"

"Really? I knew he was after them, but I didn't know he had offered a reward."

Palesa nodded. "Wouldn't that be great – lots of money, and the freedom to live in the city as an honoured resident; who wouldn't want that?"

"Sure, that would be anyone's dream, but not at the cost of having Kanda and Rais thrown in prison … or worse."

The girl's eyes narrowed as she contemplated her next move. "If we get caught in their company, we could all end up in prison."

"Mmm … I hadn't thought of that."

His hesitation spurred her on and, choosing her words carefully she said, "What would you do if it looked like we were about to be caught ... hand them in or go to prison?"

"I couldn't hand Kanda in. I would fight to protect her."

"But what if there was no way to save them, would you just go to prison too?"

"What are you saying, that you would hand them in? Really, Palesa, I thought that you liked Rais?"

Deciding she had better choose her words carefully, she said, "I do... I did... but now... he seems interested in that pale imitation of a person, Caria... so..." Not sure how far to go, she paused.

Leopold was gazing off into space. "I wonder what Yaholo wants with them. What would happen to them if they were captured? I wouldn't want Kanda to get hurt."

Palesa could see that Leopold was getting upset, so, stumbling over her words, she added, "If Briador decides to take the twins back to the city, I don't think we will have any hope of sneaking in without getting caught, so... if it looks like we will... get caught, I mean... we could please Yaholo by handing them in, then you could plead with him to save Kanda's life and let her live in the palace. It would be a way of making sure she was safe."

Leopold's brow furrowed as he considered her words. Then, he shook his head. "No way. You couldn't trust that snake. We have to keep them safe."

"Of course." Palesa smiled grimly as she turned away. *Safe in prison for the rest of their lives.* Frustrated by the outcome of their talk, she moved back to her bed. She didn't want to be seen talking to Leopold when Rais came to take his place. Everything hinged now on getting back into Rais' good books, so she could carry out her plan.

Rais lay on his bedroll watching this scene. He wondered what they had to talk about – especially now that Leopold had made it obvious that he favoured Kanda. *She is so two-faced. One minute she is begging me to forgive her and then next she is sneaking off to have private conversations with Leo. I can't make her out. I really thought she was special.*

CHAPTER ELEVEN

Furry Fiends in Their Gangs

Over breakfast, they discussed the next clue in the warning verse. Yanis frowned in concentration. *"Furry fiends in their gangs'*, what could that mean? There are no furry animals down here that I know of."

Leopold peered into the passage ahead. "What about on the surface of the mountain, we must be getting close now?"

"Not sure what lives out there. Father does bring home the meat and fur of an animal called a cassum, but I don't think they're dangerous."

"There is the liogon of course," Kanda said as she stroked Nobosi's head thoughtfully.

Rais stared at Nobosi. "Yeah. I never think of them as savage because they are so easily tamed, but I guess there could be wild ones on the other side of the mountain."

Markos rose to his feet. "We don't have time to discuss this. Let's be on our way and be cautious. If we don't reach the surface soon, we'll run out of food."

"Father said it is two suns walk to the surface from our home. I'm sure the time that has passed is close to that. We should reach there soon if we pick up our pace," Yanis said as he shrugged into his backpack.

They moved cautiously past the dead croragons in the next cave and into a passage as dark and narrow as the previous ones. Kanda had handed her torch to Palesa and walked with Leopold. He took her offered hand and smiled, but he was distant and moody. Palesa pushed past and his grip on Kanda's hand tightened. Kanda glanced up. His expression was grim as he glared at Palesa's back. The others were close, so she didn't ask what was wrong.

After walking for some time, the path became steeper. "We must be getting close," Yanis called from the lead. They gave a shout of joy and their spirits lifted with each step.

Kanda looked back at Markos and could see that he was tiring. She left Leopold and took his arm to help him. Finally, she called to Rais to stop for a break. Markos' body folded wearily, and he sank to the floor.

Rais hurried after Yanis, who was out of earshot, to tell him they had stopped so Markos could rest. Before he reached him, he heard a shout and increased his pace. He hurtled around the next corner to find Yanis' backpack in the middle of the path. A track continued on the left, but footprints led into the narrow passage to the right. Rais moved forward cautiously. As he took a step around a curve, he yelped in surprise. He teetered on the edge of a huge hole in the path. He threw himself backwards, recovered and crawled to the rim. Peering over, he saw the still bodies of Yanis and a stranger.

The hole was about the depth of four strides. Rais searched frantically for a way to climb down. He called Yanis' name, but he didn't stir. He raced back to the others, calling for help.

Leopold came to meet him and Rais told him what he had found. "We need a rope to lower one of us into the hole. I think Markos has one."

They hurried back to their guide and explained the situation. He rummaged in his pack and produced the rope, then went to rise.

"You stay here. We can manage," Rais told him. He and the rest of the group disappeared down the passage; except Kanda, who hesitated to leave Markos.

The old man gratefully resumed his rest. "You go with them, Kanda, they will need you. Here take my pack, some potions are in there. They are named and the uses will be explained in your book."

Clutching her healer's pendant nervously, Kanda said, "I guess I had better go, in case I can help. Will you be okay?"

Markos smiled reassuringly. "I'll be fine. I'll catch up soon. Just be careful."

When Kanda reached the scene of the fall, they were about to lower Rais into the hole. Leopold stood well back, with the rope tied around his waist. The two girls were holding the end behind him. Kanda hurried to the side of the hole and watched Rais' progress.

Her brother looked up. "Kanda, there's a strange smell in here – a bit like sulphur, but stronger."

She lay down and put her head into the hole to sniff the air. She pulled back quickly gasping for fresh air.

"Leopold! Stop lowering him. Get him up. There's gas at the bottom of the hole. That same smell came from the cave where you were poisoned!"

Leopold stopped and Kanda called to Rais. "They're bringing you up."

Rais' head lolled, but he nodded. He tried to use his feet to help them, but he was too groggy. With great effort, they managed to bring him to the edge and Kanda helped him onto the ground.

Rais tried to sit, but he couldn't do it. "Sleepy," he whispered closing his eyes.

"No, Rais, you mustn't go to sleep," Kanda cried, shaking him.

Palesa stood back watching, trying to harden her heart against the anxiety she was feeling.

Caria knelt beside him.

"Caria, keep him awake while I find the potion. There's no time for me to find the right spell," Kanda said.

The potion that Markos had used for Leopold was still near the top of the bag and Kanda recognised the label. Taking off the stopper, she mixed a few drops in a bowl of water and held it to her brother's mouth. Rais lifted his head and swallowed, then slumped back onto Caria's lap. Caria turned an anxious face to Leopold. "That is my father down there with Yanis. We must get them out."

"We will. Don't worry," Leopold assured her.

Rais sat up shaking his head. "How can we get down there? The gas starts halfway."

Then a voice behind them spoke. "You can do it, Kanda. You can create an air bubble around you, so the gas has no effect on you."

102

Kanda gazed at Markos, a look of wonder on her face. "I can?"

"Yes, it is sure to be in the book. On one occasion your mother created an air bubble that enclosed her and your father."

"Then I'm going with her," Rais stated.

"No, it is too soon after your treatment. However, Leopold can take the chance, as he will still have some immunity."

Leopold had already walked to Kanda's side. "No problem. I wouldn't let her go without me anyway."

Kanda had been searching through the book; she looked up and smiled gratefully. "I found it. I need room to perform this spell. The wider the space the bigger the air bubble I can create." The group backed away and pressed up against the walls, leaving her with the most space they could in the narrow tunnel.

She read the spell again, reached into her backpack for a wrap and stood straight. "I hope it's long enough to create a big enough bubble to enclose both of us." She held it at arm's length, clutched her pendant and started to twirl. The garment swished through the air around her. The rest of the group threw themselves to the floor as it threatened to decapitate them. As Kanda gathered momentum, she started the chant:

Oh, spirit of the winds
I call on you today
to purify the air around me
and keep the gas at bay.
Give us your protection
to complete the task at hand

till we return to this spot,

the one where I now stand.

As she spoke, a blue glow appeared and spun with her, encircling her from head to toe and out as far as the end of her flying wrap. When she had finished, she stood in a glowing blue cocoon. Her heart raced, her head spun, and she swayed on her feet.

Outside the circle of air, the floor's loose surface swirled as if churned up by a whirly-wind. Her companions rose to their feet, shielding their eyes from the flying dirt and stones. They backed away as the fierce wind threatened to blow them into the cave-in. Kanda called Leopold. He tried to push through the blustering wind, but it was too strong. Just as he felt his feet lift off the ground, Kanda reached out and took his hand, pulling him to her. He stumbled into the cocoon, amazed at the calmness inside. Kanda clung to his arm until her head cleared. "There's lots of room in the air-lock for you too," she said with a sigh of relief.

They hurried to the edge of the hole. Rais tried to get close with the rope, but the buffeting winds almost pushed him over the edge. "How are we going to lower you? The wind is too strong for me to get close enough to hand you the rope. Besides, your combined weight would be too much for us to hold."

Kanda smiled confidently. "That won't be a problem. We don't need a rope. The wind will take us."

"What do you mean?" both Leopold and Rais said together.

"The spell allows me to float on the wind around me." They looked at her with amazement. She took Leopold's hand. "Trust me. We must hurry. Stay inside the bubble or you may fall."

Leopold wrapped his arm around her, holding her tightly to his side. Taking a deep breath, he said, "This will be safer. If you're sure… let's do it."

Her heart pounded with excitement, but strangely, she had no fear. "I'm sure," Kanda said and they stepped off together. They floated to the bottom of the hole, dust swirling around them, and moved quickly to the injured pair, covering them with dust and pebbles until they were standing over them. Kanda crouched down, pulling Leopold with her. As they crouched, the air bubble expanded and surrounded Yanis and his father as well.

"What have you found?" Markos called.

Wiping the dust and gravel from Yanis' face, Kanda replied, "Yanis is still breathing strongly, but I can't find Wason's pulse. He hit his head on a rock when he fell. There's blood under his head."

"Give Yanis the potion that I gave Leopold. Then place your hands on either side of Wason's head and seek his life-force. If he is alive, the healthy sections of his body will glow pink, and show red where he is injured."

Kanda frowned. "You mean like trying to read his mind?"

"Yes, but seek further. It will work if you are strong enough."

Kanda wasn't sure what he meant but was willing to try. She forced Yanis to drink the mixture then turned to Wason. Clutching each side of his cold head, she concentrated on seeing inside his body. "Nothing," she called to Markos.

"Try it on Yanis. That way you will know if you are doing it right."

Nervously, she held Yanis' head and repeated what she had done. Suddenly his body glowed pink, with deep red over his lungs. Her skin crawled with excitement. "It worked! His lungs are red, but the rest of him is pink." She again placed her hands on Wason's head. "There must be something I can do ..." She tried again. Still no result. Above, she heard Caria's sobbing and Rais' murmured sympathy.

Leopold put his hand on Kanda's reassuringly. "He's gone, Kanda. There's nothing you can do."

She nodded sadly. "How will we get them up there? Could we tie them to the rope one at a time and let Rais and the girls haul them?"

Leopold shook his head. "They are a dead weight. Rais and the girls won't be strong enough."

"We'll have to wake Yanis so he can help." She shook Yanis, but he didn't respond. Kanda sighed and reached into her bag and drew out the bottle of dawning dew and the bowl. "Well, I guess I'll have to use my healing spell here. I hope it works if I am kneeling, because if I stand, the bubble won't be big enough for all of us." Opening her book to the right page, she silently rehearsed the chant. Her body sang with energy.

She kneeled beside Yanis and pictured him standing before her, healthy and strong. Sprinkling the dew, she said,

"The healing light I call to me
To heal the wounds that I can't see
Make Yanis as he was before

106

And immune to this poison forever more."

Kanda experienced the same euphoria she had felt the first time. The white healing light flowed from her and surrounded Yanis. Then the light disappeared, and she slumped to the floor. Leopold held her while her strength returned. She remained a moment longer, revelling in his loving touch, pleased that he was no longer distant. Brought out of her daze by Yanis opening his eyes and trying to sit she said, "Yanis, thank goodness. How do you feel?"

"I… don't know. Fine, I guess, but what happened?" Seeing his father beside him, he cried, "Father! Is he okay?" He shook his head as his memory returned. "The path had caved in. I saw him down here and jumped down. I left my pack on the path as a warning, and so you would know I was still nearby. But then I don't remember anything."

"The cave-in is full of gas. I think the same one as in the cave back there. You passed out from the effect of it," Kanda told him.

"What is that light?" he said, noticing the glowing blue air bubble for the first time.

"We are in a protective air bubble created by Kanda's healing magic," Leopold told him, adding, "but you shouldn't need it. Kanda healed you and made you immune."

"What about Father? Did you do a healing on him? Why doesn't he wake up?"

Kanda bit her lip anxiously. "I think he may have been down here too long, and he has hit his head. I sought his life-force but found nothing."

Yanis put his head on his father's chest listening for a heartbeat. "He can't be dead. We must get him to Mother. She will heal him." Tears came to his eyes and, sobbing, he slumped over his father.

Finally, Kanda brushed away her tears and said, "Come on, Yanis – we'll take him out of here and see if your mother can do anything to help him."

Yanis picked up his father's body and walked through the blue light. He staggered as the wind hit him but gained his balance and strode to the side of the hole. Leopold and Kanda followed, the swirling air bubble throwing dust and gravel all around them. It pelted Yanis' legs, but numb with grief, he didn't notice.

"Throw down the rope," Leopold called to Rais.

The rope snaked down the wall and landed at Yanis' feet. As he tied it securely under his father's arms, Leopold said, "Rais won't be able to haul him up on his own so Kanda and I will go and help. Now that we are standing, unfortunately, the air bubble is not large enough to take you with us. Once we have your father out of here, we'll throw the rope down to you."

As they floated to the surface, Leopold held Kanda tightly. Tilting her face towards his, he said, "You were fantastic down there. You are so incredible."

A tinge of pink flushed Kanda's cheeks as a warm glow spread through her body. "Thank you, but I didn't save Wason. I guess I'm not much of a healer."

Markos heard her remark and, as the wind abated, he hugged her and said, "No-one can bring someone back from the dead, Kanda. You did very well to heal Yanis."

Kanda brightened a little, but still turned troubled eyes to a sobbing Caria. Rais sat beside her, lost for words, his hand stroked her back, his face contorted in shared grief.

Kanda turned to look for Palesa. The girl stood back leaning against the cave wall, picking at her nails, trying, unsuccessfully to look unconcerned.

"Come and give us a hand, Palesa," Kanda called. The girl grunted but came forward to help.

Working together, they soon raised Wason and Yanis. After he was safely at the top, Yanis gently hugged his sister. "Come, Caria, we will take Father home." Turning to Rais he said, "I'm sorry, but you must go on without us. It is not far now. Take that left path and it will take you around the cave-in, and then take the right path at the next fork." He eased his father's body over his shoulder and strode off in the direction of their home. Caria hesitated, turning to Rais.

Rais hugged her. "I'll come back as soon as I can. You must help Yanis with your father."

Caria kissed his cheek, and brushing away tears, hurried after Yanis. Rais stood for a moment staring after her, then, raising his head, and taking a deep breath he said, "Let's go."

Palesa's eyes had misted as she watched the kiss and the loving gaze on Rais' face as he watched her walk away. *He used to give me the same look,* she thought. Anger soon replaced jealousy. Biting her lip to stop an angry remark, she turned her back and stalked ahead. The rest of the group, all saddened by the death of their friend's father, walked soberly into the left passage.

The surface was more rugged, dry, and dusty on this rarely used path. The walls were narrow. Jagged rocks protruded from them and down from the ceiling. The gradient was steep, and the group moved cautiously, dodging the obstacles. At one point, the passage was barely wide enough for one person to pass through at a time. Kanda closed her eyes and clung tightly to Leopold's hand as she squeezed through the gap ahead of him.

Panic gripped her body as her clothes caught, trapping her. "I can't move. The walls are closing on me. Get me out! Please get me out!" she screamed as she struggled to free herself.

Leopold squeezed her hand. "Kanda, stop struggling. The walls are not moving. I can't free your clothes while you are wriggling. Take a deep breath and stand very still."

Trembling, Kanda stood, eyes closed, as Leopold worked to free her.

"Okay, move forward now," he said quietly. Kanda opened her eyes and tentatively moved forward. She stumbled out the other side and collapsed on the path.

Leopold joined her and held her until the trembling stopped. Concerned, Rais and Markos stood waiting for her to be ready to move on, but Palesa, still seething with jealousy, scowled and paced impatiently. "We'll never get to the surface at this rate. What with little Miss Fearful and the old man, we'll die of starvation before we make it."

Rais turned smouldering eyes on her. "If you want to go on by yourself, feel free. Then we won't have to listen to your whining any longer."

Palesa glared at him and stalked off. "Seems as if you couldn't care less if I'm safe, so I'll just do that," she shouted over her shoulder.

"Palesa!" Markos called, "It's not safe to travel alone in these passages."

She didn't stop or bother to reply and soon disappeared out of sight. Rais sighed. "She won't go too far ahead. She's not that brave. We'll soon catch up."

Rais was right. When they turned into the right-hand passage at the next fork, there she was, sitting leaning against the wall chewing on her last piece of dried fish. "Just wanted to make sure you took the right path," she muttered.

He just nodded and swept past. She jumped to her feet and fell in beside him. "Rais, I know I have upset you, but can't we please be friends again?"

He didn't take his eyes off the path as he replied, "Friends work together. They don't think about only their needs; especially in dangerous situations."

"Yes, I know. Please, please forgive me!" She slipped her arm through his and looked longingly at his face.

Rais shrugged her hand free and increased his pace. He was not ready yet to listen to her pleas for forgiveness.

Markos stepped up beside her. "Once trust is gone it can only be earned, not asked for, Palesa."

She turned on him, a sharp retort on the tip of her tongue, but she bit it back and instead said, "I know. I guess I'll have to work on it won't I?" He nodded.

The gradient was steeper now and the path well worn. Rais was sure that they were back on the main path to the top and increased his pace expectantly. However, many tiring strides later, no sign of the entrance appeared. They were all growing weary, so Rais called a halt. "This path must be a lot longer than the usual one. We should have

111

been there by now. We'll rest here and eat a little of our last supplies."

Grateful for the break, Markos stretched out and closed his eyes. Soon he was sound asleep. Nobosi curled up protectively by his side. Rais smiled fondly as he watched Markos sleep. "I think it may be a good idea if we all try to get some shut-eye. We'll need all our strength when we reach the surface. We have no idea what we will find. There could be troops waiting for us."

The group didn't need any more prompting. Leopold laid his head on his backpack and encouraged Kanda to rest her head on his shoulder. She accepted gratefully. The familiar warmth and tingling sensation spread through her body as she snuggled into his side. She had never experienced this before and found it exciting and calming at the same time. She felt safe, and was soon fast asleep, his arm protectively around her.

Palesa moved to Rais side. "I'll keep first watch while you sleep, Rais. You must be tired after being injured, and all the hard work you have been doing."
Rais nodded gratefully and fell back on his pack. Palesa checked both directions for any sign of life then settled to watch the passage ahead. Soon her eyes grew heavy. She fought to stay awake but sleep over-powered her.

***

Sometime later, a furry body rubbing up against her arm woke Kanda. Thinking it was Nobosi she reached out to stroke his back, without opening her eyes. Her hand felt air where his body should have been, and she sat up puzzled.

She screamed as she saw a small furry animal with a wide thick tail and tiny beady eyes lift its head from rummaging in her backpack. Her scream startled the creature and it scuttled away, joined by half a dozen more that had been busy raiding the other backpacks. The rest of the group woke at her cry and witnessed the retreat of the creatures. Nobosi raced after them barking furiously.

Palesa yelped and jumped to her feet as one of the animals ran over her foot in its bid to escape. "Hell! What was that?" she asked breathlessly.

Markos was the only one who answered. "A gang of cassums. They live near the river on the upper slopes of the mountain in West Nevaah."

Rais' face lit up. "Then we must be close to the surface."

Kanda could still feel the fur on her arm and shuddered. "Are they dangerous, Markos?"

"No, they are not flesh eating – well not animal or human flesh anyway. They prefer fish."

Rais lifted his pack confidently. "They won't have got mine. My arm was on it." But when he checked he found his food sack empty. "Hell... they burrowed in the top under my arm and ate the last of my fish." He rummaged around in what remained in his bag. Shaking his head, he said, "Yep, they got the lot."

The rest of the group checked their bags with the same result. Rais turned angry eyes on Palesa.

She dropped her head in shame. "Oh Rais, I'm sorry I let you down. I must have been more tired than I thought. Oh no, it is all my fault," she said, tears springing to her eyes.

Rais' heart went out to her. She seemed so upset that he moved to her side to console her.

Leopold eyed her suspiciously. Knowing what she was prepared to do to save herself and get the reward if they were captured, her expression of sorrow didn't impress him.

Kanda noticed Leopold's look of disdain and her eyes narrowed. *I wish I had mind-reading powers on everyone,* she thought, *I would love to probe her mind and see what she is really feeling.* Markos hauled himself stiffly to his feet. "Well, with no food, we had better hope that we are close to the top. Let's get moving."

They had only moved a short distance when Nobosi came loping back. Kanda reached out to pat him and gasped with pleasure. "He's covered in leaves. The entrance must be close. He was only gone a short time."

With renewed vigour, they hurried forward – Rais in the lead. A whoop of joy escaped his lips as he stepped out of the passage and into an external cave. He blinked at the bright sunlight then stared at the vista before him. West Nevaah lay at his feet. He had never seen a more spectacular sight. On the slopes of the mountain, tall trees reached for the sky, and under them, a tangle of ferns and small bushes fought for space. The Plains of the Shifting Sands hugged the base of the mountain and stretched out to meet the fertile farming district. A patchwork of fields, in many shades of green and yellow, marked the farms, with the occasional farmhouse roof nestled contentedly between them. To the left, snaked the sparkling water of The River of Safe Passage. The sunlight bounced off its running water like fireflies skipping on the surface. In the far distance, the city's stone towers were just visible.

Kanda and Palesa cried out in delight and hugged Rais, Leopold and Markos. "We made it. We got past all the danger," Kanda cried. Her heart felt like it would burst with pleasure, and the relief of being out in the open again.

Markos held a hand up for silence. "We must be careful. The troops may have guessed we escaped into the Passage of Death and be keeping an eye on the exits."

Rais nodded his agreement. "We'll go scout around; you stay here." He headed for the entrance and gestured to Leopold to accompany him.

CHAPTER TWELVE

Captured

Kanda sat hugging her knees and looking with wonder at the view. Her eyes strayed to the far distant city walls. She wondered if there was a quicker, safer way to travel there than across the plains below. They would be easily spotted by the troops if they had to go that way. She watched Palesa pace the entrance impatiently. *I would love to know what she is thinking. I wonder if I could read her mind.* She clutched her pendant and started to probe the girl's mind, but blushed guiltily as Markos turned to her, as if he knew what she was doing. She stood and walked to the entrance.

As she paced, Palesa was deep in thought. She was trying to harden her heart against any feelings for Rais. Her jealous anger made her eager to reach the city and determined to have the reward in her hands. But she knew she needed more time to get back in favour with Rais and convince Briador to go there. Now that she was sure Leopold wouldn't help her, she could see he would be a problem. She bit her lip anxiously as her scheming mind got busy plotting her next move.

If Kanda had read her thoughts at that moment, it would have saved them all a lot of trouble.

Markos was planning his next move, but his was on a more positive note. *We are close to Briador now. It won't be long before they are safely with him.*

Lost in thought, the three didn't hear the stealthy approach of danger. Suddenly, Nobosi flew towards the side of the cave barking furiously. He met the same sound and sunk his teeth into the neck of a larger liogon. Two more of the wild creatures charged into the cave, snarling. They advanced towards the three humans. Hearts thumping in fear, Kanda, Markos and Palesa backed towards the wall of the cave, drawing their spears as they moved. Markos placed himself in front of the girls and ordered them into the passage. Palesa froze, fear paralysing her.

Kanda stood her ground. "No, we can't leave you to fight them on your own." She moved beside him, aimed, and threw her spear. It hit the closest creature in the chest and the liogon buckled to the ground.

"Good shot," Markos said, and let loose his spear. The other liogon changed direction and the weapon hit it in the front thigh and bounced off. Injured and enraged, it flinched and rushed towards them with a roar. Kanda grabbed Palesa's spear out of her shaking hand. As the wild creature leapt for her throat, she plunged the weapon into its heart. The power of the animal's charge forced the spear deeper into its chest. The momentum threw her back against the wall, the liogon on top of her. The handle of the spear pierced the ground beside her. Stunned, she fought to throw the creature off; still not sure it was dead. At that moment, Rais and Leopold raced in and flew to their side.

"Kanda!" Leopold cried as he hauled the dead animal off her. He pulled her trembling body to him. "Are you okay?"

She burst into tears and clung to him. "I am now. But I thought we were dead this time."

After checking everyone was okay, Rais hurried to Nobosi. Teeth deep in the throat of his adversary, Nobosi shook the creature with all his might. The wild liogon was not fighting back. Rais placed his hand on his pet's back, calling his name. The animal let go, but continued to stand over his dead foe, growling.

"It's okay boy, you killed him," Rais said hugging him. The liogon licked his face then turned his attention to the other dead animals, checking them carefully before going to Kanda. "Good boy, Nobosi," she cried hugging him.

The adrenaline subsiding, the group leaned against the cave wall in complete exhaustion. Finally, Kanda asked, "Did you see anything out there? Any sign of more danger, or troops?"

Rais nodded. "Yes, there are well worn tracks along the ridge line; looks like they are patrolling the caves to watch for us."

"Then we must hurry and conceal ourselves before they come back. We will head to the cave at the mouth of the river where Briador lives. I don't think the troops know about it. It is well hidden," Markos said.

As they stepped out into the bright sunlight, Markos in the lead, they cautiously scanned the area around them. No sign of danger showed. They headed for the river, scrambling over rough, uneven ground, and squeezing between large boulders. Soon the terrain became much steeper as they went down the slope to the river. Rais could see that the tired old man struggled to stay on his feet on the stony path. He called a halt and they squeezed in behind some large boulders to rest.

Rais took Leopold aside. "We will have to take turns carrying Markos on our backs. He can't make it much further under his own steam."

To Rais' surprise, the youth readily agreed. After a short break, Rais approached Markos. He knew that the man's pride would be hurt but could see no other way. "When we leave, hop on my back. I'll carry you a way," he said casually. Markos protested, but as Rais insisted, the old man's shoulders slumped in defeat. "Now I really wish you could leave me," he muttered.

Palesa had been watching from the top of the boulder. She ducked down. "Someone should scout ahead," she said, looking at Leopold.

"Good idea, I'll go," Leopold said. He squeezed through the gap and bounded over the obstacles on the path with ease.

"Cautiously, Leopold," Markos called, shaking his head.

"I don't think he knows the meaning of caution," Rais said.

Palesa watched as he disappeared from sight then slid down and joined the others.

After a short rest, Rais' loaded Markos onto his back and they headed for the gap in the rocks. Just as they went to step out, a shout ahead startled them. "Leopold," Kanda cried her hand over her mouth. She headed for the entrance. Rais stopped her and told the girls to hide. Markos slid off his back and they crouched, listening for any more voices.

Kanda sat beside Rais holding his arm tightly. "What if they got him? We have to see," she whispered. Rais just shook his head and put his finger to his lips.

After a short silence, Rais decided he would go and check if Leopold was okay. Just as he was about to move, they heard a scuffle, and raised male voices.

Her heart twisting in her chest Kanda gripped Rais' arm. "Leopold must have been seen by the troops," she whispered.

He raised his hand for silence as they heard the approach of heavy feet. They peered through the gap in the rocks. Soon two troops came into view, one of them carrying the struggling Leopold. They stood half as high again as the tallest of the Nevaahions. Their well-muscled bodies scrambled with ease over the rough, uneven terrain. Even though Leopold was tall and well-built, his captor carried him with ease.

Rais and Kanda watched until they were out of sight. Kanda's fingernails bit into his arm as she suppressed the urge to call Leopold's name and go to his defence. Her twin gritted his teeth to stop from crying out from the pain of her grip.

Palesa stood behind them a grin of satisfaction on her face. *That got him out of my way.*

Removing Kanda's fingers and rubbing his arm, Rais said, "I'll follow and see where they take him. You wait here."

Palesa rushed forward and grabbed his arm. "No, Rais, you mustn't. If you get caught, we will have no one to protect us."

Rais shook off her hand and moved towards the path. "I have to."

Kanda grabbed his arm again. "I want to come too."

He shook his head and removed her hand. "I will travel swifter and quieter on my own."

Markos nodded. "He's right. We will wait here. But be very careful not to get captured too. It is important you make it to Briador. Lives depend on it."

Rais paused. A thousand questions swirled in his mind after Markos' last remark. He shook his head. He knew asking them would do him no good. He moved cautiously in the direction the troops had taken.

Still undecided, Kanda glanced from Palesa to Markos. The thought of leaving their guide with only the surly girl for protection made her stay. Rais soon disappeared.

Palesa paced as she fretted about what would happen to Rais. She didn't want him to get captured too. Confusion over her feelings for him and the fear that his capture would leave her without the reward battled for prominence in her mind. She looked to where Kanda sat hugging her knees and biting her lip anxiously. *I've still got little Miss Fearful. She must be worth something*, she thought.

Overcome with anxiety, Kanda had slumped to the ground. Panic consumed her and her muscles tensed as she fought the urge to follow. *The two people who mean the most to me in danger, and I have to just sit here!*

CHAPTER THIRTEEN

Torture

Rais swiftly caught up with the troops and followed them at a safe distance. They took Leopold to a sturdy log hut, hidden by low bushes, not far from the mouth of the cave where the group had emerged. From the shelter of the bushes, Rais peered through the open window. He could see that it was the troop's residence. Bunks lined two walls and in the centre of the room were a crude table and a few chairs. The aroma of a meaty stew cooking on the fireplace made Rais' stomach growl with hunger.

The guardsman who had carried Leopold, tied him to a chair. Rais crept closer and pressed himself up against the back wall of the hut.

"Where are the others?" a loud gruff voice demanded. Leopold didn't reply. Rais cringed as the sound of a fist striking a body reached his ears.

"It will do you no good to resist. We will get the truth out of you eventually. And, if you die before you tell us, that will be no loss. We seek the twins. We *will* capture them. We know the mountain like the backs of our hands."

"You will never find them. They are smarter than you idiots," Leopold said.

Rais cringed before the blow this time, feeling Leopold's pain. He squeezed his fists in anger and controlled his urge to leap through the window and go to his aid. He knew he would be captured too if he tried. *Leo's only hope is for me to remain free to rescue him.*

The brutal interrogation went on for a little longer, with Leopold remaining silent. Rais' estimation of him rose with every blow, along with his anger. Finally, the interrogator kicked the chair. "The weakling has passed out. We must get back to the river end of the path to search. The twins won't be too far from where we found him."

Rais felt his pendant warm and knew that Kanda was trying to contact him. He blocked the connection. He didn't want her to find out what was happening to Leopold. He retreated to the shelter of a nearby bush and waited impatiently for the troops to leave. After he heard footsteps disappearing down the path, he cautiously crept back to look through the window. Leopold slumped in the chair, his chin on his chest, eyes swollen, and blood trickling from his mouth. Rais checked the room to see if the prisoner was the only occupant. Finding it clear, he was just about to haul himself through the window, when he heard footsteps coming his way. "Hell! One stayed behind," he muttered. He swung through the opening and flattened himself against the inside wall.

The guard strolled by. Rais crouched and ran to Leopold's side. "Leo," he cried shaking him gently. Leopold's eyes opened a slit and he started when he saw Rais kneeling there. "Get out of here. Get back to Kanda and keep her safe," he mumbled between swollen lips.

Rais was busy untying the ropes. "I have to get you out. Can you walk?"

"I think so. But they left a guard. He will be back any second."

As Rais tossed the ropes aside and pulled Leopold to his feet, they heard the guard round the end of the cabin. Half carrying his staggering friend, Rais hurried out the door. They hid in the nearest bushes; fearing travelling a further distance would alert the sentry to their presence.

The trooper looked in the door as he marched by. Seeing the prisoner missing, he charged into the room. The youths moved deeper into the undergrowth. They crouched in hiding as their enemy scouted the area briefly. He then ran down the path, shouting to raise the alarm.

Rais, assisting his injured companion, went further into the dense bush, staying low and looking for shelter. They found it in the form of a giant tree. From the widespread, above ground, root system, two trunks grew and joined a few strides from the ground. The section where they met was hollow. Rais scrambled in on top of the roots and hauled Leopold up beside him.

Squashed into the small space, they held their breath as the troops searched the area. Relief fought with the desire to flee as Rais forced himself to remain calm and still. Leopold collapsed against him. Rais whispered, "You okay?" A slight nod was all he received in reply, but that was enough to reassure him. He hated to admit it, but he admired Leopold's strength. He was not sure he could have withstood that kind of beating without giving something away. Grudgingly he said, "I don't know how you held up during that beating. Thanks for not giving us away."

Leopold muttered, "I did it for Kanda, not for you. But thanks for getting me out."

They lapsed into a brooding silence. Leopold's weight against him increased and Rais checked his pulse to establish that he was still alive. He was reassured to find it strong. He hoped that meant he was asleep, not unconscious, but he was not game to wake him to check. The sun was sliding into darkness before Rais was game to move. The troops had returned in the direction of the hut, and he prayed that meant they were giving up until suntime. He shook Leopold awake and they jumped down from their hiding place. Their muscles stiff from the enforced inactivity in the cramped space, they groaned as they stretched.

Rais noticed Leopold clutched his chest, his breathing ragged. "You okay?"

"My wounds are throbbing, and every movement is painful. I took a few heavy blows. Might have a cracked rib I think." He took a deep breath before continuing, "But I'll be okay. We must return to Kanda and the others. The troops may find them."

"You sure you're okay to head back? You don't look so good."

Leopold grimaced as he moved, but said, "Just try and stop me."

As quietly as possible, they crept past the hut, noting with relief that the troopers they had seen earlier were there, eating a meal. Rais paused long enough to check the hut for signs of prisoners. To his relief there was no evidence they had captured Markos or the girls.

Leopold's face contorted into a look of loathing as he passed. "You'll pay for that," he muttered.

In the faint light from the cabin, Rais could see bruises' appearing on his companion's battered face and body. The enforced rest would have given him time to regain some strength, but Rais was concerned about the severity of his injuries. He walked hugging his chest. His eyes were just slits, and he seemed to have trouble focusing, but he knew his determination would keep him moving.

After a short time, his breathing became laboured and Rais worried that he would not make it back to the others. He kept a close eye on him as they trudged through the darkness jumping at shadows; startled by every noise. Once they reached the open area where the troops had captured Leopold, the moonlight guided their way. Rais paused to stare at the moon's surface, his face grim. *Looks like we lost about 4 suns in that passage. If we have far to go, we may not make it now.* Their steps quickened in anticipation as they moved closer to the group's hiding place.

Suddenly, a shadow fell over them and they dropped to the ground, hearts racing. Then it landed on the boulder beside Rais. "Owl! Man, am I glad to see you," Rais said, sighing and stroking the bird.

With Owl perched on his shoulder, they quickly covered the rest of the distance and slipped in between the boulders where he had left Markos and the girls. They were not there. Rais sank to the ground in despair. "Where could they be? They weren't in the hut."

"Maybe they moved on to a safer place," Leopold suggested.

Rais chewed his lower lip. "Wherever they are, I hope they're safe."

CHAPTER FOURTEEN

A Flight to Safety

As soon as Rais was out of sight, following Leopold and the troops, Markos struggled to his feet. "We must find a better hiding place. They will soon be back looking for us."

Palesa shook her head. "I'll wait. If nothing happens soon, I'm going after them."

Markos opened his mouth to protest, but Kanda beat him to it. Anger flared as she turned on the girl. "Palesa, quite frankly, I couldn't care less what you do. I have had it with your selfishness. Putting yourself in danger won't help anyone. The troops will soon capture you, and then Rais will have to rescue you as well. Besides, I hate to think what those men would do to you if they caught you. If you're not worried about that, go right ahead."

Palesa hesitated for a moment, a look of shock on her face. Kanda took Markos by the arm and left the shelter of the rocks. As she moved away, she glanced back, to see a sulky-faced Palesa two steps behind. Kanda nodded in satisfaction. She understood Palesa's urge to go find the boys; she wanted to do that too, but her common sense told her that going with Markos to a more secure shelter was the right thing to do.

Palesa strode angrily behind her, eyes shooting daggers into Kanda's back. *She is really starting to drive me crazy. Just wait until I turn her in – then we'll see how smart she is.* Then her conscience sunk its teeth into her. She stumbled along behind Markos and Kanda, eyes down. *I know I owe them for saving my life, but I have to turn them in; without the reward I will have nothing.*

Kanda helped Markos to negotiate the rocky terrain as they headed for the dense forest that bordered the river. Once in the shelter of the trees, Kanda stopped. "I'm going to contact Rais to see what is happening."

"It won't work if he is more than a few hundred strides away," Markos warned.

Palesa stood nearby watching Kanda anxiously, hoping that they would soon have some news. Kanda clutched her owl pendant and concentrated hard on Rais. Her heart raced when she received the panic in her brother's mind; then he blocked her contact. "He won't let me in," she wailed.

Markos put a reassuring hand on her arm. "There must be a good reason for that, Kanda. Maybe he is worried you will distract him from whatever he is doing. Leave it now. We must hurry to the cave."

Tears sprang to Kanda's eyes and a feeling of complete helplessness consumed her.

Palesa, her hopes dashed, and her heart heavy with worry and confusion, followed blindly as Markos led the way, urging the girls to hurry. The urgency of their situation, and the fact that the girls only had him for protection caused adrenaline to surge through his tired and frail body, giving him extra strength.

The forest undergrowth grew thicker the closer they got to the river. Flowering bushes filled the cool air with fragrance and Kanda paused for a second to breathe it in. The terrain was smoother here, but the gradient was steep. Giant trees reached for the sky, creating a dense canopy. Small shafts of sunlight managed to sneak through between the leaves lighting the tops of the foliage below and creating shadows that danced around them like pixies as the trees swayed in the breeze.

Normally, Kanda would have loved this walk through the forest, but not this time. She and Palesa glanced about them nervously, but Markos hardly took his eyes from the direction they had to follow. Nobosi roamed around them, staying close, but sniffing for any sign of animals or danger. The undergrowth of tough thorny bushes and vines was becoming impenetrable. Kanda saw that their guide was struggling to push through, so she moved in front of him, using her spear as a barge pole to clear a path for them. Palesa was quite content to stay back and let her and Markos lead the way.

Soon, Kanda's legs were growing weary, and scratches covered her face and arms. When she heard falling water, her spirits lifted. "I hear the waterfall!" She picked up her pace and soon came to the rocky bank of the river. As she stepped out of the forest, a light mist drenched her hair and settled on her wrap. She ducked back. From the shelter of the bushes, she stared in awe at the power and majesty of the waterfall in front of her. It leapt roaring over the precipice like a ferocious ogre; confident that it could consume all that stood in its way. It dived about 300 strides down into the pool below, where the water bubbled like a boiling cauldron.

Markos came up beside her. "Follow me," he said. He stayed in the edge of the forest and climbed in the direction of the falling water. Soon they passed the growling giant and headed up the slope towards its birthplace, the precipice. Markos stopped, and struggling for breath, he pointed up the rocky hill. "See that big boulder; we have to climb to there."

As they stepped out of the cover of the forest, Kanda looked around nervously. She took the old man's arm, and with Palesa following, they finally reached the landmark. Markos stopped for a breath, and they took the time to look around. They were about halfway to the top of the falls and the view to the valley was breathtaking.

"Wow, from here you can see all the way into the edge of the city," Kanda said. She traced the journey of the river monster as it thrust hungrily through gorges of the soft rock, constantly devouring them. She lost sight of it as it disappeared for a time over a rise not far below. In the distance, she could see where it snaked through the Plains of the Shifting Sand, then along the edge of the farming district before it veered away from The Walled City.

The only place visible that you could join its journey was a small, relatively flat area on the other side, not far below the bottom of the falls. Then it plunged between high rocky cliffs that protected its travellers from sight. On the plains below, it had consumed the sand and created the same high banks on both sides. It finally returned to the surface on a rocky outcrop just before the farming district.

"It is not hard to work out how The River of Safe Passage got its name when you see it from here, but why are the sandy plains called the Plains of the Shifting Sands, Markos?" Kanda said staring into the distance at the river.

"You will, unfortunately, find out if Briador takes you that way. Come, we mustn't stay too long on the slope. We are totally exposed," Markos said. He moved towards their destination with Palesa close behind.

Kanda frowned then shrugged. *It can't be that bad, surely.*

She would change her mind about that.

She took one more look at the vista and turned to find that her companions had disappeared. She hurried forward and stood uncertainly at the side of the boulder. It was hard up against the solid rock behind it. There was no sign of them. She spotted Nobosi rummaging amongst the rocks a little further down the slope and called to him. They were alone. Even though the air was cool, beads of nervous sweat formed on her lip and forehead, trickling down her face and back. Shivering, she called, "Markos?"

Nobosi joined her as a voice from below Kanda's feet answered. "Down here, Kanda."

She knelt and saw Markos and Palesa staring up at her through a small crack where the boulder sat on the rocky slope. "How did you get there?"

"Around the other side, under the bushes, there is a narrow fissure just wide enough to slip through."

Kanda rounded the boulder and lifted the bushes. She looked into the deep dark hole below and her skin crawled with panic. Another man had joined Markos and Palesa. *Briador?* They were about three strides down, their faces pale in the shaft of sunlight that streamed through the gap. "Jump, Kanda, it's not far," Markos called.

Nobosi sensed her fear and nudged her forward. Taking a deep breath, she forced herself to sit down and slip through the gap. Her pet squeezed in behind her. She landed on her feet and looked around. Nobosi landed beside her. The hole was only a couple of strides wide and a few strides long. The three people waiting had moved back to allow her and her pet room to land. Stalagmites stood like sentinels in the gloom, and stalactites hung from the ceiling. Over time, some had joined, creating columns that crowded the space. She could see no way out. Cold, musty air surrounded her. The fist of fear squeezed her chest and stole her breath away. The more she stared, the closer the walls became. She shivered and closed her eyes. Panic crawled up her back like a giant spider, threatening to devour her. "How do we get out," she whispered.

Markos took her arm reassuringly. "This way." He moved to the end of the hole and around a large limestone column. This led them into a narrow passage. They followed the tunnel for a short distance and stepped out behind an opaque screen of water. A powerful roar greeted them, as the ogre announced its presence.

"Wow! We're behind the waterfall!" Kanda said. The clamour of the powerful gush was thunderous. They moved to the right to peer at the riverbank below. Here, the water flow eased to a slightly lighter veil. Owl sat on a tree not far away. Markos sank to the floor of the cave gratefully.

Kanda studied the other man. He was of slight build. His face was weathered and tanned like old leather. His long grey hair and beard came to his waist. But his brown eyes were bright as he studied her. He stepped forward and bowed. "Miss Kanda, welcome to my home. I am Briador."

"At last! Do you know why we are here?" Kanda asked.

Briador looked at Markos. "Markos quickly filled me in on the reason for your presence. But where are Rais and Leopold? I thought they were with you."

"Leopold was captured near the cave entrance and Rais went off to see if he could free him. He hasn't come back. Even if he does free him, how are they going to find the way to this cave?" Kanda said biting her lip.

"I gave Rais a map, remember. He will be able to find us," Markos said. "Don't worry too much. We'll settle here and watch for Rais and Leopold. Owl will scout the area. When he lets us know they are near, you can try to connect again."

"But, what if … what if … they are both captured?" She turned to Briador. "I tried to contact him with my pendant, but he blocked me. Should I try again?"

Briador smiled. "Oh good, you have worked out how to do that. Well done. We may be too far from him now, but you can try."

Kanda nodded. "I learnt how to do it totally by accident." Kanda clutched her pendant and focused on Rais. Even though the white light streaked back in the direction they had travelled, it soon died. She turned to Briador, tears flowing down her face. The lump in her throat was so large she could only shake her head.

Briador placed a reassuring hand on her shoulder. "Mmm … as I thought, you have put too much distance between you. Don't worry, the boys are resourceful, or at least I'm sure Rais is, they will find a way of escaping." Looking at the moon he added, "I hope they make it soon. We are running out of time."

Palesa had watched Kanda's effort hopefully. Now she was fighting back tears of frustration. She wandered to the other side of the falls to hide her panic. Confusion continued to wage a war in her mind. Whatever she decided about turning them in, she knew now that she didn't want Rais to be hurt, after all, he had saved her life. She slumped down against the wall. Exhaustion soon claimed her, and she sank into a deep sleep.

Kanda sat beside Briador and Markos, leaning on her pack, her back against the wall and her eyes glued on Owl. Intermittently, he flew away, then returned. Nobosi curled up beside her. Kanda tried to keep her vigil, but soon the strain of the last few suns crept up on her and she dozed. Nightmares of Rais and Leopold tied to a tree and surrounded by troops disturbed her rest.

She woke with a start. Through the light veil of water, she could see that the sun had started its descent behind the mountains that divided Nevaah and Gantis. The sky was the colour of fire as it signalled its time of rest. Soon the only light would be from the moon as it returned to its duty. Kanda shivered and looked around. The scent of the flowering bush beside her filled the air and she breathed in the fragrance. The rush of the growling waterfall blocked out all other sound. She looked to where Briador and Markos had been sitting. Her heart leapt in dread. She was alone. "Markos, Briador!" she shouted. But the roar of the falling water drowned her call.

As she bounced to her feet and hurried towards the other side of the cascade, a welcome aroma drifted towards her, making her stomach growl in hunger. Following the enticing scent, she rounded a limestone wall, formed over millions of years by the joining of stalagmites and stalactites. Briador and Palesa cooked fish on sticks over a fire while Markos watched. Nobosi looked up from his feast, his tail wagging in welcome.

"I was just coming to see if you were awake," Briador said smiling. He held up the fish he was cooking and indicated more on a rock beside him. "Palesa and I have been fishing. We didn't dare light the fire over there. It might have been seen from the bank."

"Fish?" Kanda looked around. "Where did you find fish, the pool below is too far down?"

Briador indicated behind her. Close to the cascade, gouged in the rock by the constant assault of the flow, was a deep pool. Kanda wandered over and peered into its depths. She could see the silver glint of the fish as they swam in the crystal-clear pond. The spray soaked her face and arms and she hurried to the fire, warming her hands gratefully. "Is there any sign of the boys yet?"

Briador shook his head. "No, Owl is still checking. We'll eat; then check again."

When they returned to the other side of the cave the sun had disappeared and soft moonlight bathed the bush. Owl was missing. They paced as they waited for him to appear. As the time since they had last seen him increased, they became optimistic. Then, he flew back, circled a couple of times screeching, and disappeared again. The girls danced in joy. He had obviously found at least one of them.

CHAPTER FIFTEEN

The pursuit

Rais stood undecided. Did they go on, or wait here? He searched the area for signs of a struggle and found none. He looked for an indication of the direction they had taken, with the same result. Owl had flown off towards the river and returned while they searched. "I guess they've gone to the river. Markos said Briador lives in a cave near there. I have a map here somewhere." He searched through his bag and pulled out the map. They stood examining it for a moment in the faint light of the moon. "That shouldn't be too hard to follow," Rais said looking towards the river.

Leopold nodded and stepped out from behind the rocks. "We had better get moving before the troops decide to continue their search."

They hurried along the path towards the river. The moon was high in the sky when they entered the dense forest that grew on its bank. As he was about to step into the forest Rais checked the moon. "We're running out of time," he muttered.

Total darkness enfolded them as they stepped under the trees. They stopped to get their bearings and allow their eyes to adjust. Rais peered into the gloom anxiously. "We don't dare light a torch; it may be seen from the mountain."

They stumbled along in the darkness. Owl led the way, the intermittent rays of moonlight stealing through the foliage reflecting off his white feathers. Rais could hear Leopold's muffled cries of pain as the branches of the dense undergrowth assaulted his wounds. Soon the canopy became so thick that they couldn't even see Owl. The undergrowth in front of them seemed unyielding. They stopped to rest. "This is hopeless. I'll try contacting Kanda," Rais said. He clutched his pendant and sought the mind of his twin. The white band of light streaked out before him and soon he was in her mind. *Kanda, thank goodness, we are in the dense part of the forest heading your way, but it is too dark to continue. Are you in the cave?*

Tears of joy flowed down Kanda's cheeks. *Oh Rais, are you okay? Is Leopold with you?*

Yes, he is. We're okay, but we're not game to light a torch, and the forest is so dark and dense here that we can't continue without light.

Kanda relayed the message to Briador. His face showed the relief he was feeling.

"Tell Rais to hold the mind connection and follow the white light that is flowing between you. You will have to concentrate too and not let anything distract you."

Hope flooded Kanda's face. "Will that work?"

"Yes, it is a faint light, but it's better than none."

Kanda excitedly passed on the message. The glow had disappeared as Kanda spoke to Briador but returned when she reconnected.

Rais looked doubtfully at the white light; it was so faint he wasn't sure it would be much help. Clutching his pendant, he took tentative steps forward. Kanda sat concentrating on Rais. They exchanged thoughts about what had happened since they parted, but Rais was careful to play down the beating Leopold had taken. He didn't want his sister to become too upset and break the connection.

Once the youths located the track that the other group had taken, the going was not as hard, and they made good time reaching the edge of the forest. The light now led to the centre of the waterfall and Rais paused. *How do we get to you?*

Go further on, to the big boulder on the side of the slope. We will be there with a torch to show you the way.

Rais peered up the slope trying to locate the boulder in the faint moonlight. As soon as Kanda broke the mind connection, to explain to Briador what they needed to do, the light between them disappeared and he was once again lost. Even here, clear of the forest, the moonlight was not bright enough now for them to see very far. Then Owl appeared and flew up the slope screeching. Rais realised he was once again guiding them and followed.

The climb was difficult in the dark. Every foothold was precarious. Rais could hear Leopold gasping for breath and knew he was struggling to continue. Then his companion cried out as he lost his footing and tumbled down the steep slope. Rais raced after him. As he helped Leopold to his feet, the youth grimaced in pain. Rais held him by his arm to steady him as he swayed. "You okay?"

"Yeah, I will be in a minute. I fell on my sore ribs. It knocked the wind out of me."

Leopold took a deep breath, which seemed to Rais to cause him more pain, then slowly, fighting for every breath, he began to regain the ground he had lost. Rais slipped his arm around his back and half carried him up the slope. Soon they could see Owl perched on top of the boulder.

They stopped to regain their breath. As Rais let go of his friend, Leopold staggered and clutched his chest, gasping for air. He slumped to the ground, his head in his hands. "I can't breathe. I feel dizzy."

Rais panicked. They were too exposed where they were. "Just a bit further, Leo, I'll help you hide behind the boulder." Rais lifted his friend and guided him to shelter. The connection with Kanda returned and Rais sighed in relief. She had arrived at the entrance. He received instructions on how to get down to her.

He eyed Leopold doubtfully. *Kanda, Leopold's not well. He is feeling dizzy and is having trouble breathing. He is not up to jumping into the hole.*

Alarm screamed through Kanda. She turned to Briador. "Leo is hurt. He can't jump down. What are we going to do?"

Markos placed a reassuring hand on her arm. "You'll have to resort to magic, Kanda."

"How? There's no way for me to get there. There are no footholds."

"Harness the wind spirit. Where is your book? The instructions are in there. You can create a cushion of air for him to descend on. Look in your book for the spell. It's like the one you did at the cave-in, Kanda," Markos said.

Markos explained to Briador what she had done. Briador shook his head in amazement. "I knew she would inherit her mother's healing powers. But I didn't expect them to be this strong already. This is an easier spell than that one."

As Kanda was searching through the book, Rais stuck his head through the entrance. "There are two torches coming through the forest. We must hurry. I've helped Leopold to hide behind the boulder, but he has passed out."

Briador held his torch closer to Kanda's book. "Hurry, Kanda, the troops are following the trail we left through the underbrush. We must get the boys down here before they clear the trees."

Kanda was in such a state of panic that she was having trouble focusing on what she was reading. Visions of Leopold unconscious on the slope were clouding her concentration. Briador's plea for urgency didn't help. After what seemed to them to be a long time, she sighed and said, "I've found it."

She donned her healer's pendant and shivered as the power surged through her, once again creating a feeling of confidence and strength. She shouted up at Rais, "I'm going to create a cushion of air for Leopold to descend on. When the blue cloud appears under the hole, lower him onto it." Following the instructions in the book, she waved one hand in a circle over her head, clutched the healer's pendant, and chanted:

Oh, spirit of the winds
I call on you today
to make a cushion with your sacred breath
on which our friend can lay.

Deliver him to us now, out of harm's way.

When she had completed the chant, wind swirled in front of her, chilling the air and filling it with small stones and dust. The gusts finally abated, and a glowing blue cloud formed. Shielding her eyes from the particles that still hung in the air, she waved her hand skyward. The cushion of air moved to the top of the hole and drifted there. Kanda sank to the floor exhausted but concentrated on the cushion to keep it floating.

Briador shouted, "Now Rais – lower Leopold onto the cloud."

He gratefully moved to obey. "Good timing, the troops are at the edge of the clearing. Put out the torch."

Briador extinguished the torch. Using the faint glow of the cloud to guide him, Rais pulled Leopold's body to the gap and as gently as possible lowered him onto the air cushion. Kanda rose to her feet and gestured in a downward motion, and it drifted down to sit on the floor, delivering Leopold's unconscious body safely to them. Rais joined them and they crouched in the dim blue light from the cloud. Kanda peered at Leopold. She gasped in horror at the injuries to his face. Tears welled as she lovingly stroked his swollen lips and eyes. She bent down to kiss him softly and her tears spilled onto his cheeks. She gently wiped them away.

Palesa stared at his injuries. Guilt flowed through her like acid. *Oh, this is all my fault. I thought they would just take him to the city. I didn't think they would hurt him like this.* She moved forward and stroked his hand. As Rais landed, she rushed to him and threw her arms around him. "Oh Rais, I was so worried. Are you okay?"

"Shhhh, they are close," he whispered. He sank to the ground, exhaustion folding his body. Palesa huddled beside him.

Kanda placed her hands on Leopold's head to search for his life-force. The group drew in a shocked breath at the result. From his waist up, his body glowed with patches of red. The ones that concerned Kanda the most were on the right side of his chest and his face. She heard Briador muttering in dismay. Tears streaming down her cheeks, Kanda whispered, "What happened to him? His face is badly damaged, and his ribs and right lung are glowing red."

Rais quietly explained the ordeal that Leopold had undergone and told them how he had fallen down the hill and exacerbated his injuries. They cringed as he described their friend's beating. He ended by saying, "Leo took the beating without saying a word. I never thought I would say this, but he is braver and more loyal than I thought he could be."

Kanda sobbed as she listened. She placed her head on Leopold's chest. "His breath is faint and gurgling. I think his right lung is punctured. We must get him to a warmer and lighted position so I can heal him. I'll try to move him using the cloud. We may do more damage if we try lifting him." She wiped away her tears; determined to be strong. He needed her now more than ever.

Moving him proved no problem. The cloud followed Kanda's direction. At the exit of the tunnel, they hesitated. If the troops were on the slope nearby, they would see the faint blue glow of the cloud.

Rais held up his hand in a gesture to stop. They huddled there as he went to the side of the cave and searched for the troop's torch light. He hurried back, an anxious expression on his face. "They're further up the slope. I hope they don't know about the entrance."

Briador shook his head. "I don't think they would. Only locals know about it, but I suppose some fool may have told them."

"The troops are huge. I think they are too large to fit through," Markos said.

Rais stood at the side of the cave, Nobosi at his side. "I'll keep watch."

The rest of the group cautiously made their way through the cave to the sheltered position behind the rock wall. The fire was still burning. They were grateful for the warmth of its glow.

Kanda positioned the cloud on a bedroll and dismissed it. Leopold's unconscious body sank gently onto the soft hide-covered straw. Then she reached into her bag for the dawning dew and performed the healing spell. She slumped down onto his chest so she could listen to his breathing and heart rate as she recovered her strength. A smile played on her face as she heard his breathing clear and his heart rate improve. "He's getting stronger," she told the others.

Rais suddenly appeared. "They're at the edge of the waterfall. I heard them shouting to each other. Briador, is there somewhere we can go that is more secure than this?"

"Not with Leopold still recovering. Serious physical injuries like his broken ribs and punctured lung can take some time to heal completely. He needs more time before we move him. We'll have to make a stand. Did you see how many troops there were?"

"Only two torches, but that doesn't mean only two troops."

Briador nodded grimly. "I think we can take on two, but any more than that and we are in trouble."

Rais' eyebrows lifted. "I don't want to be disrespectful, but you, Briador? How could you take on two oversized Gantians?

Briador shook his head doubtfully. "I have some magic powers... if I still remember how to use them; and if my strength is sufficient. But I'm hoping you have inherited much stronger powers from your father, Rais. Unfortunately, there is not much time to learn and practise them now."

"Who is my father? Markos wouldn't tell us anything. We discovered on the journey that our mother has healing powers and Kanda has inherited them, but we still know nothing about our parents or why we were hidden away. Markos said you would tell us."

Kanda looked up hopefully, but her heart slumped again when he said, "I will, but there is not enough time now. For now, all I can say is your father has amazing powers and I hope you have them too."

"Then show me what you want me to do. I've left Nobosi guarding the entrance so we will know when they get close."

Briador gestured at Rais to give him a minute and closed his eyes. He sought the magic power he had long suppressed and felt it flow through him, giving him confidence and energy. He rose stiffly to his feet and nodded at Rais. "I can't actually demonstrate, as I don't have the power we need, but I'll explain how it works. Follow my instructions, but don't complete the last action as the sound and flash would attract attention. Understand?" Rais frowned but nodded and Briador continued, "Concentrate on that log on the edge of the bush down the slope. Point your hand at it and imagine a lightning bolt flashing down your arm and causing it to explode into splinters. You would then flick your hand strongly but hold back that last action this time."

Rais mimicked his instructions and allowed his imagination to visualize the explosion. A strange sense of power flowed from his mind to his fingertips. He dropped his hand and gasped as his arm quivered with the suppressed force. Briador saw the look of surprise and his face lit up with hope.

Kanda watched in awe. *I wonder if I will be able to do that.*

Nobosi barked a warning. Palesa had wandered off into the cave and rushed back. "I've been over to check the other bank. They're still out there. What if they find the entrance?"

"Smother the fire and stay as still and quiet as you can. Rais, you come with me," Briador instructed as he moved into the cave. Palesa crept after them, pausing at the end of the rock wall, not wanting to miss the excitement of a fight. Markos joined her, taking Kanda's spear as well as his own with him. He knew he wouldn't be too much help if it came to a physical fight, but he could still throw a spear with accuracy.

Kanda tried to stifle the flames with hands full of dirt, but it was too hot and strong. "Palesa, come and help me," she hissed. Palesa didn't hear. She was too close to the thunder of the falls. Kanda increased the amount of dirt and her speed of application, but it was no use. The fire just flickered and then flared again. She stared into the flame. *It must be magic fire.*

Then she thought about the magic she had performed and what Briador had just shown Rais. She decided to try smothering the fire with magic. She stood over it and imagined a heavy wet skin dropping, covering it completely. She gestured her hands over the fire and drew them down. Suddenly a surge of power flew down her arms, the flame disappeared, and blackness engulfed her. Her heart pounded and her hands tingled from the energy rush. *Wow. That worked.*

She huddled on the floor, her head spinning from the exertion of casting the spell. Nobosi barked a warning and she moved in front of Leopold protectively. Palesa crept back towards her, stumbling over rocks in the darkness. "Sit down where you are and be still," Kanda hissed.

Rais had gone to the fiercely growling Nobosi and was restraining him from charging towards the troops. Briador signalled Rais to leave the entrance. "We must try not to let them know we are here. Even if we noiselessly take out one, the other will alert the rest of the troops."

Dragging a reluctant Nobosi, they retreated behind the wall again. Briador and Rais stood watch as one of the men grew closer to the side of the falls, peering into the darkness of the cave. "I must extinguish his torch," Briador muttered. He concentrated hard on the flame and with a sweep of his hand, sent a strong gust of wind that blew out the torch.

The soldier stopped in confusion as total darkness swallowed him. He pulled back a little and listened for sound, then shouted, "My torch has gone out. I can't see a thing. A liogon barked as I came closer, but now I can't hear any movement," he shouted.

"The torch would have frightened him off. Wild liogons are afraid of fire," the other trooper called.

The man glanced over his shoulder nervously. Rais took Nobosi to the end of the wall, his hand holding his collar firmly. As he spotted the troopers on the bank, Nobosi let out a ferocious bark.

"There may be a pack of them living there."

"Okay, I guess if there are wild liogons, our fugitives won't be there. They must have gone further up the slope."

Briador sighed with relief. They stayed huddled quietly in the darkness until they saw the glow of the remaining torch disappear up the hill.

"Putting out his torch was good thinking, Briador," Rais said.

"As was making Nobosi bark again. We must avoid a fight with these people for as long as we can. We don't want them to know that you and Kanda have already developed your powers. Yaholo would increase the number of troops looking for you if he knew. And we have to stay here for now. I need time to teach you to use your magic skills. Besides, Markos said you told Varn we would meet him here. We can't wait more than a day though; we are running out of time."

Rais had forgotten about Leopold's guardian. He wondered if he would make it. His injury may have healed quickly, but he still had to deal with the trip over the mountain; and the troops when he arrived on this side. Rais hoped they didn't have to wait too long. He no longer felt safe here.

They walked back to the girls. Kanda sat shivering in the chilly darkness. "Briador, is it safe to light the fire now? I'm worried about Leopold getting cold."

"Yes, I'll light it again."

He gestured magically towards where the fire had been. Nothing happened. He frowned and approached the spot feeling for the logs with his foot. He found them and tried again – nothing. "Kanda, how did you extinguish the fire?"

Biting her lip nervously Kanda said, "At first I tried to smother it with soil, but it wouldn't go out, so I err... used magic, and imagined smothering it with a wet skin. It worked. Did I do something wrong?"

Briador chuckled. "No, you didn't do wrong. I'm thrilled you could do that. But would you mind undoing it now. I can't start the fire again while your spell is in force."

"Oh, sorry err ... what do I do to undo it?"

"Just reverse whatever you did."

Kanda waved her hands over the fire-pit, imagined the wet skin, and as the power surged through her, gestured in a lifting motion. The flames flared and burnt strongly. She sank to the ground as the blaze consumed the darkness.

"Well done!" Briador said. His heart overflowed with happiness as he beamed at his two charges. "You both have your father's power. That is incredible." A feeling of confidence settled over him. *I just have to teach them to harness and direct that power in a fight. I hope that we have enough time to do that.*

CHAPTER SIXTEEN

Reunited

When the troops had disappeared, Kanda said. "Briador please tell us now who we are and where we come from."

"It's a long story, Kanda. It will have to wait for the dawning. We all need some sleep."

Kanda opened her mouth to complain but realised he was right. Markos had already fallen asleep and by the look of him, Briador wouldn't be far behind. She looked at Rais. He smiled sadly and shrugged.

Before they settled down, Kanda checked Leopold and found his heart rate and breathing had improved some more. He hadn't woken yet, but Briador assured her he was better off sleeping. He would heal faster that way.

Rais and Nobosi took first watch at the end of the wall. Palesa waited for the others to fall asleep and crept over to Rais. Encouraged by his acceptance of her last intimate contact, she tentatively snuggled up to him and placed her head on his shoulder. "I was so worried about you. I'm glad they didn't capture you too."

Rais stiffened a little. He already felt guilty about taking comfort from her last embrace. "Thanks, Palesa, but you had better get some sleep. You're next watch, aren't you?"

Palesa felt his tension and tears came to her eyes. "Yes," she said quietly and crept back to her bed by the fire. She sobbed herself to sleep, hoping no one else was listening. The worry about the boys, Leopold's injuries, and her confusion over whether to turn the twins in had exhausted her emotionally. The rejection by Rais was just too much.

Briador was still awake and heard the whole thing. He shook his head in sympathy. "She is a spoilt brat, but she isn't a bad kid," he muttered.

If he knew what she had been planning, he wouldn't have been so sympathetic.

Rais sat brooding. He had been so smitten by Palesa that he was still not immune to her charms. But his heart now belonged to Caria. *I miss her so much. It's as if I left a part of me behind.* He decided that when he woke Palesa to replace him as guard, he would tell her how he felt. He hoped they could still be friends.

He settled to his watch, his mind on Caria. He was now used to the constant roar of the water ogre and it, and the scent of a flowering bush on the other side lulled him to a state of complete relaxation. He struggled to stay awake.

Rising to his feet, he walked to the other side of the falls to stretch his legs. As he stood staring at the picturesque sight of the countryside bathed in soft moonlight, he caught a glimpse of a torch glow approaching. He tensed as he watched the silhouette of a man move towards the slope.

He was soon close by, peering into the dimness behind the falls. The youth slunk back behind the flowering bush. He parted the branches a little and stared at the intruder. As the man held his torch in front of him to see more clearly, Rais recognised him. His body relaxed. It was Varn. Just as he was about to call to him, the man retreated and climbed towards the boulder.

Rais fetched a torch from beside the fire, lighted it and made his way through the tunnel. He arrived at the entrance at the same time as the visitor. He raised his torch and called, "Varn, it's Rais."

Varn poked his head through the opening. "You're still here, good. I was afraid you had moved on by now."

"We had a bit of trouble, but everyone is safe."

Varn jumped down. As he landed, he took a deep breath and held his injured leg for a minute. "I had a bit of trouble myself. There are troops everywhere out there. I had difficulty avoiding them."

"Yeah, they're looking for us. They captured Leopold and gave him a hell of a beating before I managed to rescue him."

The older man's eyes widened in shock as he listened to the tale. "Hell, poor Leopold, is he alright now?"

Rais explained that Kanda had healed him, and he was still unconscious, but recovering.

Varn nodded thoughtfully. "So, Kanda has healing powers… that's great."

Rais nodded and led Varn through the tunnel to their camp. "I wouldn't wake anyone now if I were you, they need rest."

Varn nodded. "I'm pretty wacked myself. Do you mind if I catch some shut-eye too?"

"No, go for it, I'll be relieved soon anyway."

When Rais could no longer keep his eyes open, he woke Palesa with a gentle shake. She stirred and took his offered hand to rise. Half asleep still, she snuggled into his chest for a hug. Rais hugged her briefly, took her by the shoulders, and gently moved her away from him. "Palesa, we have to talk."

The girl almost tripped over Varn as she backed away. "Who the hell is that?" she said.

"Varn has caught up at last. He arrived just after you all fell asleep."

She nodded absently, and he walked with her to the guard position. Palesa tensed and sank sulkily to the dried grass mat; her back to Rais as if to shield herself from the hurt she knew was coming. She knew she had lost his affection forever.

Rais stared at her, picking up the fact that she knew what was to come. Taking a deep breath to still his own butterflies he said, "You know I still admire you, right? You are the most beautiful girl I have ever seen."

Palesa met his eyes for just a second. The hurt and doubt there almost stopped Rais from continuing, but determined to set things right he said, "I'm sorry, but I love Caria and as soon as we find out who we are and get settled somewhere, I'm going back for her."

This time Palesa didn't lift her head. She stared down at her hands in moody silence.

Rais shuffled his feet. "We can still be friends though, can't we?"

Palesa restrained herself from screaming at him and beating him with her fist. She lifted her eyes and stared into his. She did little to veil her sarcasm as she said, "Friends, Rais… of course we can."

Rais flinched from the malevolent glint in her eyes as she spoke. "Palesa... I..."

The girl turned away, to stare into the darkness. "You had better get some sleep."

Rais stumbled back to his bed, his skin crawling with a feeling of apprehension. *She is not someone I want to have as an enemy. I will have to keep a close eye on her.*

He slumped onto his bedroll and lay on his side where he could watch Palesa.

The girl turned as if she knew he was watching her. *That pale girl will never have Rais, I'll make sure of that,* she thought as she glared at him.

Rais turned away from her glaring eyes. Occasionally, he dozed, and woke with a start, anxiously checking that she was still there.

Palesa spent the moontime brooding. *At least I won't have any trouble turning him in now. He'll be sorry when he is thrown in a cell.*

As the first light of dawn painted the sky, Leopold woke and sat up, staring at his surroundings. "Where the hell am I? What happened?" he asked. His voice and movement woke the group and they stared at him, smiling. Kanda rose and went to his side. Before she could speak, he spotted his guardian and his face lit up with pleasure. "Varn, you made it."

Briador, Markos and Kanda looked with surprise at Varn.

Briador smiled. "Varn, I'm glad you made it. Any trouble?"

"Not much. I managed to avoid the troops. But I can tell you, they were out in force, searching every inch of this side of the mountain until the moon was high. I wasn't game to light a torch until I saw them disappear towards their camp."

Varn moved to Leopold. He inspected him carefully. His charge's face still showed signs of the beating he had taken. Faint bruises coloured his cheeks and a fading scar showed that his lip had been split. "You okay, I heard you had been through the wars."

Leopold looked around him. "The last thing I remember was falling down the slope. Then I woke up here."

Kanda hugged him. "Leo, I'm so glad to see you awake at last. Are you feeling okay?"

"My chest hurts a bit when I breathe, but apart from that, I think so. What happened? How did I get here?"

Kanda explained what had occurred from the time he fell down the hill. He listened in silence, his eyes glowing with love and admiration as she explained her part in the events. A pink glow flushed her cheeks as she observed his loving expression.

He reached out to hug her. "I think I'd better be more careful next time I head out on my own. I walked right into their trap."

Briador nodded. "Good idea, Leopold. Next time you may not escape so easily."

"Will you ever learn to be cautious, lad," Varn said shaking his head. He didn't miss the adoring look that Leopold gave Kanda. "That could complicate things a little, if we return to the City," he mumbled.

Palesa was sitting next to Varn and turned curiously. "What do you mean?" she asked.

"Oh, err ... nothing," he stammered.

The girl's mind surged with hope. *Is it possible that I could have an ally in Varn? Maybe he has plans of his own.* She moved forward to give the boy a hug. The guilt she had felt was lessened by his swift recovery. "Don't do anything that stupid again, I'm sick of worrying about you."

Leopold laughed and hugged her back. "Me too. Kind of over being saved. As Briador said, next time they may not spare me. There's no price on my head."

As Palesa moved away, he remembered that she had been the one who had been on watch and had suggested he scout ahead when he was captured. He shook his head as the idea that she might have sent him out knowing the troops were near, nagged at his mind. *Oh, surely not,* he thought, but he decided to keep a closer eye on her.

"I will be off, Briador," Markos said, "I will let your guardians know that you two are safely with Briador," he said looking at the twins.

"Thank you for bringing us here, Markos. We are so grateful for your help and protection," Kanda said giving him a hug.

Rais hugged him and shook his hand. "Yeah, thanks. We couldn't have done it without you."

Leopold started to get up, but Markos waved him to stay where he was. "It's okay, boy. I'm glad you are okay. You had us worried for a while."

"Thanks, I'm sorry I was such a handful. It seems I owe so many people for saving my life that I will be forever paying off the debt," Leopold said looking a little ashamed.

Briador handed Markos a bundle of food that he had gathered as they were talking. "Thank you for bringing the twins to me. I hope you have a safe trip back. Which way will you go?"

"The safest way will be over the top of this slope. I know a couple of tracks that way. The troops are focussed on finding you lot over here, so I should be safe."

Markos walked over to Kanda. Reaching into his bag he said, "Take these potions with you. They are clearly marked. Leo may need the pain one when he starts moving."

Kanda shoved them into her pack. Briador smiled. "No need to worry, Markos. I have everything we need in here." He held up his backpack.

Kanda smiled. "So, do you want them back, Markos. You might need them."

He shook his head, waved, smiled, and started for the entrance. "Kanda, would you help me get out, please. A ride on your cloud to the top of the entrance would be great?"

Kanda hurried to do as he asked. Proud that she could help.

After he had gone, they settled down to have breakfast. As he dished up grilled fish and damper, Briador said, "I guess I had better fill you two in on your destiny before we go any further."

"And what our urgent mission is," Rais said.

"Yes, that too, but first you must know who you are."

All eyes turned to him as he started the tale.

CHAPTER SEVENTEEN

The Invasion

Wriggling into a comfortable position he sighed and began.

'Your father is Baldasarre, a powerful and magical oracle. He was chief advisor to King Marbon, the ruler of Nevaah, before the invasion. I was your father's personal assistant. Did you know that you are both mirror images of your mother?"

The twins' eyes grew wide with amazement. They nodded and said together, "Markos told us that. Our father's an Oracle? And our mother is a healer... wow."

"Yes, she is a spiritual healer and alchemist. Please let me finish," Briador continued, "You were taken to Adaya over a decade ago, after the invasion and overthrow of King Marbon's rule."

"Yeah, we know about that event. It was in our lessons. Were you there when it happened?" Rais asked.

"Yes. And the story is one you need to know. It is, sadly, a story of deceit."

The twins moved closer and stared at Briador with rapt attention as he began his tale. Palesa and Leopold listened with great interest.

"One sun before the invasion, your father, Baldasarre, and I stood with the king's sentry in the guardhouse at the palace gate, watching a rider in guardsman's uniform approach. The soldier identified himself as Yamat, from the Gantis Border Guard Post One. When asked to state his business, he responded by saying that he had a message for King Marbon from Yaholo, chief advisor to Ogma, King of Gantis.

"The guards raised the gates and Baldasarre and I escorted Yamat to the receiving hall. He handed your father a message. It went something like, '*Yaholo, chief advisor to King Ogma, esteemed ruler of Gantis, requests an audience with Marbon, King of Nevaah to discuss a peaceful solution to border issues.*'

"Baldasarre showed me the message, and said, 'I don't trust this man; he is as sinister and untrustworthy as a snake. Still, it is not my position to decide. I will take the message to the king'.

"We hurried to the court. When he read the message, the king asked your father if he believed it a genuine attempt at peace. I watched him struggle with his reply. Finally, he explained that as all previous attempts at peace had failed and led to further border hostilities, he didn't believe it was. At that time, raiding parties still attempted to steal animals and grain from our farmers at the base of the dividing mountain. Our border patrols struggled to keep them out.

"The king nodded thoughtfully. He spoke of the change that had taken place in Gantis in the last century. As their food supply had diminished, the people of the original race of giants had shrunk with each generation, but their citizens were still larger than our race. Spies had informed him that only three giants remained – Ogma and two of his guards.

"Respectfully, I told him that while I knew this to be true, I believed Ogma to be bedridden and not long for this world. And, as he had no sons to carry on the sovereignty, Yaholo was touted as the next Head of State of the Kingdom of Gantis. I explained that my spies had told me Ogma's chief adviser was charged with the task of proving he was up to the challenge, by finding a way to help the population out of its famine.

"The monarch considered my information and nodded thoughtfully. I remember him saying to your father, 'Then maybe the purpose of the visit is to broker a peace with our nation by accepting our last offer of trade – our food for their minerals. I think we must see him, Baldasarre'.

"I could see your father was not convinced, but he bowed and said, 'As your majesty wishes'. We returned to the receiving room, and, against his better judgement, the Oracle sent Yaholo an invitation to proceed. He instructed Yamat to ensure that the emissary's party was small and accompanied by a troop of Nevaah guardsmen."

Rais and Kanda sat mesmerised, their mouths open, trying hard to believe what they were hearing. Palesa's eyes lit up as she learnt more. The desire for the reward doubled as she realised how badly Yaholo would want the twins.

"I stood with your father watching the envoy arrive at noon the next suntime. In the group were Yaholo, the two giant guards and half a dozen Gantis guardsmen. A troop of a dozen Nevaah border guards accompanied them. We met them in the guardhouse just outside the palace gates.

159

"The giants stood to attention. They towered over the rest of the party like trees, standing the height of two men. Their shoulders were three arm widths wide, and their powerful arms ended in hands the size of platters. By nature, the original race of giants was peaceful. Many times, your father and I speculated that the raids on Nevaah were not on the orders of King Ogma, but on those of his chief adviser.

"I observed Yaholo greet your father with a short bow, and tell him that, as a gesture of peace, he would leave the giant guards outside the palace and proceed with just his personal guards. He requested time to rest and refresh before his meeting with King Marbon. The Oracle reluctantly agreed.

"Ushering them to the visitors' quarters, I posted a guard outside the suite. Your father came to me and said, 'I tried to probe his mind when he arrived, but he blocked me'."

Rais looked at Kanda, his eyes wide. "So, our father has mind reading skills."

"Yes, that is one of his skills. I remember your father and the other advisors were pacing impatiently by the time the emissary emerged. Your father and I stood to one side of the king's court as Yaholo entered. His guards followed instructions to remain in the hall. King Marbon and his personal guards arrived, and the king took up his position on the throne, flanked by his advisors. As Yaholo bowed low to our monarch, your father muttered to me, 'Did you see that fleeting smug expression as he began his bow? Trust me, he is up to something. I must read his mind and see what it is. I'll wait until he is distracted'.

"He waited until the discussions were under way. While the king spoke and Yaholo was relaxed and concentrating on the conversation, I saw your father tune into Yaholo's mind. He gasped as the chief advisor's treacherous thoughts became clear to him. A frown of concern on his face, he turned to me and said, 'It's a trap; his troops are coming'. He then recited Yaholo's thoughts to me. As closely as I can recall, they were, '*Where are our troops? They should have overcome the border patrol by now and reached the walled city. I am tired of playing this game. This pompous ass actually believes that I want peace. Well, peace is what he will have, locked up in the tower for the rest of his life'.*"

Rais and Kanda gasped and moved closer. Wide-eyed, Palesa stared at Briador. "Wow, I heard about the overthrow, but I didn't know you were there."

Briador smiled grimly at her and, looking at the twins, continued, "Your father instructed me to alert the Royal family and tell Edalene to gather you both and leave the palace at once. Fearing he would need me, I sent a messenger and stayed to help. I watched as Baldasarre turned to the king's guards and ordered them to arrest Yaholo and secure the gates to the palace and the city. We rushed to the king's side. Your father, with a wave of his hands, wove a protection spell around him. He explained the trap and the plan to take over the land by force. He told him Gantis troops were fighting the border guards at that moment, and should they be successful, they would storm the palace. The king jumped to his feet in horror.

"I was amazed to see Yaholo laugh as the guards seized him. He then stood placidly and smiled smugly at Baldasarre. I will never forget his mocking words. 'Your magic tricks will not save your king this time my friend, it is too late for that'. He went on to say he had been training a troop of soldiers that outnumbered our army by ten to one and that they would soon arrive at the palace. He boasted that now Ogma had gone, no one was left to stop him. Calling his deceased king an old fool who had grown soft in his old age, he said that if he had listened to him sooner, they could have ruled Nevaah long ago.

"I had never seen your father so enraged; he raised his arm, pointed at the evil visitor, and flicked his hand. A red flame flew towards Yaholo, but a stride from him it bounced back, hit the floor with the sound of an exploding ember and died. Puzzled at his failure, your father raised his arm to try again, and I moved to help, but Yaholo just laughed at us. 'Do your best, Oracle. You are not the only one with magic tricks. The Oracle of Gantis has placed a spell around me that will ward off any magic you might try'."

"Wow! I hope I have that power," Rais said remembering his earlier attempt.

Briador smiled and said, "I hope so too." Then he continued, "Just then, an almighty crash from the front gate of the palace startled us. The evil one laughed victoriously and said, 'No point locking the gates when my giants are around. It's like breaking matchsticks to them'. It was then clear to us why he had left the giants outside.

"Baldasarre, the king's guards and I, placed ourselves in front of the king as the thunder of battle reached the court. As it grew closer, Baldasarre turned to me and commanded me to go and ensure that the Royal family, Edalene, and you two had fled to safety. I sped to the king's chambers. Only you two and your mother were there. I enquired after the royal family and your mother told me they had gone with Markos. 'We must go now', I told her. Your mother shook her head decisively and declared that she would not leave your father and the king, as they may need her healing. I protested and told her of your father's protection spell for the king and his orders that she should leave, but she would not listen. She told me to take you to safety. I remember her exact words. 'I pray it will be but a short time until this madness is over', she said as tears streamed down her face. She hugged you both and added, 'God speed, stay safe my loves'."

Kanda brushed tears from her cheeks as she listened. The image she had seen when she looked at the mannequin in the shop window appeared in her mind and she realised who it was. Her mother.

"I took you by your hands and hurried you into a secret tunnel that led us underground and out into the forest well clear of the castle. You screamed and yelled for your mother at first, but I had calmed you by the time we reached the end of the tunnel. We travelled through the farming district and skirted the Plains of the Shifting Sands. We journeyed for three suns on chinows given to us by one of the farmers, sheltering at moontime in farmhouses on the way. Travel between the states was easy then, as the Passage of Recourse on the border between East and West Nevaah was open to all travellers. Yaholo's guards now patrol the border and movement is restricted. We crossed to East Nevaah and on to Adaya. I told the mayor what had transpired and of the need to find you sanctuary until the hostilities ceased. He led me to Nona and Pap."

Kanda brushed away more tears as Briador paused.

Rais lifted his head as if coming out of a trance. "What happened at the palace after we left?"

"Refugees told me that the king's guards had surrendered because of the overwhelming odds, and their fear of the giants who now stood guard at the palace gates. Many people fled the city. You and your parents were among the exiles, Palesa. And you and your mother, Leo. They informed me that the king, Baldasarre and Edalene had been imprisoned, and Yaholo had assumed control of the land. Any attempt to rescue the king by his royal troops, or his loyal followers outside the palace, have been blocked by the giants.

"Yaholo is a cunning snake; he controls your father with threats of harm to your mother. She is now Yaholo's personal healer and only allowed out of his chambers to oversee the preparation of his food.

"I attempted to return to the city to see if I could help, but Yaholo's troops were scattered through the farming district and there was no way through. They robbed the farmers of food and grain stocks to feed the people of Gantis. All that remained were meagre rations, and just enough grain and seeds to replant. I had no choice but to return to Adaya. Anyway, I knew that your father would want me to be close to you, so I could keep an eye out for your safety. When the troops came looking for me, I came over here."

Rais listened to this narrative with a frown. He could feel his face getting hotter as his anger grew with every sentence. Then he exploded. "The rotten bas..." He stopped himself from swearing, took a deep breath, and paced the confined space of the cave like a caged animal. His nostrils flared with anger, and the veins in his neck stood out like train tracks as his eyes narrowed. "There must be a way to free them and get rid of Yaholo. What can we do?"

CHAPTER EIGHTEEN

Their Task Revealed

Palesa watched Rais as he paced. *"Son of the Oracle, now that is more interesting. Maybe it would be better if I could win him back. He did say I was beautiful. Living in the palace could be even better if I was the wife of the next Oracle."* As she stared, the brown peasant's clothing disappeared, replaced by the gold trimmed grey uniform, worn by the warriors in her storybook of ancient Nevaah.

Briador looked thoughtfully at Rais and Kanda. "Actually, something can be done, and unfortunately you two are the only ones who can achieve it. We were hoping it would be when you are older, but it has now become urgent. That is why Yaholo is so set on finding you."

"The messenger said we only have until the full moon to complete some task and save someone's life. Was that what they meant… saving our parents and the king?" Kanda exclaimed.

"Yes, in a way. I'm sorry to have to tell you this, but your mother has been put in the dungeon and is due to be executed on the evening of the full moon."

Kanda and Rais stood still, eyes wide with shock.

Briador continued, "We must go as soon as we can. I will try to teach you what you need on the way. Once your powers are developed, hopefully we can save your mother and overthrow Yaholo's rule."

Rais shook his head as if to clear it. "Why was she imprisoned?"

"The king's health was failing. The protection spell only saves him from physical harm. Yaholo had made sure he didn't get sufficient nourishment and he became ill. Your mother sent a vial of medicine to him hidden in his meal, but the guards were alerted and confiscated it. It seems Yaholo has a spy in the kitchen."

"Oh hell! How long do we have now?" Kanda said biting her lip.

Briador grimaced. "Not nearly enough time. I think about 5 or 6 suns."

"Then we had better go now. We have to save her," Rais said getting to his feet and pacing the floor.

"What other powers will we have? Do you think I might have more of father's powers?" Kanda asked breathlessly.

Rais' eyes lit up with excitement. "I think I will be able to blast people like Father tried to do to Yaholo. What other powers are we likely to have? Maybe we have them now and don't know it?"

"It seems you will, Rais. Yes, Kanda. The way you smothered the fire suggests that you will have power from both parents. It has happened before. During our journey, we will test your powers to see what you can do. But I think it would be best to leave this cave now. When the troops find no sign of our tracks on the mountain, they may well come back to search the cave in the sunlight. Besides, we have to prepare for our journey."

"How will we get to the city?" Rais said.

"We will go on the river as far as it will take us during moontime. It will be the fastest way and we will have more protection. We'll move to the forest on the other side of the river now and test your skills."

Kanda and Rais looked at each other with growing excitement.

Briador encouraged Leopold to take a short walk to see if he was capable of travelling. He sauntered around the cave checking out their location. "This is a cool hiding place."

Briador nodded. "It has been a safe and comfortable place for me, but it is time to move on. The only place to cross the river is through this cave, so we won't be easily followed."

Kanda looked over the edge of the cliff on the side of the waterfall where they had camped. "How do we get down? The banks are steep here."

"We'll abseil down on a rope. Then we'll have to go down the riverbank about five hundred strides to get to calm water where we can bathe and fetch water to drink."

Rais walked to the cliff face and looked down. "Good idea. It will give us time to hide in the forest down there before the troops come snooping around. If we are going to the city on the river, we'll have to build a raft before it gets dark."

Briador nodded. "We'll have to clean up all traces of our occupation before we go."

Kanda started to clear the debris of the fire away, but Briador motioned her to stop. "I can do it much more simply. All of you go stand by that rock please."

Raising his hands and circling them over the floor, he muttered a spell. The fire and all their footprints disappeared. The group watched in awe.

"How did you do that? What was the spell?" Rais and Kanda asked.

"One I will teach you later. We must be on our way."

Varn raised an eyebrow in surprise. "You think these kids will have powers already?"

Briador regarded them proudly. "Yes, indeed. And I suspect they will be quite strong by the time we make it to the city."

Varn nodded thoughtfully. "That's amazing." He moved to secure the rope over the pinnacle of rock jutting up from the floor.

Palesa joined him. She looked over the cliff nervously. The ground was about nine or ten strides away. Her fear of heights kicked in and her head spun as she looked down. She backed away and turned to Briador. "Couldn't you use a spell to get us down there?"

"Yes, I could, but it is best we abseil this time."

Palesa pouted. "What about Kanda's cloud? We could all float down on that?"

Briador's face showed his impatience as he explained. "Yes, but if we resort to magic for every little thing, we will grow weak. Every spell takes strength from our bodies, and it takes time for that strength to return."

Kanda nodded in agreement. She remembered the dizziness and exhaustion she felt every time she cast a spell.

Varn reached out and patted Palesa's shoulder. "You'll be fine, there's nothing to it."

The girl smiled gratefully and gave him a hug of thanks. But even this gesture was not without intent. She smiled slyly. *Never too soon to get into his good books in case I need him.*

Briador encouraged Rais to go first so he could help the others land safely. Varn followed and set off to investigate the safety of the terrain. Palesa had been cowering behind them, her heart beating furiously as she visualized falling to the rocks below. She nervously moved forward. "I've never done this before. How do I do it?"

Leopold moved to her side. "You'll be fine. Just hold tight to the rope over the knot, we will let it out a little at a time. Use your feet to kick out before every descent or you will scrape against the rocks. Kanda you go next and show her how it's done."

Kanda clutched the rope and lowered herself over the side. Confidently, she dropped down the cliff face to land beside Rais.

They watched anxiously as Palesa appeared over the side. They were both thinking the same thing. They didn't need anyone else hurt. Even with Kanda's healing powers, it would take time to heal and slow them down too much. Palesa stumbled as she landed and Rais caught her before she fell. "Thanks," she said. She hugged him and smiled sweetly. Apart from a few scrapes, she had managed the descent.

Leopold followed, wincing as his arms took the weight of his body; the strain on his chest muscles caused pressure on his still tender ribs. By the time he reached the bottom, he was gasping. Kanda moved anxiously to his side. He waved her away. "I'm okay." He took a deep breath and winced again. Kanda reached into her pack, took the painkiller potion Markos had given her, and poured him a dose. He swallowed it gratefully.

Briador paused to clear their final footsteps before he climbed down the rope using the knots as footholds.

"What about the rope, do we just leave it there?" Rais asked.

"We can't leave it. It will show the troops our escape route and give them a way down. We will have to resort to magic. But I'm not feeling strong enough; you'll have to do it, Rais."

"What do I do?"

"Call to your mind the image of the rock where Varn looped it. Flick the rope and imagine it flying off and dropping to your feet."

Rais tried twice but failed. He swore softly.

"Want me to help?" Kanda asked.

"No," Rais snapped. With more determination, he concentrated harder and repeated the action. This time the power surged, and the rope dropped. He whooped with joy as he caught it.

Briador beamed with pride, but cautioned, "Quietly please, the troops may be near."

As they moved down the bank, their mentor strode with confidence. *The twins are showing signs that they will be as powerful as their parents. I will have the few suns it will take us to get there to complete their training. We may well pull this off.*

CHAPTER NINETEEN

Taming a monster

The group made their way down the side of the river, staying just inside the shelter of the trees; all the while watching the other bank for signs of the troops. They stopped below the worst of the rapids. The terrain flattened here as the water monster rested for a short distance.

"We are exposed here on the bank. We'll head into the forest. Once we are on the river we will be out of sight of the troops."

They moved further into the forest to find suitable logs to construct a raft.

Rais gazed at the huge trees around him. "How are we going to cut them down, Briador?"

"We'll have to use magic. This will be a good start to your lessons. We'll choose some of the smaller, straighter ones."

Rais and Kanda's eyes lit up in anticipation. Deep in the forest, Briador chose the first tree. "Rais, remember what I showed you last moontime? Repeat those actions, but this time, don't pull back. You need to make sure it falls away from you, so visualize the trunk breaking in one small place, about a hand's span from the base, and then push it away from you." He held up his hands and showed the gestures needed.

Rais' and Kanda's eyes locked. The excitement they were experiencing took their breath away and made their heads spin.

"You first, Rais," Briador said, pointing at the tree.

Rais' hand shook as he raised it and pointed at the base of his target. But once his visualization started, a feeling of confidence and power surged through him. He flicked his hand. His arm quivered with the force of the spell and a red bolt charged through the air. The base of the trunk exploded with a huge boom. Splinters flew in every direction, and it started to topple towards them.

Ducking the deadly fragments of wood, Kanda raised her hand, concentrated, and repeated the pushing gesture Briador had shown them. It changed direction and fell harmlessly away from them.

Rais collapsed on the ground beside his mentor, pulling splinters from his legs. "Thanks, Kanda. Sorry about that. I think I used too much power – and I forgot the second part."

Briador shook his head in despair. "Just as well Kanda was listening. Next time try to tame the blast a little. You've almost destroyed half the tree and that blast could be heard for a great distance."

"Sorry, is it still okay to use?"

"Yes, we will need a shorter one for the cross beam. Come on; we had better try to find a few more suitable trees. Practice makes perfect."

"Your turn, Kanda. See that tree there, repeat what Rais did, but remember to push it away if it falls this way."

Kanda raised her trembling hand and pointed it at the tree. She turned to Rais for support. He smiled and nodded.

Taking a deep breath, she visualised the tree breaking and falling. She flicked her hand with confidence, but nothing happened. Devastated, she turned to Briador.

"Did you feel a surge of power when you visualised the tree breaking?" he asked.

She shook her head sadly.

Briador smiled a sympathetic smile and patted her arm. "Well, it looks like that is not one of your powers… yet. It may come later."

Kanda dropped her head in anguish. "Then how will I be able to help in the battle?"

"Don't worry, I have something that will help with that. Let's get on with travelling to the palace."

Kanda looked at him questioningly, but he turned and walked away. She shrugged and followed.

They roamed the forest, Rais and Briador taking turns felling trees and resting. Briador was impressed with the force of Rais' magic. He smiled in satisfaction. *Rais will be very powerful when he learns control. We will be in good hands with him and his father guarding the palace.*

Once Rais learnt to use the appropriate amount of energy, he recovered quickly between spells. Leopold and Varn followed them, dragging the fallen logs to a clearing and marvelling at the demonstration of magic. Kanda collected vines off the fallen trees to help tie the raft together.

Palesa watched with awe. She was staggered by the force of the power Rais possessed. She bit her lip anxiously. *If I do have to turn them in, maybe it won't be as easy as I thought.*

Briador saw her watching and gave her a knife. "You can help Kanda gather some thick strong vines to tie the raft together."

She flounced off muttering.

Back at the clearing, Kanda and Palesa delivered their vines and Varn and Leopold began the construction. Rais and Briador rested to recover their strength.

Briador checked the raft plan that Varn had drawn on the ground and nodded his approval. "Make sure you tie securely and that we have sides and a cross beam to hold onto. There are a few hairy rapids before we reach the base of the mountain."

After a short rest, Rais began to feel guilty for sitting down while the others worked on the raft. He went to help. Briador gave the girls the fishing net and sent them to catch more fish for their last meal of fresh food before their long and arduous journey. He then roamed around gathering fungi and herbs for his potions.

The sun was on its dive towards the horizon when the raft was completed. Briador had dozed while the boys completed the task. The girls returned and set a fire behind a couple of boulders to cook the fish.

After they had eaten, they settled down to gather their strength before the trip down river. Rais placed the remaining fish filets on the hot rocks to dry for travelling supplies. Briador's head nodded wearily. He told the twins that he would take a short nap and suggested they do the same. Leopold moved closer to the bank to keep watch.

***

As the deep red of the sky announced the sun's departure, they headed for the river.

Rais stared at the rising moon, his face grim. *No more than 4 or 5 suns to go by the look of that. I hope we make it in time.* Kanda saw the direction of his stare and walked over to him. They hugged in silence, both having the same grim thought.

Dragging the raft through the trees was no easy feat, but soon they were standing on the bank gasping for breath from the effort. They quickly loaded their backpacks, tying them securely to the crossbeam. The stream ran swiftly here, but a small area between two boulders was relatively calm. They pushed the raft onto the water there and climbed aboard.

"Everyone, please tie yourself to the cross beam. We will be going over some serious rapids just over that ridge," Briador instructed, throwing them all a length of rope. Kanda tied Nobosi between her and Briador. Palesa tied herself close to the edge beside Kanda. Once they were all secure, Rais and Varn took a position on each side of the raft with a pole to push them away from the bank and any boulders on the way that may upset the raft. Leopold sat at the rear, his pole secured between the log and the base of the raft to act as a rudder.

Briador and the girls sat clinging to the crossbeam. Taking a deep breath for courage, Rais said, "Everyone ready?"

Terror at what they were about to do stole their ability to speak. They nodded.

Rais pushed them away from the bank into the swift stream.

The raft bucked as the river monster gleefully dragged them into its clutches. The girls and Briador grasped harder to the cross beam, their knuckles white. An icy spray drenched them all, but Rais and Varn were too busy to notice. They had not anticipated the force of the water, and both overbalanced as the raft became a wild animal trying to buck them off. They threw themselves to the floor of the craft, seizing the side rails to stop their slide into the icy grip of the water creature.

The excitement of the wild ride soon consumed their fears and they whooped as the raft slid onto the first rapid. The river's path curved ahead, and Varn knelt at the side ready to push them off the rocky cliff face where they were heading. He was grateful for the rope that secured him. "Stay alert, Rais, there are rocks ahead. We will have to steer between them."

Leopold was struggling with his rudder. The bounce of the craft meant it was mostly out of the water. He pulled it from its place. "I'll be more use up the front," he called. He inched forward using his rope. Just as he was climbing over the crossbeam, the vessel bucked, and he fell heavily onto Palesa. Leopold put a hand on her to steady her as he glanced towards the front of the craft. "You okay," he asked, then glanced up. They were hurtling sideways towards the cliff face. There was no time to check if she was hurt. "Hell, sorry, I have to go help," he muttered, crawled over her, and headed to the front of the raft.

Palesa yelped and held one arm to her chest. The strain on the other was too great. She felt her grip failing as the raft leapt into the air once again. She threw herself lengthways over the beam, hanging on with her legs and one arm.

Kanda reached out to hold her but realised she was safe now. "You okay?" she called but wasn't sure Palesa heard her over the roar of the ogre. She frowned in concern but gripped the rail again as the raft bucked.

Leopold reached Varn's side just as they were about to slam into the cliff. Both he and Varn used their poles as battering rams. The force of the rods hitting the solid rock vibrated through their bodies and knocked them backwards. They tumbled to the deck, but soon resumed their positions. Relief flooded their bodies as they saw that the impact had pushed them once again into the centre of the stream.

The passage between the rocky cliff faces was dark and gloomy. The moon was shirking her duty, shining at only half strength from behind clouds.

A boulder rose out of the water like a sentinel challenging Rais to a duel. As if he was a knight on a white charger, he readied himself as they hurtled towards it. He hit it full force with his pole. Rais toppled to the floor of the raft, but the fiend stood its ground as if mocking his puny strength. Leopold and Varn cheered. The raft tilted, but to their relief it slid past without over-balancing. In the faint moonlight, Rais' eyes scanned the water for the splashes of white foam that signalled the danger of submerged rocks. Adrenalin coursed through him as the desperate need to fight for survival replaced the first flush of exhilaration.

Then it appeared, right in front of him – a rock twice the size of the last. It loomed like the Grim Reaper, determined to take them to a watery grave. Varn and Leopold screamed a warning and scrambled towards him to help but the river monster had other ideas and for every step forward they slid back as far.

Shock froze Rais for an instant. It was huge. Too wide for the pole to help get them around it. Instinctively, he raised his hand and used the spell he had used to fell the trees. But this time he didn't hold back on his power. The bolt of red light hit the rock seconds before the raft reached it. The rock exploded, showering them all with flying debris. The raft bucked as the force of the explosion lifted it from the water.

Varn lost his grip and slid over the side. The only thing that saved him was the rope tied to the centre beam, but they knew the line would soon snap from the force of the water against his body. Leopold reached for him but missed. Grasping frantically, Varn had managed to grip the rail with one hand as he slipped off. He hung precariously over the side, the waves and force of the rushing water buffeting his body as the river monster tried to drag him into its deadly depths. Seeing his peril, Rais dived to the side and grasped his hand just as it lost its grip. "Leo, help me," he screamed.

As the raft righted itself, Leopold threw himself to Rais' side and grabbed Varn's wrist above Rais' hand. Together they hauled Varn closer to the raft and he clutched at the rail with his other hand. Leopold let go and grabbed the hand. Pulling together, they managed to drag an exhausted Varn onto the raft. He gasped for breath as Rais and Leopold collapsed beside him.

Kanda and Briador had watched all this in horror. Kanda had tried to go to the aid of the males, but she couldn't let go. She had hung on tightly for so long that her hands felt numb. The scraping of the bottom of the raft against the submerged remnant of the rock threw her into panic as she waited for the vines to snap and the raft to split to pieces. Then they passed into clear water again. Relieved that the raft was still upright, and the boys were safe, she tried to relax.

The river continued to toss them about as they flew through the passage of high cliffs. Every muscle in her body ached from the strain of trying to remain upright, as the watery violence did its best to dislodge them. The malicious creature's call assaulted her constantly as it roared and hollered. It was as if the craft and the river monster conspired to send them to an early grave. The constant force of fighting the plunges and bucks had driven the breath from her tense body. Drenched to the skin, she sat huddled beside Nobosi, trying without success to use his body to stay warm. Her teeth chattered as cold seeped into the very core of her body.

She checked on Briador and was startled to see him swaying wildly, his eyes closed. Spots of blood covered his arms and cheeks where the fragments of the rock had rained on him. Alarm bells shrilled in her mind. *Is he unconscious?* She glanced back at Palesa. She was huddled over the beam clinging on, her face grim.

For a brief second the raft hit a comparatively smooth stretch of water and Kanda took the opportunity to reach out with her foot and touch Briador. His eyes opened and he looked into hers. "I'm okay. Stop fighting the movement of the raft, Kanda, just hang on and allow your body to move with it – as if you and the craft are one."

As the raft once again became a wild bucking animal, Kanda relaxed her body and tried Briador's suggestion. It worked. The tension melted from her limbs, and she started to enjoy the sensation of being a part of the vessel. After checking the boys, she closed her eyes and swayed with the motion.

The river wound its way, crazy and rampant, down the side of the mountain. The boys and Varn were back on their feet and on constant alert, using their poles to save the raft from being shattered on the rocky cliffs on either side, or on submerged boulders that made a sudden appearance out of the foam. Fortunately, no more the size of The Grim Reaper appeared. They were at the point of collapse when the gradient eased, and the ride became smoother. Rais relaxed a little. *It's as if the monster has finally conceded defeat,* he thought.

They glided along flat water between sandy cliffs. The river became an ally and carried them gently, at a strong but steady pace. Even the moon was assisting them as it emerged from the clouds to shine its bright light on them like a benevolent benefactor.

Rais, Leopold and Varn collapsed on the raft, their strength spent by the ride of horror.

Nobosi rose and shook the water from his coat. He licked Kanda's face, before going to Rais to repeat the greeting. Kanda tried to let go of the log again, but at first, her fingers wouldn't obey. It was as if they were frozen in place. When they did start to move, she wished they hadn't, as a deep pain seared through them. She rubbed them together to increase the circulation, then tucked them under her arms to warm them. She pushed the pain to the back of her mind. "Everyone okay?" she asked.

Everyone except Palesa answered in the affirmative. Kanda went to help Briador, who was having the same trouble removing his fingers as she had. She gently prised them off for him – feeling his pain as he winced and groaned. She rubbed them gently, then tucked them inside his wet wrap, under his arms. He smiled his thanks and slumped to the floor. Nobosi moved to his side snuggling in against him as if to warm him.

Kanda moved to Palesa. The girl's body was still wrapped around the crossbeam. She hadn't moved for some time. "Palesa, are you okay?"

When she received no answer, she gently shook the girl's shoulder. Palesa started to rise, whimpered, and fell back. Kanda panicked. "Rais, come and help me move Palesa. She's hurt."

Battered and bruised, Rais moved stiffly to his feet and staggered on legs like jelly to Kanda's side. Groaning at every movement, Leopold joined them.

He took Kanda gently in his arms, kissing her cold lips. "You okay?"

"Yes; you?"

He nodded.

"Something is wrong with Palesa."

Rais and Leopold lifted her still body off the log and laid her gently on the floor of the raft. Except for another deep groan, the girl remained motionless; her eyes closed; her body limp.

Leopold frowned and blushed guiltily. "I hurt her when I fell on her. She yelped and clutched her arm, but I didn't have time to check that she was okay."

Kanda tenderly felt the arm that Leopold indicated. Just below the elbow, it bent at an awkward angle. "It's badly broken." Now comfortable in her role as healer, Kanda sought Palesa's life-force to see if any other damage showed. Her body glowed a healthy strong pink – only red where the break had occurred. "It's just her arm; she's probably unconscious from the pain." Kanda reached for the backpack, removed the healer's book and, in the light of their benefactor, started looking for instruction on how to heal a break.

Briador watched Kanda's confident movements with pride. *She is so like her mother, and her healing power just as strong.* His heart was heavy as her image reminded him of the unrequited love he felt for Edalene.

Kanda quickly found the right spell and instructions. After asking permission, she searched Briador's pack for the potion needed. She raised her eyes to the hovering boys. "As I apply the potion and begin the spell, will you two please hold opposite sides of the break. When the bones start to move, gently guide them towards each other." The boys gingerly took hold of the patient's arm as Kanda clutched her pendant and started lightly massaging the mixture onto the area of the break. At the same time, she began her healing chant.

Rais' and Leopold's eyes locked in awe when they felt the power surge through the arm, causing the bones to move in their hands. They steered the broken ends together, removed their hands and sat transfixed. Both beamed with pride.

Kanda's trance was deep this time, and her strength compromised by the wild ride and the adrenaline from the danger they had faced. As soon as she felt the healing begin, she slumped to the floor, totally spent, and collapsed, unconscious. Leopold rushed to her side, lifting her head onto his lap. "Briador! Is she okay?"

Briador nodded wearily. "Yes, she is just spent like the rest of us, and using the energy she needed to heal Palesa was just too much for her. Let her sleep. Let them both sleep."

Rais fetched the girl's bedrolls from their packs, removed Palesa's wet coat and lifted her head onto her swag, covering her with a dry skin from her bag. He then moved to Kanda and with Leopold's assistance, did the same for her.

Rais rose stiffly to his feet, arching his aching back and rubbing his sore leg muscles. "Briador, Varn are you okay? Any injuries?"

"Just a bit cold, but nothing serious," Briador responded. Rais helped him remove his wet wrap and draped the skin from his bedroll around his shoulders. Varn rose and staggered over to them. "I didn't realise how cold it was until I relaxed."

Soon they were all rugged up and resting. Exhaustion crept up and carried them off into a deep sleep. Nobosi moved to the front of the raft and set himself up as guard, but he needn't have worried. The high cliffs of sand on both sides protected them from view from the plains.

It was as well they had no time to contemplate the danger they would face the next sun; even exhausted as they were, they may not have slept so soundly if they had.

CHAPTER TWENTY

Unexpected danger

The sun's brilliance as it taunted the moon for its now weak glow woke them from their slumber. One by one they struggled to rise, stiff again from the period of complete inactivity. Rais rubbed his growling stomach. "Time for food," he said and reached for his pack.

Kanda had woken to find her head resting on Leopold's chest and looked up to gaze lovingly into his concerned eyes. He smiled. "Hello. Feel better now?"

She sat up and gave him a light kiss. "Yes, thank you." Then she moved to Palesa. "Has she been awake?"

"No, Briador said to let you both sleep."

Kanda gave Palesa a gentle shake. The girl opened her eyes. "What?"

"We're safe now. How is your arm?"

Frowning, Palesa sat up. Remembering the pain, she rubbed her arm where it had been broken. "It's fine now. Did you heal me?"

"Yes. You had passed out from the pain and exhaustion."

"Oh, arrr … thanks." Palesa bowed her head. She bit her lip anxiously. Now she owed Kanda a debt too – she didn't like that.

After they had all eaten, they stretched out in the sun, allowing its healing rays to warm them. "How far does this stretch of the river go?" Rais asked Briador.

"With the river running at this swift pace, it will take the rest of the suntime before we reach the area where the sand banks drop away, and we can leave the river. That will give us time to rest and heal our bruises and bumps."

Varn stared over the side. "There would be good fish stocks in the river here. We can catch a few and dry them. The trek to the palace will take a couple of suns at least."

"Good thinking, Varn," Briador said.

Palesa groaned. "I'm so sick of fish."

Leopold shook his head. "Well maybe you can think of something else we can catch here on the river. We're all over your whining, Palesa, be grateful we feed you at all."

Varn lightly slapped Leopold on the side of the head. "That's enough of that, boy, no need to be nasty. I'm amazed it's not you complaining."

"Maybe I grew up a bit since we started. Shame she didn't," Leopold muttered.

Briador reached into his pack for the net he had fashioned earlier, and they threw it over the side. The movement of the raft through the water soon filled it. Retrieving the wriggling fish as the net hit the deck, Rais placed them in a pile between the backpacks, so they couldn't escape. Kanda knelt beside him to help, with Nobosi crouched beside her, snapping at every one that moved. As Briador started to kill and fillet the catch, he called Palesa over and instructed her to place the fillets at the front of the raft on a skin to dry. Grudgingly she obeyed – pulling faces as she touched the raw flesh and washing her hands after each trip.

Suddenly, Kanda let out an ear-piercing scream. She hopped around the deck shouting, "Get it off me – get it off me, now."

A strange creature hung off her calf. Its thin slimy body, about a foot's length, writhed in pleasure as its sharp fangs bit into Kanda's leg and sucked her blood. Nobosi lunged for the creature, but Rais pushed him aside.

He grabbed at it to reef it off, but Briador shouted, "No! Don't pull it, Rais."

Rais stopped and turned to Briador. "What the hell is it? I've never seen one before."

"It's a Zargon. They live on the riverbed. The net must have scraped the bottom. They have long sharp fangs to suck blood from their victims. If you pull it off, you will tear a deep chunk out of Kanda's leg. We have to kill it where it is."

Kanda continued to hop around screaming in pain. Nobosi circled her, barking furiously.

"How?" Rais and Leopold shouted at the same time.

"Burn it off. It's the only way."

Rais looked around in despair. "What with?"

"Magic flame, Rais! We'll need to light two torches with a spell. I'll light one and you can light the other. We'll have to use a red flame." Briador reached into his pack for two bundles of dry twigs and grass. He handed Rais one. "Hold the bundle in one hand and use the other to create the spell." He held it in his left hand and placed his right hand at the base. "Now stare at the end of the bundle and imagine it burning with bright red flame. Then move your hand slowly towards the tip as you say the word 'endescardo'." As he spoke his hand moved slowly to the top, when it arrived there, he said the magic word. The bundle burst into flame. He handed it to Leopold who was holding Kanda tightly to stop her hopping around and falling overboard. Kanda clung to his arm saying, "Oh, oh, oh," and biting her lip.

"Hold this until Rais is ready. It will take the heat of both torches to make the Zargon let go."

While he was speaking, Rais had tried to light his torch and failed. He was staring at Briador in frustration. "Here, light this one too. I can't do it."

"Yes, you can, Rais. Calm your mind. Take a deep breath and try again. Look at the flame on my torch. That will help you imagine the flame you need.

Rais took a deep breath, stared at the other torch first, then stared at his, imagining the same flame on it. He moved his hand slowly to the tip. As he felt the power moving down his arm, he chanted the magic word. The torch burst into fire.

Rais stared in awe. "Wow, I did it. Now what do we do to get rid of that creature."

"You must try to hold the torches near the tail of the creature without burning Kanda. Once it feels the pain of the burn it will let go."

Rais held his head in panic. "Will that work? What if we burn Kanda?"

"Do it Rais! Do it now," Kanda screamed.

Her brother rushed to her side. "Varn, hold her ankle to keep her leg still. Leopold, aim your torch at the tail and don't burn Kanda."

Varn clutched at Kanda's ankle. "Sorry; it will be off soon. Please stay still."

Kanda clutched Nobosi's fur and froze. Even though the pain was so great that she wanted to shake her leg to get the creature off, she was worried Rais and Leopold would burn Nobosi or Varn if she moved.

Nervously, Rais and Leopold pointed their torches at the creature. It screeched and writhed as the heat seared its flesh. Finally, it fell to the deck. Rais immediately stomped on it and the screeching stopped. Nobosi grabbed the creature, but Leopold took it from him and tossed it over the side.

Kanda watched in horror as blood poured from the wound. Leopold caught her as she swooned onto the deck. Briador checked the wound and grabbed a potion and some dry herbs out of his pack. He cleaned the wound with the potion, packed it with the dried leaves, and then wound a clean bandage around it.

Kanda woke while he was tending her and watched gratefully. She had no trouble healing others, but when it came to her, she was glad to have Briador around. "Will my healing spell work on me?" she asked.

"I don't see why not," Briador said smiling and handing her dawning dew.

Kanda used her healing spell and rubbed her leg above the bandage. "It feels better, but I think I'll leave the bandage on for a while."

When he was sure his sister was okay, Rais went back to sorting the fish in the net. Only this time he did it from a standing position, using his spear. Nobosi growled menacingly as one of the creatures appeared. The other Zargons he found were mercilessly slaughtered and dispatched to a watery grave.

The rest of the suntime passed uneventfully as they relaxed, taking turns to keep a watch on the banks. When the sun had retreated and the moon was again their only source of light, they began to sort and pack all but the warm wraps that they had managed to dry in the heat of the sun. Without its comfort and warmth, the air was growing cold. The fish was once again divided into equal quantities and packed into their food sacks. They filled their water bladders and prepared to leave the safety of the river.

Kanda trailed her hand in the water, smiling at the irony of life. The river monster, who had threatened their very survival at the beginning of their journey, was now a kind and gentle saviour, feeding them and safely delivering them to their destination.

The high banks began to shrink, and rocks appeared at the river's edge as the moon reached its highest point in the sky. As soon as they came out of the shelter of the cliffs, a strong wind buffeted the raft, pushing it to the side of the stream. Rais, Leopold, and Varn jumped to their feet, grabbing their poles to stop the craft from crashing into the rocky bank.

Soon the plains around them were visible. They stared in awe at the vastness of them. As the river started to curve away from the direction they needed to take, they used their poles to guide the craft into sheltered water between two large rocks. They jumped off and dragged it onto the sand behind shrubs. The strong wind whipped them, and the sand assaulted their bare skin like a thousand tiny needles as they unloaded.

Shielding her face with her hands, Kanda asked Briador, "Why do they call it the Plains of the Shifting Sands?"

"Unfortunately, you will soon find out," he replied, his face grim. "I think we had better find a spot to sleep for the rest of the moontime and start our journey at dawning. I don't want to face the dangers of this plain in the dark."

Sand continued to assault them as they searched the area for a sheltered place to camp. Stumbling along the banks blindly, they came to a rock formation that had a solid wall facing the direction of the wind. They gratefully threw themselves behind it. Kanda's body folded and she sat rubbing her leg above the wound. Nobosi licked her face reassuringly.

Kneeling on the bank, the others washed the sand from their faces and eyes. "Does the wind ever stop, Briador," Palesa moaned.

"Sometimes. It's not so bad during suntime. We'll see what dawning brings. I suggest you get as much sleep as you can. Next sun will be eventful."

"Can we light a fire?" Kanda asked, shivering.

"Best not to do that. The troops might have figured out that we have escaped on the river by now?"

Unrolling their sleeping blankets, they found a comfortable spot in the sand and settled down, piling their spare clothes on top of them to stay warm. Varn took first watch and Nobosi settled beside him at the entrance to their hideaway.

CHAPTER TWENTY-ONE

The Plains of the Shifting Sands

At dawning, the sun's rays bouncing off the water woke Kanda. Confused for a moment, she sat up and took in her surroundings. *The tops of the waves on the river look like dancing water sprites*, she thought, smiling as she stretched her aching body. The howl of the wind whistling through the gaps in the top of the rock wall intruded on the moment, and she remembered where she was. Dread at the thought of travelling over the unknown landscape of the plains chased away the appreciation of the beautiful sight before her. She looked for Leopold who had been sleeping beside her. His sleep mat was empty.

Rising slowly, she stood and tested her sore leg. To her amazement the pain had gone, and she could stand comfortably. She removed the bandage and checked the wound. A faint line where the teeth had sunk in was the only evidence that she had been wounded. She strolled down to the river for a drink and to wash away the sleep.

As she bent down over the water, a large shadow appeared below the surface. She leapt back, her heart racing. Then a head rose out of the water.

Leopold grinned as he hauled himself onto the bank. "Come in for a swim. It's a bit cold, but it's great."

Kanda clutched his arm. "What about the Zargons? You could have been attacked?"

Leopold shook his head and chuckled. "The water is very deep here. They live on the bottom. It's safe. Come on, come for a swim," he said, as he reached for her hand.

Kanda took a step back and studied him. She blushed as she took in his appearance. All he was wearing was his underpants. A light growth of hair covered his well-muscled chest. His arm muscles rippled as he brushed the water from his face. She dropped her eyes, not knowing where to look. Her heart was racing and that tingling feeling she had when he was close was coursing through her body. She backed away as he went to embrace her. "I had better wake the others," she stammered, turning, and hurrying back to the camp. She was surprised to see that only Palesa was there, still sleeping.

She hurried back to where Leopold stood looking out over the plains. "Where are Rais, Varn, and Briador? Their packs are gone."

"They went for a look around. Look, Rais is up there on that sand dune. Briador went with him and Varn took Nobosi and went down the river a bit to see if he could catch some fresh fish for breakfast."

Kanda stepped out from the shelter of the rock wall, shielding her eyes against the wind. She waved to her brother, and he waved back. "The wind is still strong," she said, turning back to Leopold. Just as she did, he leapt forward, his hand flying to his mouth in shock. She turned to see what he was looking at and couldn't believe her eyes. The high sand dune that her brother had been standing on had disappeared. A deep hollow had replaced it. "Rais! Oh, hell! Where is he? What happened?"

"The sand shifted. I have never seen anything like it. It moved like a wave on the ocean and flattened over there." He pointed to a spot about fifty strides away and started running towards it, calling to Rais as he ran.

Kanda was right behind him. "Rais, Briador, where are you?" she screamed.

They raced to where her twin had been standing and stared in horror at the hollow in the sand. *"Rais!"* Kanda screamed in anguish. Her heart was pounding and a feeling of dread she had never felt before swept over her. She clutched Leopold's arm as her legs threatened to fold.

His arm encircled her protectively as his eyes frantically searched the landscape. Then they heard a faint call from their right and started towards it. Hope flared in Kanda as she recognised the voice of her brother. As they climbed the dune, they saw a hand waving at them. A few more steps and they could see his head sticking out of the sand.

They charged towards him. Kanda's head spun as the shock and fear at seeing her twin buried up to his neck gripped her. He was struggling to push off the sand with his one free arm, but the wind was too strong, and the hole quickly filled again. They threw themselves down beside him. "Don't worry, we'll soon get you out," Leopold said. Kanda brushed sand from Rais' face and asked if he was okay.

Rais nodded. "I'm okay, but, boy, am I glad to see you."

Their backs to the wind, Kanda and Leopold dug desperately, uncovered the top of his body, and released his other arm. He joined the effort to dig the sand from around him. Then they realised he was buried in a standing position, and the hole would have to be deep and wide. The space they had made around him was now filling with sand.

As quickly as they dug it out, the wind forced it back into the hole. Realising the futility of their actions, Leopold took hold of Kanda's arm to stop her frantic digging. She slumped down beside him, brushing the sand from her twin's face as they searched for ways to get him out.

Rais moaned. "Even if we throw the sand out in the direction the wind is blowing, the hole will still fill from it blowing in on the other side. It's hopeless. Go and find Briador. He was standing at the bottom of the dune when it moved. I'm really worried about him."

Kanda's heart sank at the thought of Briador in the same predicament as Rais. She knew he would be too frail to help himself, even as much as her twin had. She rose to her feet and searched the area around them, but there was no sign of the old man. She shook her head. "No, we can't give up. We have to keep digging. The wind would eventually cover your head with sand. We will look for Briador when we get you out." She resumed her efforts, throwing the sand in the direction the wind was blowing.

"We need a wind break to stop the sand blowing in. What can we use?" Leopold said, searching the horizon.

Kanda struggled out of her wrap, her eyes lighting with hope. "I'll create a bubble of air to stop the sand," she said as she started to twirl it.

"Kanda, it's not long enough to make a bubble big enough to enclose all of us and allow me to throw sand out of the area. Do you have any other spells you can use – either of you?" Leopold shouted.

Kanda stopped and slumped to the ground. "I don't, and without Briador or my book, I can't do anything else."

Rais shook his head. "I only know how to use the lightning bolt spell, and if I try that, I'm likely to bury us all."

"Where is your book? If you fetch that we might find something that will help."

Bowing her head in despair, Kanda replied, "Back at the river. There is no time to go back for it." She buried her head in her hands. "How are we going to get him out without Briador?" she said, groaning.

Striding over to where Rais said Briador had been standing, she searched the ground again for any sign of the old man, but nothing remained. Shoulders slumped in defeat she went back to Rais and Leopold. She didn't need to tell them the result, the crushed expression on her face told them.

Examining the scene again, she muttered, "Maybe if I hold the wrap up to stop the sand from coming in you will be able to clear it more quickly." She held it up to block the wind, but the sand slid in under it. Thinking quickly, she buried the bottom of it in sand and tried again. This time she managed to stop the sand at the spot where her wrap was, but it blew in around it. "It's not big enough. We need a sleep mat. I'll go back and get one – and Palesa to help me hold it. You keep digging." With one last anxious glance at the boys, who nodded acceptance of her idea, she raced back toward the camp.

Palesa was sitting on the bank of the river, trailing her hand dreamily in the water. She looked up as Kanda charged in. "Where have you been? I was getting worried that you had all gone without me."

Kanda grabbed the sleep mat and ran towards her. "Quick, we have to save Rais. He is buried in the sand."

Palesa jumped to her feet. "Rais! Where is he?" But Kanda was already running back towards the boys.

Palesa's stomach knotted in anxiety as she tried in vain to keep up.

Kanda was a lot swifter and was stomping her feet impatiently by the time the other girl, panting, fell beside her. Kanda could see that Leopold had made little progress and was almost exhausted. Rais had stopped digging and closed his eyes in fatigue and defeat.

"Rais! Are you okay?" Palesa shouted. She knelt and stroked his face, brushing the sand away.

Rais opened his eyes and smiled faintly. "Just help Kanda, will you," he said softly, his voice thick with weariness.

Kanda held one corner of the sleep mat. "I could try to create the air bubble with this. It's long enough," she said and tried to twirl it around her head. But the wind was too strong, and she became entangled in it as the wind wrapped it around her. Impatiently, she untangled herself. "Come on! Take hold of the mat at the other end and hold it up like a shield," Kanda screamed at the other girl.

Palesa jumped to her feet and clutched the end of the mat. They stretched it along the edge of the hole. Leopold stopped long enough to bury the bottom in the sand at their feet, before resuming his digging. Biting her lip, Kanda watched his efforts weaken as exhaustion took hold. "Leopold, you hold the mat, and I will dig," she shouted.

He shook his head at her and tried to increase his efforts. The girls struggled to hold the heavy mat. They swayed on their feet as the force of the wind tried to snatch it from their hands.

"I can't hold on much longer," Palesa moaned. Her knees buckled and she fell to a kneeling position.

"What the hell!" a voice shouted from behind Leopold. They looked up to see the welcome sight of Varn and Nobosi racing towards them. Pushing his charge aside, Varn took his place.

"Varn, boy, am I glad to see you!" Kanda said.

Too weary to speak, Rais weakly slapped him on the shoulder to show his appreciation. Leopold collapsed beside Varn for a moment to regain his breath then joined in the digging. Working together, they soon had the sand piling up behind them. Barking furiously, Nobosi circled the group until Varn snapped at him to shut up. He moved in to lick Rais' face and then burrowed in beside him.

"Just a bit longer," Kanda said to Palesa. Hope surged through her. Her shoulder sockets were screaming in pain, but she was determined not to let go. Palesa struggled to her feet and braced herself against the force of the wind.

Kanda anxiously searched the terrain around them for signs of Briador. A picture of him buried like Rais and struggling to hold his head above the sand haunted her. At one stage, she thought she saw a movement on the horizon towards the farming district but dismissed it as a mirage.

The girls struggled to hold the mat high as the force of the sand piling up behind it made the weight unbearable. Just as they felt they couldn't hang on any longer, Varn stopped digging. "Okay, we've reached his knees. We should be able to pull him out now." He clutched Rais under the arms. "It will take all of us working together. Leopold, you reach in and grab him around the chest. Girls, take hold of his arms at the elbow and when I say lift, pull with all of your might. Rais, start moving your legs to help free them."

The girls dropped the mat over the pile of sand and slipped their hands under Rais' bent elbows. Leopold joined them as Varn shouted, "Now!"

Panic screamed through Rais' mind as he tried in vain to move his legs. They wouldn't budge. It was as if the sand was sucking him down. The group continued to pull but he didn't move. "It's hopeless. Go find Briador. He might know a spell to help," Rais muttered. As he spoke, a slight tremor shook them and the sand around the hole moved.

Varn jumped to his feet. "Rais, try to wriggle your legs now as we lift." He shouted to the others, "Pull!" They put all their strength into the effort and, as the ground trembled, the suction disappeared. They fell in a heap as Rais was released, panting from the struggle. But Varn jumped to his feet and shouted, "Run for the camp. The plain is about to move again."

Propelled by the urgency in his voice, they jumped up and raced for the camp. Nobosi barked behind Kanda, and she glanced back to see Rais struggling to run, his legs still numb from being buried. She screamed at Leopold, "Help me. Rais can't make it on his own."

"Go without me. I'll be okay," Rais shouted.

"No way! We didn't go through all that effort to see you buried again," Leopold said as they each took one of his arms.

Varn came striding back. He lifted the boy over his shoulder and shouted, "Run! There's no more time." The sand was slipping away. They staggered and stumbled as the ground trembled under their feet. Gaining their balance, they sprinted the last few strides to the camp. Leopold and Kanda threw themselves behind the wall as the ground disappeared beneath them. They turned anxiously to see if Rais and Varn had made it and were relieved to see them stumbling to their feet not far from Palesa and Nobosi.

Palesa moaned, "Oh, that is so scary." She rushed to Rais' side.

"Briador!" the twins said at the same time.

Varn shook his head in despair. "I'm afraid there's not much hope for him now. After two shifts, he will be well buried. We will look for him as soon as it is safe."

"What if we don't find him? How are we going to learn any more magic? We need him. What if he is ..." Kanda's voice trailed off as panic at the thought that was on everyone's mind strangled her voice.

They had all dropped their heads in anguish when he said there was no hope for their mentor. "Does anyone know how far apart those shifts were?" Varn asked.

Leopold looked at the sky. "The sun is high now, so at least half the sun-time has gone. The first shift happened when it was just about a quarter of the way, so a quarter of the sun-time. Is there some kind of pattern to them?"

"Yes, it varies depending on the season, but it is consistent. When it stops, we will go and look for Briador."

They watched silently from behind their shelter as the last of the sand fell into place. Their minds were already on the search for the old man – each imagining the worst outcome.

When Varn indicated it was safe, they hurried out and stood looking into the distance. Sand dunes nearby blocked their vision.

Leopold glanced at the rock wall beside them. "I'm going to climb onto the wall and see what I can see from up there."

Varn gave him a leg-up to the first foothold and he scrambled up. He stood looking into the distance for a while, turning to check each way. Then he shouted, "Varn, I can see some movement over there, in the direction of the farming district. It seems to be too big to be one person, but the haze creates illusions, so it is hard to tell."

Kanda shrugged. "It's the only lead we have. We'll go that way and see what we find."

Rais shook his head. "I think we should go to where you found me. Briador was standing beside the sand dune I was on. As my dune swept away, another formed where the old man was. It most likely buried him. That will be gone now. Maybe he is still there ... or at least his ..." Rais stopped himself from saying the word that was on everyone's mind, 'body'.

"The sand doesn't always go back to the way it was. The dunes could be in a totally different place," Varn said.

With looks of despair, the group moved silently towards the area where Rais had been found. The landscape had changed again, and they were confused about where he had been buried. They searched the area. Finally, Kanda looked back towards the river and declared, "I'm sure it was here. I could see that boulder just behind the edge of the rock wall when I looked back towards the river. So, this dune has replaced the hollow where Rais was."

Nodding, they stood and looked carefully at the terrain around them. Kanda walked down the dune to where Briador had been standing before the first shift, then in ever-increasing circles around the area. Panic caused her thoughts to scramble. Mentally she slapped herself. *I must focus. If I seek his life force, I might find him.* "Rais, I have to seek Briador's life force to see if he is near. Come and shelter me from the wind so I can concentrate. We have to find him. We will never be able to save our parents without him," she called.

Rais rushed to her side. Kanda pictured Briador and concentrated. She sent her mind out seeking his life force.

"Anything," Rais asked as she relaxed.

"No," Kanda muttered, shaking her head.

Nobosi prowled around behind them, sniffing the ground, and scratching at the sand every few feet. They searched for some time, walking further away, but always returning to the spot Rais was convinced Briador had been standing.

"It must be nearly time for another sand shift," Varn said looking anxiously for shelter. Sand dunes surrounded them. He shook his head in dejection. "I'm going to climb that huge dune over there and see if I can see any sign of him."

They watched expectantly as he reached the top. Suddenly, he dropped to his stomach and slid down towards them. Scrambling to his feet, he gestured at them to be quiet, and raced towards them. "Troops! At least ten," he hissed.

Nobosi lifted his head from where he had been sniffing and growled. Kanda quickly silenced him.

They looked frantically about. Nowhere to hide!

"How far away? What do we do?" Palesa whispered, clutching his arm.

"About 500 strides. There is nothing we can do, except hope the next shift buries them." Varn stared frantically around as his mind searched for a possible way out of this predicament.

The earth trembled beneath them.

"Or buries us," Rais said.

On her knees, head bowed in defeat, Kanda searched her mind for a way to save them. She went through the spells she had used. Then she jumped to her feet. "I know! I can save us!" she shouted.

"Shhh ..." they all chorused.

Clutching the healer's pendant, she waved her hand in a circle over her head, and started to chant:

Oh, spirit of the winds
I call on you today
to make a cushion with your sacred breath
on which we all can lay.
Deliver us now out of harm's way.

When she had completed the chant, wind swirled in front of her, chilling the air and filling it with a veil of sand. The gusts finally abated, and a glowing blue cloud formed. Shielding her eyes from the particles that still hung in the air, she gestured to the ground, and the cloud settled beside her. Kanda sank onto the cloud, exhausted.

"Quick hop on," Varn shouted as the earth shook and the sand started sinking below them.

Leopold jumped on beside Kanda, helping her as she struggled to sit up. When they were all aboard, Kanda gestured upwards to make it rise well above the highest dune – just as the sand mound they were on disappeared – a hollow taking its place.

Sitting up, she imagined a cloak, the colour of the sky, enveloping them, hiding them from view. A veil of blue settled around them. They huddled together, hoping that the troops didn't end up anywhere near them.

As the sand settled, they peered out. The troops were further away now – still on their feet. "How do they stay on top of the sand?" Kanda muttered.

"They are a lot bigger and heavier than us. You'd think they would be buried," Palesa said.

"Look, that one is lying down. They use their curved wooden shields to ride the sand waves like the ocean people ride the waves of the sea on their dug-out canoes," Varn said in amazement.

"That's what we need," Palesa exclaimed.

"No, we don't. Thanks to Kanda we have just what we need," Leopold said hugging her.

Varn looked towards the farming district. "We're not far away now. If we head to that hill over there, we can hide in a cave that I know. Can the cloud take us there, Kanda?"

Kanda bit her lip anxiously. "I'm not sure how long it will last. The last time we used it was a very short time. We have to go back for our backpacks. I will need my book of spells and potions. And what about Briador? We can't leave without him."

"You're right," Rais muttered. They all nodded.

They watched as the troops headed back in their direction. Kanda lowered the cloud to the ground. "We haven't got much time before they reach us," Varn said.

As he jumped to the ground Nobosi started sniffing the surface, growling, and digging frantically. Kanda put her hand on his collar and stared at the ground. A slight hollow formed where he was digging. As she stared, a vortex started in the sand and a funnel-shaped hole formed. Nobosi jumped back, growling. The sand at the bottom of the hole continued to cave in, as if it was being sucked down by the vortex. "Look, the sand is swirling and caving in. What can be making it do that?" Kanda whispered.

Nobosi dug at the edge of the hole, barking furiously. Rais took hold of him to quieten him and stop him jumping into the hole.

"Sand worms!" Varn exclaimed.

"What?" they chorused.

"Huge worms that live under the sand. If there is something buried, they will create a hole to expose it so they can eat it without sand."

Kanda's hand flew to her mouth. "Briador!"

They stood surrounding the hole and watched in horror. The cloud melted behind them, but they didn't notice.

Nobosi barked and continued to scratch at the top of the hole.

"Kanda, stop Nobosi from making that noise. The troops are not far away," Varn said as he glared at the animal.

Kanda dropped her hand on the liogon's collar and dragged him away. As quickly as it had started the whirlpool stopped. They moved forward as one and peered into the hole. There, at the bottom of the cave-in, was Briador. Varn restrained Rais as he stepped towards the edge. "No, the sand worms will get you too. There has to be another way."

"Kanda, create the bubble you made to rescue Yanis, and we'll go down and get him," Rais said.

Handing control of Nobosi to Leopold and asking them all to form a wall to protect her from the wind, Kanda quickly used her wrap to make the bubble around her and Rais. They stepped off the edge and drifted down towards Briador. A huge worm's head appeared beside Briador, and Kanda stopped their descent. "Quick, what will we do? We don't want the worm in our bubble. And we have to stop him from getting to Briador."

Instinctively, Rais raised his hand and sent a controlled blast of power at the worm. He feared he would create a cave in, but his aim was perfect this time. The creature flew out of the sand, dead. It dropped to the bottom of the hole and its head landed on Briador. A little sand covered their mentor's body but didn't bury him.

Kanda continued the descent and soon they were crouching beside him, the bubble surrounding him. While Kanda brushed away the sand, Rais grabbed the worm. "It's huge," he exclaimed. "The body is as thick as my thigh. Help me lift it off him, Kanda."

Kanda shuddered as she grabbed its head. The teeth were razor sharp. Struggling with the weight, they lifted it off Briador. Rais picked up their mentor. "We have to get him to the surface before more of them come."

Kanda grabbed his pack from beside where he lay, and they quickly rose to the surface. Rais lowered Briador gently to the ground. Nobosi broke away from Leopold's hold to lick his face.

"Rais, there are more worms. They're coming towards us," Palesa shouted.

Panicked, Rais turned and sent a power blast that shook the earth and filled the hole. A cloud of sand dust filled the air around them.

"Hell, boy, that blast was so loud that it will attract the troops. Look at that sand cloud. You may as well have sent up a sign saying, here we are. What were you thinking?" Varn shouted.

Rais lowered his head, but his eyes blazed. "I was trying to save our lives – that's what I was thinking."

Leopold ran to the top of the nearest sand dune to locate the troops. "You're right, they are coming this way. We have to get out of here." He scuttled down to where they were gathered around Briador.

Nobosi licked his hand while Kanda checked for pulse and respiration. Her hand flew to her mouth as deep sorrow swept through her body. "He's gone. There is no pulse and he's not breathing. I'll seek his life force."

Varn had been checking Briador while she spoke. He took her by the arm. "There's no time. He is gone. There is nothing you can do to save him. We have to go now."

Tears clouded Kanda's vision as she looked imploringly at Varn. "We have to take him with us."

"He will slow us down too much. The troops will bring his body to the city to claim the reward. We can get him back there and give him a decent burial." He took her by the arm and turned to where the cloud had been. It was gone.

"Kanda, quick create the cloud again," he said.

Leopold was lying on top of the dune watching the troops. He slid down and whispered, "No time. Run for the rock wall."

Rais stood for a moment undecided. He didn't want to leave their mentor to the mercy of the troops, but he could do nothing. Staying wouldn't help. He picked up Briador's backpack.

"Let's go, Kanda. We have to. Now there is only us to save our parents and free the land."

As they threw themselves behind the rock wall, panting, Varn said, "They will stop to recover Briador's body. That will buy us a little more time. But they won't all go back with it. We have to get out of here." He looked towards the farming district. "We're not far away. If we stick to this side of the rock wall and head to that hill over there, we can hide in the cave I mentioned. Grab your bags and bring everything with you. We will have to run for the shelter of the rocks at the bottom of the hill. The cave is just behind them. We can make it across the short strip of sand before the next shift if we hurry."

They scurried around and gathered up their things, then started towards the cave. Rais hesitated. The vision of Briador lying on the sand at the mercy of the troops flashed into his mind. Nobosi too seemed reluctant to leave. Rais finally sighed and turned away. He flung Briador's pack over his shoulder with his and raced after the others, Nobosi at his heels. At the end of the wall, Rais paused and crept up on the nearest sand dune to see what the troops were doing.

They were just coming down the last dune. Seeing Briador's lifeless body, the soldiers stopped to check on him. One of them got down on his knees and listened for a heartbeat. He looked up at the others and shook his head. He stood and lifted Briador onto his massive shoulder. 'We'll take him back for the reward. The others must be close," he shouted.

As they started to scan the area, Rais slid down. Nobosi was waiting for him and licked his face in pleasure. They sprinted after the others.

Staying as close as they could to the edge of the sandy plains, they raced for the shelter of the forest. Behind them, they heard a shout and realised they had been spotted. Varn looked back and saw their pursuers standing at the top of the last dune they had climbed. He looked forward. They were only 100 strides away from the edge of the forest and the cave in the hill. "We can make it if we pick up our speed," he called.

Kanda was already holding her side as a stitch cramped her muscles, but the sight of the large men rushing towards them was enough to make her forget it and increase her speed. Desperate to escape and carry out their mission, they sprinted on without looking back. By the time they reached the first of the trees they could hear the footfalls of the troops. Varn led the way and they dashed through the trees, threw themselves into the mouth of the cave and ran towards the rear.

He paused to look back. The troops had reached the cave entrance. "Follow me; there is a tunnel ahead that the troops won't be able to fit in."

Struggling to continue, the group dashed after Varn. Palesa had dropped behind. As the rest of the group sprinted into the passage she tripped and fell in the entrance. She struggled to rise. One of the troops threw himself to the ground, shoved his hand in the passage, and grabbed her by the foot. She screamed in panic and clutched the nearest rock to stop him dragging her back. Rais, who was just ahead of her, stopped, and looked back. "They have Palesa!" he shouted as he rushed to her side.

Nobosi followed Rais and was nipping at the soldier's hand when Varn and Leopold arrived to help. Knowing the soldier couldn't enter the narrow passage, they took out their spears and attacked his hand and arm. Yelping with pain, he let go and slid back.

Hauling Palesa to her feet, Rais half-carried her further back to safety.

Palesa fell where Kanda had collapsed. She grabbed Rais and pulled him down in a hug. "Thank you. I thought they had me," she said, sobbing.

Rais patted her back. "That's okay," he muttered.

As he stood, she laid back on the floor with her hands over her face. *Now I owe him for saving my life twice. I owe them both now. What am I going to do? I can't hand them in.*

"I can't go another step. Can we stop here for a rest? It'll be dark soon. Maybe the troops will go back to camp," Kanda said groaning and clutching her side.

"They won't leave. They will wait at the entrance for us to surrender when we get too hungry to hide. We must get further in. They could crawl to here while we were sleeping," Varn said.

Leopold pulled Kanda to her feet and lifted her into his arms. "I can carry you for a bit." His face flushed with pleasure as she snuggled her head into his shoulder and closed her eyes.

"Just for a bit then," she muttered sleepily.

With Varn in the lead they slowly moved deeper into the passage. "Where does this lead, Varn?" Rais asked.

"I don't know. I have never been in this far. I hope it leads somewhere."

Peering at the ground, Leopold said, "It doesn't look used. Maybe it doesn't go anywhere."

The group stopped and stared at him in horror. Kanda slid out of his arms.

"Then we're trapped. We will have to surrender. We only have enough food and water for a couple of suns," Palesa said frowning.

Rais paced the floor anxiously. "And we need to get to the city before then. We'll have to fight them. I'm sure I could take out the two of them."

"By now there could be many more," Varn said shaking his head.

Varn peered into the dark passage ahead. "We have to keep moving and hope it does come out somewhere. Do we have anything we can turn into a torch? As we go further in, it will get very dark in here."

Kanda dug into Briador's bag and found one of the torches they had used on the raft. She decided she would try the spell Briador taught Rais. She held it up, and concentrating, she moved her hand slowly along the bundle and said the spell that lit it. It burst into flame. Her face flushed with pleasure, she handed it to Varn. The rest of the group applauded, and she blushed as she bowed.

Following the glow of the torch, they moved after Varn. The passage became narrower, and the ceiling lower the further they went. The air was musty and cold. Soon they were stooping and only able to walk in single file. Kanda's heart raced as she glanced at the walls. To her amazement they weren't moving. Feeling more confident, she continued behind Leopold. Nobosi followed her protectively.

Leopold paused and asked, "Are you okay?"

She nodded, smiling, but not yet game to look too closely at the walls.

The tunnel wove its way through the hill. Many times, they paused at a crossroads, but Varn soon made a choice and they moved on. After a long time of back-breaking travel, Varn called a rest. "We'll sleep here. We need to eat and drink to keep up our strength but try to do it as sparingly as possible. I have no idea how long we will have to keep this up."

Leopold and Palesa sank to the floor gratefully, but Rais and Kanda stood looking at each other.

"We don't have time to stop. We have to keep moving. We have lost too much time already," Rais said pacing. Kanda nodded in agreement.

Varn hesitated, then said, "We will be no use to anyone if we arrive exhausted. We must take a rest."

Rais' and Kanda's shoulders sank. Their faces showed the frustration they were feeling.

They sank to the pebbled floor of the passage. Digging into their packs, they chewed hungrily on dried fish and sipped water. Kanda snuggled into Leopold's shoulder. Images of her mother being hung alternated with images of her being beheaded and she shook her head to clear them. *We must get there. I'll rest for a short time then I'm going on with or without them.* Finally, she burrowed into Leopold's body, now slumped in sleep, and drifted off.

Palesa looked for a place to sleep. There weren't too many dry spots. Water trickled down the walls of the tunnel in small rivulets and created a couple of puddles on the path. Leopold and Kanda had settled on the largest, dry spot available. She looked longingly at Rais, wishing she could snuggle down with him. He had wandered off and settled in the passage behind them with Nobosi at his side. She sighed. *It is no use. I don't think I will ever win him back. And now I can't turn them in. I just have to hope that someone recognises me so I can live my dream of being accepted into the palace.* Using her backpack as a pillow, she lay in the driest spot she could find, staring at the ceiling, pushing the niggling feeling of fear and rejection to the back of her mind.

Varn had been pacing since his conversation with the twins. He had moved further into the passage ahead. He came back and said, "Rais, I'm going to scout ahead a bit to make sure there is nothing close. I'm taking the torch. I'll be back soon."

Rais nodded. "Don't take too long. We don't have time for this." He checked the others. They looked like they were already asleep.

As soon as Varn disappeared around a bend, darkness fell on him as if someone had dropped a thick cloak. He had never experienced anything like it. He shivered. Not being able to see at all unnerved him and he sat up, all senses alert. The musty odour of the damp walls and ground assaulted his nostrils. Except for the breathing of Nobosi and his companions, the silence was complete. He listened for any change of sounds that would alert him to trouble. His mind wandered again to the time limit they were on. *From here we will have no idea of the passage of the sun. We have to get out of here. What if we are too late?* Images of his mother's body laid out for burial haunted him and he hung his head in his hands in despair.

Nobosi barked. He dropped his hand on the animal's collar and looked expectantly towards where Varn had disappeared. No torchlight showed. Then he heard a noise – a rustling sound as if someone was moving quietly towards them. It was coming from the passage ahead. Hackles up, Nobosi growled and strained to move forward.

Reluctant to shift in the pitch-blackness around him, Rais called to Leopold. "Leo, wake up! There is something coming towards us from the way Varn went."

"What? Where is Varn? Why is it so dark?" Leopold asked.

Kanda woke as he moved. "What's going on?"

"Varn went ahead to check and see if it was safe to sleep here. He has been gone a while. Shhh, listen."

Nobosi let out a frenzy of barking and when he stopped, they heard the noise again. Only this time it was close. Suddenly, Palesa let out a scream and jumped up. "Something just ran over my feet." She whimpered in terror as she felt her way along the wall towards Rais. "Rais! Where are you?" she screamed.

Speaking softly, he guided her to where he was. She fell against him and clung on with all her might. He held her for a moment then said, "What was it that ran over your foot? How big was it?"

"Smallish … and furry I think," she replied sheepishly.

They paused to listen again. The rustling had stopped. As they concentrated, they saw the faint glow of Varn's torch coming around a bend.

The light grew stronger the closer he came. They leapt to their feet, searching the area around them. They saw no sign of what had made the noise. Seeing them all standing with worried looks on their faces, Varn rushed to their side.

"What! What happened?"

"We heard something. A rustling sound as if something was coming towards us, then a small furry creature ran over Palesa's foot."

They searched some more but found nothing. "What did you find ahead, Varn?" Rais asked.

Varn's face was hopeful as he related his findings. "The passage narrows even more ahead. I got to a section where we will have to crawl. I couldn't see how far that went." He glanced at Kanda as he said that and got the reaction he expected. Her eyes grew wide. Fear spread over her face, and she shuddered and clung to Leopold's arm. He pulled her into an embrace and murmured reassuringly.

Varn continued, "But strangely, there seemed to be a light coming from a bend at the other end. The sun would be down now, and it seemed too bright to be the moon. I just hope it is not another cave and the troops waiting for us. Let's get as much sleep as we can. We may need all the strength we can muster next sun."

Palesa lifted her backpack to get more comfortable and the contents spilled out onto the ground, followed by a dozen hairy creatures about the size of her hand. Screaming, she hopped around as they ran over her feet in their haste to get away.

"Roatles," gasped Varn. "They mostly eat cloth so there won't be much left of your bag or what's in it," he added grimly.

Palesa examined her bag to find he was right. They had eaten through the bag and started on her clothes.

The rest of the group lifted their bags with the same result. The insects scurried for safety, their antennas waving frantically, as the group started stomping on any within reach. The hard, green shell of their flat body scrunched under foot and the acrid odour that filled the air soon had them clutching their noses. Nobosi ran around barking and snapping at any he could get near.

When they were all gone or dead, still holding her nose, Kanda said, "Let's go. I wouldn't be able to sleep with this stench, anyway. Besides, we don't have time to spare. Rais and I will go on. You can stay and rest if you like."

"Kanda's right. We're not staying in here any longer. I hope that light is the end of the tunnel – troops or not," Rais said.

Varn sighed. "We'll all go. We need to stay together."

Nodding in agreement, they all reached for their belongings. Lining the bottoms of their bags with large garments to cover the holes, they stuffed their things back in.

Leopold took the torch and went to the lead, shoving his chewed backpack under his arm.

Right behind him, Kanda stopped suddenly. "Leo, they ate the seat of your pants?" Kanda cried, her hand over her mouth trying not to laugh.

Leopold dropped his bundle as he reached around to feel his rear end. "What!' he asked. As his hand groped, he touched bare flesh. Gasping, he turned to face her, his back against the wall. "What happened?"

The group was laughing so hard they couldn't reply. Finally, Varn was able to control himself long enough to say, "The roatles. They have eaten your trousers and undies."

Leopold tried desperately to see behind him without success.

Kanda finally stopped laughing, and, sorting through the bundle of clothes at his feet, handed him a spare pair of trousers and underpants. "Turn your back everyone, while he changes."

Stifling their laughter, the group did as instructed.

When he indicated he was ready, wiping his eyes, Varn said, "Okay, we needed that. Let's move away from the stench of the roatles."

They walked to the start of the narrowing of the tunnel. Varn handed Kanda the torch. "Put this out for a minute, please, so I can see the light up there a bit more clearly."

Kanda doused the torch and they got down on their knees and peered into the tunnel.

"It looks like torchlight, but very bright – more than one torch," Rais said.

"It only seems to be a short distance to the bend – about 20 strides. Why don't we go there and see what it is? If it is troops, they might be asleep," Leopold suggested.

Kanda clung to his arm. Even though the last tunnel didn't bother her too much, the sight of the small dark tunnel before them filled her with dread.

Palesa drew back. "It's dark in there. We won't be able to use our torch in case they see us coming. What if there are more creatures? Dangerous ones. Let's wait until dawning."

"It may not be any brighter in here when it is light outside. And if the troops are there, only one will be on duty, the rest will be sleeping. Leo's right, we should go at least to the bend while it is dark." Varn looked to the others for approval. They nodded.

"I'll lead," Rais said as he got into crawling position.

Leopold took Kanda by the arm. "You go next. I will be right behind you."

Reluctantly, Kanda started crawling after Rais. She could barely see his outline in the light from up ahead. She dropped her eyes to his boots and breathed deeply as she crawled. It seemed to take forever to her, but they were soon at the corner. The tunnel opened out there and they could all stand again. They crammed into the small space, pressing against the wall. Nobosi started for the corner, sniffing, his tail wagging. Rais grabbed his collar and gestured for him to sit.

"The smell of food cooking is coming from around there. It must be the troops," he whispered.

The group breathed deeply. "Oh, that smells, so good. I'm starving," Palesa moaned.

"Shhh," they all whispered.

Rais put his hand up for them to stay where they were and edged his way to the corner. "There are bushes ahead," he whispered. He moved forward, pushed aside the bushes, and peeped out. He came back and fell against the wall, his eyes wide with shock.

"What?" they all chorused.

His face split into a huge grin as he said, "You won't believe this, but I think this tunnel comes out in the city. A gate at the end of the tunnel leads to an alley with houses. I could hear the sounds of people moving around nearby."

Varn went around the corner and looked out. When he came back, grinning, he said, "Yes, it is the city. And no one seems to be waiting for us, so I guess the troops don't know about the tunnel exit. I'll go check if the gate is locked and see if it is safe to leave."

He was soon back. "The old lock is rusted, but I can't get it to break. We'll have to squeeze out over the top. I was able to break the top rail."

They went to the gate and peered through with wonder. Coming from their cloistered world, Kanda and Rais had never seen anything like the sight before them. Two-storey buildings lined the alleyway. The delicious aroma of cooking food only just overpowered the stench of the animal manure on the cobblestones and the rubbish that was discarded in corners.

"No one is about so it must be time for moontime meal," Varn said quietly. "Let's get over this gate and disappear before we are spotted."

He climbed up the gate, and with difficulty, squeezed through the gap and dropped to the ground. Rais and Leopold hoisted Nobosi to the top and he jumped down on the other side and began a sniffing frenzy at all the new smells that teased his nose. Once they were all over, they looked around. None of the teenagers had any knowledge of the city but Varn remembered it.

"It will be safer if you all stay in the alley while I find a place for us to hide. I will climb that ladder over there to have a look around and get my bearings. Wait in that dark, recessed gateway over there." He shimmied up a ladder on the side of a building and climbed onto the roof. With a wave to them, he disappeared across the roof onto the next building.

CHAPTER TWENTY-TWO

Into the city of danger

The group huddled in the gateway listening to the unfamiliar sound of cart wheels on the cobblestones, people calling to each other and animal's hooves shuffling on stone. The gate obviously led to an animal compound. The stench of manure was very strong and within a short time both the girls were holding their noses and trying not to vomit.

"I can't stay here. I'll be sick," Kanda moaned. She walked out into the alleyway and moved away. The others followed. Nobosi chased a roatle that ran out of a pile of rubbish and Rais had to go after him to stop him racing out of the alley. The others huddled in a recessed doorway opposite the animal pen, but the stench of rotting rubbish soon chased them further. Gasping for clean, fresh air they moved to the end of the alley.

It opened onto a cleaner, brighter roadway and they stumbled forward in awe. Shops and much bigger buildings lined the street. People gathered in eating establishments chatting as they waited for their meals. Street merchants sold their wares on every corner. The teens wandered the street, sticking to the shadows, gazing in wonder at all they saw, and breathing the air that was full of food aromas that made their stomachs ache with hunger.

On the first corner, a man waved a skewer of meat and vegetable under their noses, tempting them to buy. Rais asked how much and dug in his pocket to see if the coins Nona had given him was enough for four of them. Finding with delight they were, he handed it over. They grabbed a skewer each and went on their way.

"We had better stay out of sight as much as possible. Keep an eye out for Varn. He will come back looking for us," Leopold said between mouthfuls. They headed for the nearest darkened doorway where they could keep an eye on the alley entrance. Nobosi whined and they all shared a little of their meal with him.

Suddenly, they heard shouting and the street cleared. To their horror, troops marched towards them. They cowered back further in the corner as the first of them went by. In the middle of the procession, they saw two soldiers carrying someone on a stretcher.

Wondering if it was Briador, Kanda stepped forward to get a better look. Her hand flew to her mouth in shock. It was him. He lay on the stretcher as pale and as still as death.

As Leopold grabbed her to haul her back, the nearest soldier stopped.

"Here, Miss. What are you doing out at this time without an adult?" Spotting the others in the shadows behind her, he called to another soldier. "What have we got here? A group of lost children by the look of it."

The other soldier joined him and demanded to see their papers. They stared dumbstruck, not sure what to say. Finally, Leopold said, "I ... arrr ... we forgot to bring them with us. We'll have to go home and get them."

"Why don't I just come with you? Then you won't have to come out again. The streets are not safe for you younguns at moontime."

Leopold nodded to the others. "Sure, let's do that." He set off down the road. The others followed wondering what he was up to and fearful for their lives.

The soldier strode along behind them. When they drew alongside the stretcher carrying Briador, Kanda's eyes were drawn to his still form. "Oh, Briador," she muttered. He suddenly sat up and looked straight at her. "Run," he mouthed. He slid off the stretcher.

Startled, the soldiers stopped and dropped the stretcher. Briador turned and ran as fast as he could in the opposite direction. All the troops ran after him, including the one escorting the group. Nobosi barked furiously and chased them down the road.

Stunned, the group stood stock still for a moment. Then, grabbing Leopold and Rais by the arm Kanda said, "He's alive. Oh my God, he's alive. He said, run. Let's get out of here while they are distracted."

They raced for the nearest corner and ducked into a side street, only to discover it was a dead end. They turned back but weren't game to step out. Cowering against the high stone wall, in the shadow of a tree that spread over it, they resigned themselves to being captured. Suddenly, a rope ladder snaked down the wall beside them and a young voice from the tree above called, "Quick, climb up the rope. You'll be safe in here."

They hesitated and looked at each other. With a screech, Owl landed on the wall. Taking that as a sign that it was safe, Kanda grabbed the ladder and climbed swiftly to the tree above. She found a youth and a girl about their age waiting for them.

"Jump down into the yard. You are safe here. I don't know who you are, but I was out on the street and saw what happened. If you don't have papers, you will go to the dungeons. We'll take you to the house. Mum and Dad will help you get papers."

One after the other they jumped from the tree into the yard. Once they were all over, their rescuers pulled the rope ladder up and dropped it on the inside of the wall.

The youth turned to them. "I'm Kaden and this is my sister, Enolie. Come with us and we will show you where to hide until we sort out papers for you."

As they introduced themselves, Rais said, "Thank you for rescuing us. But aren't you worried about getting caught?"

"This is a safe house. Both of our parents and I work in the palace and Yaholo thinks we are loyal. We can explain better inside," Kaden said.

They followed them to a basement door. Kaden used a key to unlock it and they stood back as he opened it. As they climbed down the stairs and stepped inside, they were amazed at the sight before them. The room was comfortably furnished with tables and chairs. Off to one side were several rough beds all covered in animal fur rugs.

"This is the meeting room for our army and a refuge for anyone in trouble," Kaden said proudly.

"Army?" they all chorused.

Kaden explained that they had formed an army of teenagers to protect themselves and each other from harm and exploitation. "We can supply you with false papers so you can go freely around the city, but it might be good to wait a while before you go out again. They will be searching for you."

"We had better get you some clean and better clothes too. You will stand out too much in those," Enolie said eyeing them up and down.

Kanda blushed as she was inspected. "We have been travelling for many suns and have been in a few messy situations."

"Where have you come from, and why are you here?" Enolie asked.

They stood looking at each other for a moment not sure how much to tell them. Rais coughed and they all looked at him. He shook his head gently as he said, "We have come from one of the outlying farm areas to look for work."

"There is not much work for teens here, except at the palace," Enolie told them.

"I'll go get Mum. She will make you welcome and get things underway for your papers. We have a meeting of the Freedom Army here later. You can meet the rest of the group," Kaden said heading for the internal stairs.

"I'll go find you some clean clothes and organise a bath for you," Enolie said smiling. She followed her brother up the stairs.

Once they were alone, Rais turned to the group. "We really don't know enough about these people to tell them who we are. They could be after the reward. Let's just play it safe until we are sure." Turning to Kanda he said, "Take off your pendant and put it in your pocket for now. That will be a giveaway."

Nodding, Kanda slipped off the pendant and pushed it into her pocket. Rais did the same.

"You're right. We must be careful. We don't want you both captured now we are so close, do we, Palesa," Leopold said placing an arm around Kanda's shoulders and glaring at Palesa.

"No, of course not," Palesa agreed blushing.

Enolie returned with clean clothes, closely followed by a tall stout woman. "This is my mum, Faizar," the girl said smiling.

The older woman eyed them up and down. Her gaze rested on Kanda and Rais and her eyes narrowed. Smiling, she said, "Welcome to our home. You are quite safe here. Girls, go with Enolie and she will take you to our bathing area where you can clean up and don clothes more appropriate to city teens. Here the teens wear the light green suits that my children wear. In your farm clothes and your worn and dirty blue outfits you will stand out too much."

As the girls followed her daughter up the stairs, Faizar turned to the boys. "Okay, tell me your full names so I can organise your papers. I know one of you is Rais and one is Leopold, but I need to know your father's name. Your papers must say, Rais, son of ... and your father's name and occupation."

Rais and Leopold had lifted their hands as their names were mentioned, but now they stood looking at each other, trying to work out what to say.

Finally, Rais stammered, "I don't know who my father was. I believe he was killed in the invasion. I was raised by an elderly couple."

"Me too," Leopold said.

Faizar frowned and studied their faces. She nodded. "Okay, then I guess we will have to make up a father's name for you both."

As she was speaking, her son returned. In his hands he carried a bundle of official looking documents.

Faizar turned to him. "From this sun forward, Rais will be known as Rais, son of Aron, blacksmith, and Leopold will be Leopold, son of Sairs, wheelmaker." As she spoke, Kaden wrote on the forms in his hands.

Faizar nodded approvingly. "Now, as Kanda is your sister, Rais we will give her the same father's name and occupation. And we will pretend that Palesa is your sister, Leopold and she can use yours."

"Mother, we need an address for them," Kaden said.

"Of course. Put down the address of the lodging house in the old town area. My friend owns that, and she will swear you live there if I ask her to."

Kaden added the information to the forms, turned to the youths and handed them their papers. They folded them and put them in their pockets. The boys looked up as they heard laughter and saw the girls coming down the stairs.

Leopold's face softened as he saw Kanda. Her blonde hair shone in the glow of the lamp and curled around her face. Her skin was pink from the scrubbing she had given it. The soft green suit hung from her body and enhanced her curves. "Wow, Kanda that colour really suits you. You look beautiful," he said.

Kanda blushed and smiled. Going to his side, she kissed his cheek. "Thanks."

Palesa looked at Rais, expectantly. He smiled and said, "You both look great." But he couldn't help admiring the way Palesa looked with her amber hair gleaming and her lightly freckled face glowing. "Green suits you, Palesa." *It's a shame she doesn't have the personality to go with her gorgeous looks,* he thought.

Palesa smiled ruefully. *I guess I will have to settle for that.*

"You look like different people," Faizar said smiling. Then she frowned and nodded as she studied Kanda. Turning to the boys she said, "Kaden, take the boys to the bathing area while I make them all something to eat."

The girls followed her up the stairs and into the kitchen. "My husband, Dagma will be home from the palace soon. He has had to work late. He hates his job as tax recorder for Yaholo. But it is only a matter of time now. Soon the army we are gathering will overthrow the evil ruler and free Edalene, Baldasarre and the King."

She watched Kanda for a reaction. Kanda's eyes widen. "What do you mean?"

"Our healer, Edalene is to be executed at sunset in 3 suns' time. So, we must act swiftly." She looked deeply into Kanda's eyes as she added, "We were hoping Baldasarre's and her children had survived and would come back to help. A messenger was sent to find them and Briador, but we have heard nothing." She nodded in satisfaction at the girl's confused and startled expression.

Kanda and Palesa stared at her. Kanda's mind raced. *Should we tell her who we are? What if it's a trap? What if they know who we are and are going to turn us in?*

"That's amazing," Palesa said. "I'm so glad we are here for that. Maybe we can help." She looked at Kanda, eyebrows raised as she spoke.

Kanda shook her head. Palesa nodded. They sat quietly, watching the older woman prepare a meal. The aroma of the food cooking made them clutch their stomachs as hunger pains cramped them.

"What do you do at the palace?" Palesa asked.

"I'm the head housekeeper. It's a good role. I get to go to all areas of the palace to supervise staff. That way I can see what is going on. I also get to deliver meals to the King and his oracle, Baldasarre." She again watched for Kanda's reaction.

"Could you get us jobs in the palace?" Kanda asked breathlessly.

"Yes, I probably could, but we need to have a long talk first about what to expect and what is expected of you."

The boys joining them interrupted Kanda's reply. She turned to Rais, eyes bright with excitement. Putting her hand in her pocket and clutching her pendant, she probed his mind cautiously. When she connected but no white light appeared, she sighed with relief. *It must be because we are so close,* she thought. She sent him a message. *They are going to overthrow Yaholo. We came just at the right time.* She said, "We can get jobs at the palace."

He frowned and walked closer. *Did you say who we are?*

She shook her head. *But maybe we should. She knows about the messenger who came to fetch us and about Briador.*

"I'm not sure that is wise. We'll talk about it later," he said quietly.

Faizar heard his comment and her eyes lit up.

A large older male came through the door at that moment. "Oh, there you are, Dagma," his wife said.

He smiled, nodded, and eyed the gathered group. "And who do we have here, then?" he said.

Faizar introduced the visitors and his children told him how they had rescued them from the guards.

"Well done," he said patting them on the back. "We have enough innocent youths in the dungeon."

"I was telling them about our plans to overthrow Yaholo and free Edalene," his wife said.

He raised his eyebrows and nodded. "It can't be soon enough for me. If I have to work with him much longer, I will personally throttle him."

"That can't happen unfortunately, his protection spell saves him from physical harm. Trying would just get you sent to the gallows and someone else would take your place," Faizar said as she dished out their meals.

"I know, but it is so hard to be a part of what is happening at the moment. The people of Nevaah are helpless against his tax collectors and have nothing more to give. The ones who can't pay are thrown in the already crowded dungeon. It will be good to get rid of him. I hope our plan works."

"Oh, I think it will now," his wife said nodding at where Rais and Kanda sat woofing down their food as if they were starving.

He turned and studied the pair. His eyes lit up with hope and he turned to her questioningly. "I believe so," she whispered in his ear as she dished him a second helping.

When the meal was over, Faizar asked Kaden and Enolie to take Leopold and Palesa to the basement and prepare the room for the meeting. "Rais and Kanda, would you please stay to help clean up?" she asked.

Their stomachs bulging with delicious food, the twins happily agreed. But as soon as they started to clear the dishes, Faizar put a hand on their shoulders and said, "Please sit down."

Puzzled they sat back at the table. Looking kindly at them, Faizar said, "We know who you are. You are the image of your mother, Kanda, and I have worked with her for a long time. You have chosen a perfect time to return."

Kanda and Rais looked at each other, but before they could reply, Dagmar asked, "Do you have any of your parent's powers. Kanda, can you heal like Edalene? Rais, do you have Baldasarre's powers and mind reading skills?"

Rais was the first to find his voice. Realising that their secret was out he said, "Yes, I do have some of Father's powers, but they are not fully developed. Kanda has healing power and has been able to master some of the skills in her healer's book and she has some of father's powers too. She has the healer's pendant and the book of spells. Briador was teaching us before he died... arrr... was captured."

"Briador was captured?" their host said together.

Rais and Kanda told them the full story of the journey to The Walled City. When they had finished, Dagma said, "So Varn is back and somewhere in the city, good. From what you say, Briador is probably in the dungeon by now.

That won't be too much of a problem. That is the first place we will go. Everyone in there is an ally and as soon as we release and arm them, they will fight to the death to get rid of the man who put them there."

"It is a shame we can't get Briador out earlier to continue your lessons. Mind reading skills would be very handy. Did he teach you that yet?"

"No, but Kanda and I can read each other's minds through our pendants."

"Oh, well that could be handy. Maybe if you can get to him in the tower your father can teach you to read minds."

"If we get jobs in the palace, we will see him and Mother, won't we?" Kanda said.

"I will see what I can do to get you a job in the palace, but we will have to change your appearance first. Anyone who knows Edalene and Baldasarre will recognise you both," Faizar said. "You had best go down now. The meeting will be just starting, and you need to meet the members of Kaden and Enolie's Freedom Army."

"Are you sure that we will be safe working in the palace?" Rais asked.

"When I change your appearance you will, as long as you are careful. Don't say who you are. We can never be sure of people's loyalty."

They rushed to the stairs, fired up now to meet the rest of the teen army and join the cause. Now that they believed that they had some chance of succeeding in their original task, they couldn't wait to start. What they saw in the basement made them stop in amazement. The room was crowded with young people. The cacophony of voices in the closed-in room was deafening. "Wow, there must be at least 20 people," Kanda said.

They slowly walked down the stairs, studying the faces of the people closest to them. Kaden spotted them and raised his hand. Silence fell on the group and all turned to see what had grabbed his attention. Embarrassed, the twins stopped and waved sheepishly.

"Meet two more new members of our troop; Rais and Kanda," Kaden said gesturing for them to finish their descent.

Applause broke out, and faces the colour of the setting sun, the twins joined Kaden, Enolie and their friends.

A tall girl had been watching them as they walked down the stairs. She came over, inspecting them more closely. "Rais and Kanda. I don't believe it. Baldasarre's and Edalene's twins," she said quietly.

Rais and Kanda turned on her. "How do you know that?" Rais stammered.

"I worked with your mother at the palace. I'm Kacia. We got on very well and she never stopped talking about you two. Rais this, Kanda that. She spent her waking moments worrying about you and speculating on your inherited talents and when you would show up. She studied the faces of all the new staff carefully, obviously waiting for you."

"Is she alright?" Kanda asked.

"Do you see Father?" Rais said.

"Yes, to both questions. I take her, your father, and the King their meals and smuggle messages to them from supporters in the palace. They will be thrilled to know you have made it safely."

Rais looked at Kanda, eyes glowing. "Faizar is going to see about getting us jobs in the palace so we can see them."

"I hope she is going to change your appearance first. You will be recognised as you are."

"Yes, she said she would, but I don't know how?" Kanda said biting her lip.

Leopold came over and the girl chatted to him for a short time then drifted away.

Rais hurried after her. "Please don't mention to anyone who we are. We need to keep it quiet… for our sake, Mother's, and this family's."

Kacia smiled. "I wouldn't dream of it. Your mother's life is important to me too."

Kanda looked around. "Where is Palesa?" she asked Leopold.

He nodded in the direction of a corner where Palesa was in deep conversation with a youth with auburn hair that matched hers.

"Who is he?" Kanda asked.

"Not sure. He works in the palace. In the washroom I think he said. Kaden said he is one of their spies."

"Oh well, Palesa looks very interested in what he has to say. Maybe now she will get over Rais."

Just as she said that, Palesa looked their way. A look of guilt crossed her face and she turned away.

Kanda looked at Leopold frowning. "Did you see that look?"

Leopold nodded, a grim expression on his face. "I had better keep an eye on those two."

Kanda tilted her head and looked quizzically at him. "Why? What do you think they are up to?"

Kaden chose that moment to come over and Leopold shook his head and muttered, "Later." The youth took them around the group introducing them to some of the leaders.

To the newcomer's surprise, there was no discussion about the overthrow, so they didn't mention it. After the meeting was over, Rais went over to Kaden and Enolie. "I thought we would be talking about the overthrow and making plans. But they were more interested in arranging social occasions."

"We are not involved in the adult's planning yet, and most of the group don't even know there are plans afoot. It's best that way. When they need to know we will tell them."

As he walked away Rais turned to Kanda and Leopold. He told Leopold about their conversation with Faizar and Dagma.

Leopold looked over to where Palesa sat staring into space. "Let's keep this to ourselves for now."

They followed his gaze. "Why, do you think Palesa is a problem?" Rais asked. They told him about her deep conversation with Thoro and the look of guilt they saw. Leopold filled them in on the conversation he had with her about turning them in.

"No… surely not, not after we both saved her life. But I have no problem keeping it from her," Kanda said glaring at her.

Rais paced. "But we are running out of time. They didn't say when they are planning to strike."

Kanda frowned. "Faizar said mother was to be executed at sunset in 3 sun's time. So, it will have to be next sun or the one after."

Kaden returned and gave them bed mats out of the cupboard under the stair to put on the cots and bid them good-sleep. They settled on their beds, confident now that they were amongst friends. As Kanda lay back and closed her eyes, she felt a hand on her arm. Opening her eyes, she found Leopold bending over her. "I ... err ... I can't go to sleep without you now. Is it okay if I join you?"

She scooted over in the narrow cot, and he snuggled in beside her. Her head resting on his chest and his strong arms around her, she was soon in a deep sleep.

Palesa felt a pang of envy and looked to where Rais lay. It was obvious now that she could never win him back. The conversation she had with her new friend consumed her mind and she lay there planning the next move in her dream to be accepted into the palace.

The next dawning, Faizar woke them to tell them she was going to work. She told them Enolie would be down soon and to stay inside for suntime. "They may have realised that Briador was trying to save you when he ran. It won't take much for them to work out who you are. I will bring home something to change your appearance before we get you into the palace next sun."

When she had gone Kanda turned to her brother. "Oh, Rais, what if they torture Briador for information. He is not strong enough to take too much punishment."

"He'll be okay. Remember, he has some magic powers so he will be able to protect himself. He won't tell them anything."

Leopold and Palesa nodded grimly in agreement. They sat in brooding silence, each concerned about the old man.

Kaden broke them out of their reverie as he too came to say he was leaving. He carried a musical instrument that

236

Rais recognised from one of his books as a Satir. "Do you play that for Yaholo?"

"Yes, it's great, actually. At every meal I help serve the food to the main table then settle in the corner playing music for them. Sometimes, I'm one of the food tasters, so I get to try what our evil leader eats. It's very interesting what conversations I overhear. This sun's offering should be good. I'll know more when I come home after sundown. See you then." With a wave, he hurried up the stairs.

A scratching noise on the basement door startled them. Not sure what to do, Rais moved to the door to listen. The scratching happened again and then a whining sound. "Nobosi?" Rais said quietly.

A loud bark was the answer. As Kanda rushed over to the bottom of the stairs, Rais opened the door a crack. Nobosi nearly knocked him down as he leapt at the door, forced it open and bounded down the stairs. Rais closed and locked the door again as Nobosi jumped up on Kanda, his feet on her shoulders, licking her face in excitement.

"Okay, boy, I get it. I'm pleased to see you too," Kanda said, trying to push him down.

When they had settled him, Rais reached down to pat him. As he ran his hand over his head he stopped. "He's hurt! There's blood on his head," he said, examining him.

They all gathered around as Rais lifted his hair to see where the blood was coming from. On the side of his head was a large welt. "The bastards hit him with those clubs they carry."

Tears came to Kanda's eyes as she checked the wound. "It must have been while he was trying to protect Briador."

They cleaned the wound and Kanda performed her healing spell on him.

"He must have followed our scent to the wall and then came around to the gate to find us. What a clever thing you are, Nobosi," Kanda said stroking him. The animal was content to settle under her feet. Finally, he fell asleep.

Enolie came down a little while later to tell them to come to breakfast. She was off to her school after they had eaten.

She stopped in her tracks as she spotted their pet. "Where did the liogon come from?"

"He's ours. He raced after the troops that were chasing Briador. He found us and was scratching at the door. They injured him," Kanda said.

Enolie came over to give him a pat.

"Is it okay if he stays in here with us?" Rais asked.

"Of course. After I'm gone, it would be best if you stay in the basement all suntime. Only go up when you really need to ... you know, for the bathing room, food and stuff."

They promised they would. After cleaning up the breakfast dishes, and using the bathing room, they retreated to the basement bringing food for Nobosi. Kanda wandered the room inspecting all it contained. She found a bookcase full of books and settled on her cot with one about the palace. To her surprise, inside were diagrams of the layout of the palace. "Hey, look what I found," she called to the others.

She took the book to the nearest table, and they poured over the internal map of the Royal abode.

"There are the basement entrances, one off the hall outside the kitchen and one from the outside."

Palesa leaned in for a close look and said, "Where is the Great Hall and Yaholo's rooms?"

Kanda pointed them out as Leopold asked, pointedly, "Now why would you want to know that, Palesa?"

The girl bowed her head as she replied. "Oh, I'm just interested. That is where Thoro said he mostly works. He is one of Yaholo's food tasters and looks after his clothes."

"Who is Thoro? Is he the guy you were talking to so closely in the corner at the meeting?" Kanda asked.

Palesa nodded, a crimson flush settled on her face and neck.

Leopold raised an eyebrow. "Food taster? Kaden said he was one of them too. Why would he need them? Is he afraid he will be poisoned?"

"He should be, it would be one way to get rid of him," Kanda said.

"But I thought he had a protection spell. Wouldn't that stop him from being affected by poison?" Palesa asked.

Kanda shook her head. "No, according to my book, it only stops him from physical harm."

Palesa nodded thoughtfully.

They spent the rest of the suntime going over the many books on the palace and the Royal Family that filled the bookshelves in the room. By the time Enolie returned home they felt like they knew the palace as well as they did the basement.

"Kaden, Mother and Dad are going to be late. Kaden slipped out during the afternoon to tell me. Apparently, there is a special meeting of Yaholo's followers to work out how to capture you two," Enolie said, nodding at Rais and Kanda.

"They know we are here?" Kanda said her eyes wide and her voice squeaking in fear.

"Well not here, exactly. They worked out who you were and Briador didn't deny it. He told them you were instructed to leave the city and hide out in the forest if you had trouble. They have searched the city and are now having a meeting about where to start looking on the outside."

"Hell! Did he say if Briador is okay?" Rais asked.

"Apparently, he is. He has woven a protection spell around himself to make him immune to their torture. They are trying to starve him into telling them more, but he has just done what he did when he was buried – shut his body down and put himself in a state of suspended animation."

Kanda nodded thoughtfully. "So that is how he did it. No wonder I couldn't find a pulse or respiration. If I had sought his life force, I would have known that."

"But surely that is dangerous. He can't fight back if he is like that. They could kill him!" Leopold said in horror.

"Not with his protection spell. They can't even touch him."

While they were eating their moontime meal, prepared by Kanda and Enolie, Faizar came home, her leather bag bulging. Out of it she pulled sacks of hair dye and skin creams.

"We'll get started on your transformation after the meal," she said.

"When do you plan to strike?" Kanda asked.

"We need time to change our plans to include you. Our troops are working on the final plan now. There will be a meeting soon. We will get you to that after we change your appearance."

"What's the news on the search and Briador?" Rais asked.

"You will have to wait for Kaden and Dagma. I was in the kitchen today and don't get to hear much in there."

After the meal, Faizar took Kanda to the bathing room and opened the hair dye. "I think we will make your hair dark brown and give your pale skin a rub with this cream. It has a skin dye that will darken it to an olive glow. That should make you harder to recognise. We will dye Rais' hair red and give him a lighter brown skin tone more in keeping with his new hair colour," she said smiling.

Kanda nodded, nervous but excited. "Whatever it takes to get me in to the palace is okay with me."

When her transformation was complete, she stared at her reflection dumbfounded. "Gosh, I wouldn't recognise me."

Faizar nodded in satisfaction. "Now it is Rais' turn."

Kanda walked nervously down the stairs. All eyes turned to watch her entrance. Their faces registered amazement. Leopold was the first to speak. "Wow, Kanda, you look amazing. I hardly recognised you."

"Does it look all right?" she asked nervously.

"Great!" chorused Enolie and Palesa.

Rais nodded in agreement.

Leopold walked over and took her in his arms. "You look stunning." He kissed her softly.

Enolie raised her eyebrow at the sign of affection. "Lucky girl," she muttered eyeing Leopold.

Her face the colour of beetroot, Kanda turned to her brother. "Your turn, Rais. Faizar is waiting for you."

"I can't wait to see what Mum does to you," Enolie said smiling.

By the time Rais came back, Dagma and Kaden had come home. Even though Kanda, Leopold, and Palesa had begged for information the minute they walked in, Dagma made them wait until Faizar and Rais had joined them.

Once they had all admired Rais' transformation and commented on it, they gathered around the table in the basement to hear the news. Just as Dagma started to speak, they heard a knock on the basement door. Nobosi growled and got to his feet. Kanda dropped her hand on his back to quieten him. Startled, Dagma raced to the corner of the room quietly calling the twins, Palesa and Leopold to follow. He stopped at the end wall, ran his hands over the carved corner of the frame of a painting of the palace. Suddenly an opening appeared in the wall behind it. "In there. I will find out who it is," he said.

The space they entered was not much bigger than a closet. They huddled in there, not game to speak or move as the door closed again. Nobosi huddled at their feet.

They heard Dagma shout, "Who's there," and a muffled reply. Then the basement door was opened and closed. They held their breath as they heard footsteps coming towards their hideout.

The door opened and they peered around Dagma to see who had arrived.

"Oh, Kacia, it's you. We thought it was the troops," Kanda said smiling.

Nobosi immediately circled her, sniffing.

Kacia dropped a hand on him to settle him and smiled a greeting. "No, the troops think you are long gone. You are safe now." She frowned as she studied the twins carefully. "Wow! You two look so different. I almost didn't recognise you. I bet your mother won't either."

"Have you told her we are here?" Rais asked.

"Yes, that is why I came. She is so excited... scared for you, but excited. She asked me to give you a message. She said to make sure you change your names as well as your appearance."

Faizar slapped her forehead. "Of course! I didn't think of that. They are using their real names. It hasn't mattered up to now as they didn't mix with anyone who was here as they grew up."

Dagma nodded. "We will have to change their identity papers with new names and make sure they are not listed as related."

Kaden went to get the forms while they tried to work out new names.

"I have always liked the name Nadie," Kanda said blushing.

"You can call me Aris. That was Pap's middle name."

"Okay, so it will be. Rais will be Aris, son of Aron, blacksmith, and Kanda will be Nadie, daughter of ..." Faizar looked around for inspiration.

"Adnah, farmer," Kaden finished for her. They nodded their approval and he filled in the forms and handed them to the twins.

"Now that is sorted, will someone please tell us what happened at the palace," Kanda asked.

Gathered around the table again, Dagma filled them in on the suntime's events. "Briador has come out of his suspended animation spell and the kitchen staff, and the other prisoners are making sure he is fed. After unsuccessfully searching the city, the troops were sent out to the forest to search for you. They have not come back yet. They may take their time with the search, as Yaholo told them if they come back empty handed, they will die. I believe they will go back to East Nevaah to see if you have gone back to Adaya. Varn was there. I didn't get to speak to him. He was glued to Yaholo's side. I heard him say he was going to join the troops to help in the search."

Palesa nodded. *I thought he was going to hand them in. I'll have to make sure I do it before he can.*

Leopold frowned. "Varn? He must be spying for us. Did you tell him we were here?"

"No. The way he was sucking up to Yaholo I wasn't sure I could trust him. He and the troops searching for you will buy us some time and get him out of our hair," Dagma said.

"That's wise. I wouldn't trust him to know. A couple of things he said made me wonder," Palesa said. She glanced at Leopold as she spoke.

Leopold raised an eyebrow and shook his head. "It is possible he went with the troops to try to save us, you know."

Palesa looked down at her feet, so she didn't show the emotion she was feeling.

Dagma nodded. "Yes, you could be right, Leo. We'll have to wait and see."

"Next intake for palace staff is next sun. We will take you all then. It will have to be one at a time through the suntime. We don't want to arouse suspicion by putting you all in the same group," Faizar said.

Palesa leaned forward. "I could go first. Thoro said they wanted more staff in the washroom. They won't know I'm with the twins. We have our new papers."

Leopold stared at her. "What's the hurry, Palesa?"

Palesa bowed her head. "Oh, nothing. Someone has to go first."

Faizar picked up the sarcasm in Leopold's voice and eyed the girl with interest. A little later, she bailed Leopold up. "Do you have a problem with Palesa?"

Leopold didn't know what to say. "I guess I don't fully trust her. She is too keen to live in the palace and... well... I'm afraid she might turn the twins in for the reward."

Faizar frowned. "Mmm, I'll keep an eye on her then."

The housekeeper lectured them on palace protocol and what would happen when they went for jobs.

They hardly slept. At dawn they rushed up the stairs keen to be the first to go to the palace. Dagma told Leopold to go in at the first intake at first sun, Kanda to go next at quarter-sun, Rais at mid-sun, and Palesa at three quarters-sun.

"What if we don't get in? What if they don't choose us?" Kanda said biting her lip.

"Faizar is head housekeeper. She chooses the staff," Dagma said smiling.

Because Leopold was going so early, he followed Kaden.

Kanda hugged him tightly as he went to leave. "Please be careful."

He kissed her lovingly. "I will. I'll see you soon."

Kanda sat at the table trying to study the book on the palace while she waited but she couldn't concentrate. Palesa joined her, closely examining the map. Rais paced the floor trying to remember what he was supposed to say.

Enolie had decided to apply for a job too, so she stayed back to show Kanda the way.

When the time came to leave, Kanda gave Rais a quick hug and taking a deep breath, walked out the door.

The walk to the palace wasn't far. As they rounded the corner and stepped onto the road that led to the palace, Kanda stopped and stared in awe at the imposing front gates of the main entrance. A high stone wall surrounded the palace grounds. *At least the height of 4 men,* Kanda thought. The gates were made of split logs and stood half the height of the wall. A thick iron crossbar at the top and bottom held them together. Standing watch were the two giant guards. The girls looked up at them. Kanda's eyes widened in shock. "They're half the size of the wall. At least as high as two men," she whispered. The girls cowered as one of them leered at them and whistled. His fellow guard laughed and smiled at them.

"Do we have to go through the gate past them?" Kanda asked, shuddering.

"No, we follow the wall around to the left and go in the servants' gate."

As they approached the servants' entrance a guard stopped them. "What's your name, girl," he said to Kanda.

"Nadie, da... dau...daughter of Adnar," Kanda stuttered.

The guard nodded, checked their papers, looked them up and down, and said gruffly, "Enolie, joining the family at last. Good luck. Although I guess you won't need it with your Mum interviewing you. Through the gate and around the corner to the left."

Enolie smiled. "Thanks, Turt. See you later."

When they were out of earshot she whispered, "He is a friend of Dad's and loyal to the king."

Kanda nodded, too nervous to speak. They followed the path that wandered through grounds of flowering trees and garden beds full of blooms of every colour. "Wow, this is so lovely," Kanda muttered as her eyes swept their surroundings. She took a deep breath, savouring the heady scent of the flowers.

Enolie nodded. "They have a wonderful head gardener. He is very particular about who he chooses to work for him and very hard on them. Not many people last."

As they rounded the next corner, they came to an abrupt halt. The line-up of people waiting to be interviewed snaked through the garden.

Kanda's eyes widened in shock. "Holy cow, there must be at least 10 people ahead of us."

Enolie shrugged. "Oh well, it's not like it matters. Mum will pick us anyway. We just have to follow the line."

A couple of the younger people greeted Enolie as they joined the line and she chatted to them, but most of the people had their heads down and were not talking to anyone.

Kanda didn't mind the wait. She was enjoying being in the lovely grounds. Paths wandered in amongst the gardens and shrubs. Beside them here and there were benches and small open huts. *I hope I get time to explore the grounds,* she thought. They shuffled their way slowly past the kitchen garden beds that grew every kind of herb and vegetable known to Kanda. She reached down to pluck the flowers from her favourite herb, lavender. As she crushed the blooms in her hand and breathed the lovely fragrance, her mind was transported to the only home she had ever known. She smiled as she remembered how she and Nona had put lavender flowers in the rinsing water when they washed the sheets and pillowcases, making the beds a joy to crawl into. The fragrance soothed her, and she smiled at Enolie and waved her hands under her nose.

Enolie breathed deeply and, smiling, reached for a couple of flowers. Kanda rubbed the fragrant oil on her hair and arms. Finally, they arrived at the back door of the kitchen. When it was their turn, Enolie nodded at Kanda to go first.

Nervously, she stepped through the door into a room so large that Kanda could only stare. 3 cooking stoves, each as big as their meal table at home, lined the back wall. Scrubbed wooden benches nestled around the other walls, interrupted by cupboards and shelves that went from floor to ceiling. 2 large tables filled the centre of the room. Staff bustled around the kitchen too engrossed in their tasks to give her more than a curious glance. Delicious aromas filled the room, wafting from the pots on the stove and from the food laid out on the tables in various states of preparation.

A middle-aged woman stepped forward. "So, who do we have here?" she said as she reached for Kanda's papers.

Shocked to see someone other than Faizar, Kanda stuttered, "I'm... Nadie... I arrr." She searched the room for her protector.

"No need to be nervous, young lady. Step through the door to the right. The housekeeper will see you now."

Kanda sighed with relief and hurried for the door. She walked into a much smaller room with a large table and at least a dozen chairs. In the corner was a desk and chair. Her relief was even greater when she was greeted by Faizar's smile. Sitting at the table beside her was Kacia. Instructed that she must pretend not to know her mentor in case someone was listening, she introduced herself, her face flushed with embarrassment. "Greetings, Mam, I'm Nadie."

"Greetings, Nadie. Tell me where you come from and what work you did there."

She searched her mind for what she had been coached to say. "I come from a farm, Mam. I am very experienced at cooking and serving food. I'm used to hard work. I have been helping at the farm since I was eight."

"That sounds impressive. Very well then, wait in the room behind this one and I will talk to you further when I finish this round of interviews," Faizar said.

Kanda curtsied and did as she was instructed. Several other youths and girls sat on the chairs there or sprawled on the floor. Kanda searched the group looking for Leopold, but he wasn't amongst them. On a table in the corner was a large teapot and cups. Plates of cake and biscuits showed evidence they had been raided. The occupants gave her a friendly greeting as she joined them. Feeling self-conscious, she smiled, slumped to the floor in the corner, wrapped her arms around her legs and waited. Soon Enolie walked in and squatted on the floor beside her.

"Leopold is not here," Kanda whispered urgently.

"He would have been taken to his assigned accommodation and position by now, as we will be before the next intake comes. Let's get a cup of tea before it is all gone." Enolie rose and reached out a hand to haul her to her feet and headed for the table.

Kanda joined her and they took their cup of tea and a biscuit and headed back to the corner. A couple of the people who knew Enolie came to sit with them, and they chatted about their expectations of their positions. One of the youths was hoping for a position working in the garden or the stables, so he was waiting for a second interview with the head gardener or the stable master.

Soon Faizar and Kacia joined them. Addressing the group, Faizar said, "This is Kacia. She will take you to collect your staff uniforms and show you where you will sleep. I will see you in the kitchen when you come down for the moontime meal. After the meal you will be told where you are to report next sun and be introduced to your supervisors."

Kacia led them through the kitchen and into a hall. They followed her up a flight of stairs onto the next level. She took them into a large room and told them to select two uniforms each from the racks that filled the room. The racks held a sea of light blue tunics and long wide legged trousers. As they hunted for their sizes, Kacia sidled up to Kanda. "Your mother is worried that she will not be able to hide her excitement and give your identity away when you take her meal. Be very careful what you say."

Kanda kept her head down and nodded, afraid that if she lifted her head, she would show the excitement she was feeling.

Clutching their uniforms, they followed Kacia back into the hallway. She paused and said, "Okay, it's boys to the left and girls to the right. As I call your name you will go into your assigned rooms, find a bunk that isn't covered, then take a sleeping wrap from the pile on the bench and put it on your bed. Hang your uniforms on the hook on the wall behind the bed. Come down to the kitchen when you hear the bell chime at sundown."

They started down the passage. Kacia paused at doorways and called names from a sheet she carried. Two or three of the group disappeared into each of the many rooms along the way. Finally, Enolie and Kanda were taken to the room at the end. Kacia hugged them both. "I'll have to go back now for the next intake. I'll see you later."

Kanda surveyed the small room. Several bunks were lined up with their head to the side wall. Between the bedheads were two shelves. The space between the beds was barely enough to allow two people to stand at once. A curtain stretched across the room just before the end wall.

Kanda chose a bunk, selected a sleeping wrap, and dropped her backpack on it. She wandered down to peep around the curtain. A tub sat at one end of the space behind it. Along the back wall was a bench with shelves full of towels and soap. Under it were two buckets. The other wall was covered with towel rails.

Enolie came up behind her. "Oh, the bathing space. I hope we get hot water; I can't stand cold baths."

Kanda frowned. "Are you staying? I thought you would go home with your mother."

"I can be of more use here." She walked back to the door and poked her head out to check the hall. When she saw it was deserted, she continued, "We'll be able to do a little spying from here."

Kanda turned to her, her eyes glowing. "Did you hear what Kacia told me in the uniform storeroom?"

"No, but it was obviously exciting," Enolie said smiling.

Kanda repeated what she had said. The girl hugged her. "How amazing it will be for both of you."

They wandered around the corridors checking out the rooms. Most were living quarters, but they found one that had wash basins and 2 water tanks with taps. "This must be the staff washroom," Enolie said. They went in and discovered that one of the tanks had a fire under it. "Arrr hot water. Maybe we get our bathing water from here," Enolie said smiling. The odour coming from the next room told them what it was. Clutching her nose, Enolie said, "The latrine room."

They stuck their head in to check it out. A half a dozen stalls lined the back wall. The overwhelming smell of disinfectant and human waste made them withdraw quickly. They didn't find anything else that was interesting, so they headed back, reaching the door to their room just as the bell rang.

Kanda looked for Rais, Palesa and Leopold as they walked into the kitchen. She spotted them all sitting at different tables and sighed with relief. She and Enolie took their seat and didn't look their way again. They had been told to pretend that they didn't know the others and not to be seen talking to them straight away. Kanda had trouble sitting still. She picked at her food; her mind consumed with thoughts of seeing her mother next sun. She whispered to Enolie, "I wonder if Rais will get to deliver the meals to the dungeon too?'

"Why don't you ask Kacia? Here she comes to collect our plates."

As Kacia bent down to take the dish, she asked. The girl nodded and moved on. Her excitement mounting, Kanda couldn't help herself. She reached into her pocket, clutched her pendant, and sought the mind of her twin. She told him how excited she was that they were going to meet their mother tomorrow. He glanced her way then put his head down and gave it a slight shake but gave no other indication he had received her message. Kanda frowned. *Why is using mind power a problem,* she thought.

Finally, the meal was over. Faizar bustled around the tables giving them all their assigned duties for the next suntime. Kanda, Enolie and Palesa were told to report to the kitchen at sunup. Leopold was to go to the stables and Rais to the kitchen garden.

As they left the table, Kanda watched as Palesa hurried over to the housekeeper. They paused to listen to the conversation.

"I thought I was going to work in the washroom," Palesa said pouting.

"Not yet. We need to keep you here with us for a while until you know the ropes. We might consider a change in a couple of moons," Faizar said and turned away.

Palesa's face shone beetroot red as she glared at the back of the departing housekeeper. She turned to Leopold as he walked by and hissed, "I know this is your fault." She stomped out of the room and headed for her accommodation.

Kanda and Enolie followed the crowd of people heading for their rooms. Kanda spotted Rais walking ahead of her. He turned into a door opposite hers. *It's good to know he is near,* she thought. As soon as they walked into their room they headed for their beds. Kanda stopped as she saw Palesa on the end bed. Her back was to them. She almost called out her name but stopped. *Obviously sulking,* Kanda thought. Soon other girls joined them. Kanda was surprised to see Kacia come in and flop on a bed.

"I thought you would be working, taking the moontime meal to the Great Hall," Kanda said.

Kacia shook her head. "No. I have been helping with the interviews, so I got the time off."

One of the group was a long-time member of the palace staff and Kacia introduced her to the girls. "This is Telitha. If you need any information and I'm not here she will be able to help. She has been here longer than me."

Telitha just nodded at them, staring as if she was concentrating on remembering their names. Kanda frowned. Something about the way she stared, unsettled her. Three of the other girls were new too so they introduced themselves and chatted for a bit. Palesa kept her back to them and didn't join in. Finally, yawning, Kacia said, "Okay, we need to get our baths and get to bed. It will be lights out soon. Someone grab the two buckets at this end of the bathing closet and all of you follow me." When Palesa didn't move, she called, "Palesa, you too."

The girl sighed deeply but got to her feet and joined them. The two girls nearest the curtain fetched the buckets and they all followed her to the room Kanda and Enolie had discovered earlier. It was filled with people busy at the tubs. Except for a casual glance, they ignored their presence.

"This is the staff washroom. You have two uniforms. They must always be clean, so you need to come in here after work to wash the one you had on that suntime. You hang them in your room to dry. Now, you two with the buckets; one of you get a bucket full of water from the hot tank and the other from the cold."

With the buckets full, it took two people to carry them. When they arrived back at the room, they went to the bathing area. "Tip in the cold water and then add some of the hot in until it is a good temperature. Soap and towels are there on the shelves. Just help yourselves. Then, when you are done, hang your towel on the racks provided. Try to remember where you put it. We will all bathe in turn. Top up with a bit more hot when it needs it. And as I am one of the senior staff members, I go first and Telitha will be next. You can all work out the order you will go in." Gathering up her sleeping gown, she shooed them all out of the area and closed the curtains.

An argument started between the others about who was next. Telitha shook her head.

Kanda held up her hand. "The best way to settle it is with a draw of straws. She reached into the end of her bed mat and drew a handful of straws. Turning her back, she broke them into different lengths, lined them up in random order in her fist, and turned back.

"The person who draws the shortest straw goes last. The rest go in order of the longest to the shortest."

Grudgingly, they all took a straw and held it up. Kanda held up the last one in her hand. Hers was the shortest and she smiled at the irony. They chatted while they waited.

Silence fell over the chatter when one of the girls asked Telitha what Yaholo was like.

The girl shrugged. "Not something you need to worry about unless you break his code of conduct. Most of you will never see him."

Told by Faizar that the best way they could help the cause was to find out who was loyal, Kanda watched her expression as she spoke. *Mmm, that answer was a little too casual. I will have to watch her.*

Telitha's eyes narrowed, and she concentrated as she searched the girl's faces. Kanda frowned. *She must have mind reading skills.* The thought alarmed Kanda. She focussed on thinking good thoughts about her new companions. She sighed in relief and turned casually away when the girl's intense gaze moved on to someone else.

By the time they had all finished bathing, it was time for lights out. Kanda laid in the dark, worrying about her mother. She kept a close eye on Telitha, concerned about her loyalty. She decided to ask Faizar what she knew about her. She finally drifted off to sleep.

The next dawning, Kanda was the first awake. She dressed quietly and hurried to the kitchen. Only Faizar was there. Rais came in soon after.

He hurried to Faizar a concerned look on his face. "When do we strike? Sundown next sun is the execution."

"Yes, and how can we help?" Kanda said.

"Yes, you are right, we must strike early next sun, or it will be too late. There will be a meeting at moontime to go over each person's role. We have gathered a large number of supporters, but we are not yet game to tell them our plan.

We are still not sure who we can trust. We are hoping you can help with that."

Kanda frowned. "How can we help?"

"We want you both to come to the meeting and read their minds as we speak about the bad things Yaholo has done and the execution of Edalene. Only then will we be sure we can trust them."

Kanda frowned. "Oh, we can't do that. We can only read each other's mind."

"Have you tried? Kacia said she told your mother about your mind connection, and she said you should be able to use the same method to read others' minds."

"We haven't tried, we have been too busy learning other skills, but if Mother thinks we can, we should try."

"Your powers have grown. Try to read my thoughts."

Kanda blushed. She sought her mind in the same way she sought life force. Her eyes flew open as she picked up her thoughts. "Oh, wow, I can do it," she cried and turned to Rais.

Rais' eyes lit up. "Wow, maybe I can too." He focused. Nothing happened. He frowned.

Kanda said, "Try to hold your pendant and connect with my mind."

He did that. She sent a thought. *Now try doing it without the pendant.* He broke the connection, let go of the pendant and tried again. She smiled as they connected. "Now try to do the same thing with Faizar."

Once again, he turned to Faizar. She smiled as she felt him connect. He picked up the thought, *Well done, Rais.* He smiled happily and nodded at his sister.

"So, we can do that, wow!" Kanda turned to Faizar thoughtfully. "Do you know Telitha well?"

"Yes, she has been here for some time and is one of my serving girls. Why?"

"I believe she has mind reading skills. I'm sure she probed the minds of all the girls last moontime. I was careful to make sure if she did probe my mind, she would only get random thoughts about the palace and the girls."

"Oh, that's very interesting. She often asks questions about what I think of Yaholo. I just tell her that I wish he would show some compassion and let your father and the king out of jail."

"Do you think she is a supporter?"

"Not sure. When I ask her the same question she asks me, she just shrugs."

"But where would she get her skills? I thought only children of an oracle like Father or magicians like Briador could have these skills," Rais asked.

Faizar thought for a moment. "You're right. But don't forget, they have an Oracle in Gantis."

"Oh… of course. I didn't think of that. She might be the spy in the kitchen who told the guard about the potion Mother sent to the king," Kanda said biting her lip.

"Did she know about the vial?" Rais asked.

Faizar nodded thoughtfully. "Yes… she is the one who took it to him. I will send her with you to deliver the prisoners' food. Try to read her mind as you go down to the dungeon."

"Do you think we will ever be as powerful as Father?" Kanda said wistfully.

"You already are. You just need a little guidance in the use of your powers. It's a shame you didn't get a bit more time with Briador before you got here."

The rest of the kitchen staff arrived at that time, so Faizar set them to their tasks. "I'll see if I can find our spy," Kanda said quietly to the housekeeper. Faizar nodded and moved away.

Kanda moved around between them reading their minds. She moved over to the preparation area and studied the people there. One of the girls glared at her as she approached. Kanda frowned. She had met this girl but had forgotten her name. *What's her problem?* she thought. When she returned to her task, Kanda tuned into the girl's mind. She frowned when she received her thoughts. *At least I got rid of the healer. I'll have to keep a close eye on these new ones. Who knows where their loyalties lie?*

Kanda hid her surprise quickly and casually said, "Hello, I don't think we have met. What was your name?"

"Duro," the girl said and continued with what she was doing.

Kanda nodded. "Nice to meet you. I'm Nadie." She picked up a completed dish and took it to the serving table. She walked past Faizar and muttered, "Duro." The housekeeper raised an eyebrow but didn't say a word. She went to where Kaden and Enolie were working and had a quiet conversation with them.

A little later she walked over to the preparation bench and said, "I need someone to go to my house and get me some supplies stored there. Duro, go with Kaden and Enolie and help them please."

Duro looked up in surprise. "Sure, no problem," she said, "Happy to get out of the kitchen for a while." Kaden and Enolie walked over, and they left, Duro beaming.

Kanda had watched this with interest. She looked at Faizar puzzled. "Oh dear, poor Duro will get accidently locked in our basement hidden room for the next sun or two," Faizar said quietly. Kanda smiled and walked away.

Leopold came in for early breakfast with the rest of the stable hands. Kanda didn't get a chance to speak to him, but they exchanged a glance and a smile as he left. She so longed to be with him, she almost followed him out of the room.

Once breakfast for the prisoners was prepared, Faizar called Kanda to the serving table. "You and Telitha take food to the prisoners." Loudly she said, "As Kaden is off on another job and I don't have another male, I will have to call Aris in from the garden. We don't like the girls to go down to the dungeon without a male to keep an eye on the guards. Nadie, you go and fetch him."

Kanda smiled gratefully. She would feel a lot safer with Rais.

Palesa was given the task of washing up and stomped over to the sink, the anger that boiled inside her painting her face crimson.

Once the food was ready for the Great Hall, Kacia took several of the serving girls and they moved off to feed Yaholo, his advisers, and his court.

Kanda went to the kitchen garden. She called Rais over and told him what he had to do.

His heart singing at the thought of seeing his mother and Briador, Rais went over to the head gardener to tell him he was called to the kitchen.

The head gardener shouted, "That is not going to happen. I'll see about that."

Rais sighed and followed him and Kanda into the kitchen. *I won't be sorry to get away from that ogre,* he thought.

Rais and Kanda waited while the housekeeper and the head gardener had a loud argument about what was happening. Finally, his boss conceded defeat. His face red with suppressed rage, he turned to Rais and said, "Don't take too long. We have work to do." He stomped out the door.

As they filled the bowls on the trays for the prisoners, they were appalled at what they were taking. "This watery porridge is not fit to eat. Is this all they get?" Rais said.

Faizar grimaced and said quietly, "It is this sun. The guards on duty are Yaholo's men. If we give them anything better, Yaholo would soon know about it. They get better food when the King's guards are on duty."

They picked up the trays and headed for the door. Telitha stopped them at the top of the stairs. "Don't trust the guards. Be very careful not to appear too sympathetic to the prisoners. You must be on your guard at all times."

The twins gave her a confident smile. "Don't worry, we'll be fine," Rais said glancing at Kanda. She nodded. Kanda read her mind while she spoke. What she picked up made her smile. Telitha's concern was genuine. She was worried about Edalene and Briador and wanted to make sure they didn't do anything to jeopardise their safety.

After greeting the guard, they walked along the front of the cells, passing the bowls of food to each prisoner. Briador was in the second last cell in the first row. Rais had kept the food he carried to hand to him. He walked up to the cell door and slipped the food through the opening in the middle. Briador was lying on the hard cot staring at the ceiling.

Gruffly, Rais said, "Here's your food."

Briador sat up slowly. "You call that swill food." He looked up, saw Rais and took a deep breath. He got to his feet and slowly hobbled over to the door. "Thanks, lad," he said not meeting his gaze. As he reached for the bowl, he gave Rais' hand a squeeze.

His heart was breaking. The old man looked so frail and ill. *We have to get him out of here before he dies.* He reached out with his mind. *We'll have you out of here soon. Where is mother?* Briador looked startled for a moment but soon recovered and sent back a message that she was in the next row.

Kanda had gone to that one so Rais wandered around as casually as he could on the pretext of checking that the girls had finished. One of the guards had risen and followed Kanda. Telitha had gone to the next lot of cells.

Kanda had just reached their mother's cell. Rais walked over and took some of the bowls from Kanda's tray to distribute to the rest of the prisoners. Their mother came to the door and took her bowl, keeping her expression blank, but Kanda could see the sparkle in her eyes as she recognised them. Kanda sent her a message. *We will have you out of here next sun.*

Her mother smiled and said, "Thanks for the food." But she sent a message back. *Be careful, my darlings. I couldn't bear it if something happened to you while trying to save me.* Rais picked up the message too and they both nodded as they walked away.

They trudged back to the kitchen and walked to the trays for the tower.

Only two staff went to the tower. As the twins didn't know the way, Faizar sent Rais and Kacia.

Rais' heart was beating rapidly as he climbed the stairs. He wasn't sure he could speak to his father without showing how excited he was.

Kanda watched him walk away, her heart full of envy.

Faizar smiled at her and quietly said, "You'll get your chance at the mid-sun meal." Kanda nodded, her eyes sparkling.

As they climbed the stairs to the tower, Kacia said. "You go on to Baldasarre's cell. I will give the King his meal."

Rais nodded, his excitement building. In the first cell, the King sat waiting for his meal. The guards were standing together outside Baldasarre's cell, chatting. Rais nodded to the guards and walked towards the door. Just as he got there, a clang sounded behind him. He looked back and saw that Kacia had dropped her tray. The dirty dish, cup, and cutlery she had just collected from the king's last meal lay scattered across the hall. The guards hurried over to help her pick them up. Kacia loudly apologised over and over.

Baldasarre was waiting for Rais. He put his hands through the bars and clutched his arms. He linked his mind with Rais and sent him a message. *My boy, oh, my boy. You have grown into a fine young man.* His eyes filled with tears.

Tears sprang to Rais' eyes, and he tried hard not to let them show. *It won't be long now.*

Behind him one of the guards shouted, "What's taking you so long. Get over here and help clean up this mess, lad."

"Be careful, boy," his father whispered.

Rais nodded and hurried over to help Kacia. Under the watchful eye of the guards, they picked up the remaining pieces and wiped up the small amount of food spill. Collecting Baldasarre's dishes, they headed back down the stairs. When they were out of the guards' hearing, Rais turned to Kacia. "Thank you for doing that. It gave me time to communicate with Father."

Kacia smiled. "That was the plan. I'm not always that clumsy."

They walked back into the kitchen laughing and headed over to deposit the dishes on the bench beside Palesa. She glared at them.

Rais gave Palesa a sympathetic smile. He and Kacia joined the other waiting staff at the table for breakfast. The kitchen staff had eaten while they were away.

Faizar joined them. "All well with the prisoners in the tower?" she asked.

Kacia said, "The king looks very ill and weak. It's tragic the way they are starved. No one could live on that swill they get."

Many of the other staff nodded in agreement.

"It won't do you any good talking like that. You'll end up in the dungeon," Faizar said sharply.

The girl ducked her head still muttering. Faizar watched her for a moment then said, to Rais, "Did your visit go well in the Tower?"

Rais grinned and said, "Well, Kacia dropped her tray while I was serving Baldasarre, but the guards helped her pick the dishes up."

Faizar realised what he was saying and gave the girl a grateful glance, but said, "That's not like you, Kacia."

Kacia ducked her head trying to look guilty.

After they had eaten, they all returned to their chores. Rais went reluctantly out to the garden. Kanda watched the clock, waiting for her turn to go to the tower. It seemed like an invisible force was holding the hands to stop them turning. She hurried with the preparation of the mid-sun trays. As if by magic when she checked again the force had lifted. The hands had finally reached the right time. Kaden had come into the kitchen to help, so he went with Kanda and Kacia to deliver the mid-sun meal to the dungeon. She walked to the first row of cells while the others went to the two back rows. Finally, she approached Briador's cell, her heart beating in anticipation.

This time he was watching who came. He hobbled over to the gate and put his hands out for the tray.

He took it from her quickly. "Thanks, lass," he said, "hang on… I'll get you my dirty dishes." He shuffled over to the bunk, put down his food, brought his dirty dishes over and slowly placed them on the tray. She sent him a message. *Are you okay?*

His eyes lit up for a moment as he realised that she could read minds and communicate with thought too. He nodded. *As good as can be expected.*

He squeezed her hand. *So good to see you are here. Practice your skills, you will need them. This will help keep you safe.* He slipped something into her hand. She lifted her eyes, and looked at him questioningly, but he just turned away and shuffled back to his bunk.

Kanda bit her lip in anxiety. *He looks terrible,* she thought. She slipped the object into her pocket.

She went around to her mother's cell with her last bowl. Edalene came to the cell door and squeezed her hands as she took the bowl. Kanda linked with her mind. *I am so thrilled to see you both are well,* her mother thought. Kanda smiled and sent back, *Next sun. We will have you out of here next sun.* She collected her dirty bowl and walked away; trying not to show the exhilaration she was feeling.

The trays for the tower were ready when they got back. She and Enolie were told to take them up. As they got to the first bend, Kanda said quietly, "Stop for a minute."

Enolie turned grinning. "What, out of breath already."

Kanda shook her head, glanced up and down the stairs and took the object out of her pocket. It was a piece of cloth with something wrapped inside. When she unwrapped it, she was amazed to find a bright red stone.

"What's that," Enolie asked.

Kanda shrugged. "I have no idea. Briador gave it to me when we delivered breakfast. Maybe Mother will know. I'll ask her when we get her out of there."

"If all goes to plan," Enolie said frowning.

Kanda wrapped it again and thrust it back into her pocket. They continued up the stairs. They had already arranged that Kanda would take her tray to Baldasarre but weren't game to stage another incident to draw away the guards. She hurried past the king's cell. Her father was waiting. "What swill do we have this time, lass?" he said as she approached. He put out his hands to take the bowl and gave her hands a pat. She had to take a deep breath to stop herself from crying. Then she felt him connect with her mind.

Even with your disguise, you are the image of your mother and just as beautiful. I have prayed and waited for this for so long.

It's so good to see you. Are you okay?

Much better now that I've seen you are safe. Be careful, my lovely. He handed her his dirty dishes.

She smiled, said thank you and turned away. The girls hurried down the stairs. Kanda felt like she was floating on air, she was so pleased that she had seen him, but her heart was troubled. Out of hearing of the guards, she said, "We have to get him out of there. It's just not fair."

Enolie gave her a sympathetic glance. "We will... next sun."

Back in the kitchen, as they scraped the dishes that came back from Yaholo's Great Hall, Kanda muttered to Enolie, "Look at this wasted food. They could keep it and serve it to the prisoners instead of the rubbish they get."

Enolie nodded. "And they won't get any more meals this sun. The prisoners only get two meals a sun."

Kanda's stood, mouth open for a second, then just shook her head in disgust. They piled the dishes up for Palesa and the other washer-ups to deal with and got busy preparing the evening meal for the court.

Faizar came over under the pretence of checking the meals being prepared. "Is your father okay?" she whispered.

Kanda nodded. "We have to get him out of there," she said through clenched teeth.

The housekeeper patted her arm. "We will. It will all be sorted at the final planning meeting."

Kanda looked at the housekeeper her expression determined. "And we will be there to read their minds."

The housekeeper nodded. "Stay back after we finish." She walked away, inspecting the other dishes being prepared.

As Kanda took some pots over to Palesa to be washed, the girl turned on her, pouting. "How long do I have to do this? My hands are wrinkled from being in the water so much. Why can't you have a turn? I could do the serving."

Kanda shrugged. "It's got nothing to do with me. You will have to talk to Faizar."

Faizar saw the exchange and bustled over. "Is there a problem, Palesa?"

"I was just saying we should take turns. I could do the serving and the food preparation just as well as anyone else. I don't see why I have to be stuck in the sink all the time."

Kanda focused on Palesa's mind while she spoke and while the housekeeper was speaking to her. All she picked up was her annoyance at having to wash up. "Oh well, perhaps we will see what we can do about that," the housekeeper said as she went back to mixing the large pot of stew she had been stirring.

Kanda bit her lip as she walked away, she didn't want Palesa loose in the palace until she knew she could trust her.

Palesa's eyes lit up and she went back to the washing up with more vigour. The washroom staff came into the kitchen for the mid-sun meal with the rest of the staff and Palesa made sure she sat next to Thoro. Heads together they started whispering to each other.

Kanda decided to check what they were saying. She linked to Palesa's mind. Her eyes flew wide as she picked up her thoughts.

I owe them both for saving my life, but the reward is too tempting. I don't want to work in the kitchen all my life. I want to live in the palace like my mother said we did before the overthrow. The only way I can do that is to turn them in. It's too hard. I can't decide what to do. What do you think?

Kanda quickly switched to Thoro's mind. He paused for a minute then replied, *The reward would be great. I'm sick of working in the washroom too. If I help, would you share it with me?*

Kanda didn't wait to hear any more. Her anger and anxiety building, she hurried down to where Rais was sitting. She pretended to be getting food and sent him a message. *Palesa is talking about turning us in. Thoro wants to help her for some of the reward.*

Rais slammed his fist into his palm in frustration. *I thought she would do this. The ungrateful cow. Now I'm sorry I saved her life. We have to get a message to Faizar.*

Okay, see you after the staff mid-sun meal is over.

As soon as the staff dispersed to their tasks, they hurried to Faizar. They went to the small room at the back of the kitchen and told her what they had learnt.

"So that is her game. I can control her during work time, but I'm a bit worried about when I'm not here, and especially when we are all at the meeting. Maybe it is time to lay a trap to see if she really would turn you in. We had better include Thoro so we can see if he would go through with it. I wouldn't have believed it of him. He has always expressed his loyalty to the king. But perhaps the reward will change that. If they fall for it, we will have to smuggle them out and lock them up until it is all over. I'll ask Kacia and one of our loyal guards to help."

Palesa had gone back to the sink. She seemed a bit happier than usual. When she saw Faizar come back into the room she approached her. "So, what do you want me to do now? You did say I could do something else."

"You will be helping with the cleaning this afternoon. Kacia will show you where to go and what to do. Go to the cleaning cupboard and the girls will kit you out."

Palesa's eyes lit up. *At last, I will be allowed into the palace. Maybe I will get the chance to carry out my plan.* She went quickly to the cupboard.

The housekeeper took Kacia aside and told her of the plan. Kacia glared in the traitor's direction as she listened. She nodded grimly as Faizar finished. "My pleasure," she muttered as she went towards Palesa.

"Okay girls, I'm in charge. Let's get going." She gave them all their assigned areas and turned to Palesa. "We'll be working in the adviser's rooms, changing bed linen, and taking it to the washroom. Bring that cart with you."

Palesa couldn't believe her luck. She quickly grabbed the cart and followed Kacia as they wound their way to the washroom to collect linen. Thoro came to help her load the sheets as Kacia wandered over to speak to the supervisor.

"You got out of the kitchen, I see," said Thoro smiling, "Where are you headed?"

Palesa could hardly contain her excitement. "To the adviser's rooms. Will they be in?" she asked hopefully.

"No, they will be in the court with Yaholo," Thoro replied.

Palesa's face fell. They didn't have time to say more because Kacia came bustling over, impatient for them to be on their way.

As they headed for the rooms, Kacia said, "The advisers won't be in. That's why we are doing this now. But be warned, the corridor we will be in leads to Yaholo's rooms so the guard in that area is loyal to him. Be careful what you say."

Palesa's scheming mind got busy working out a plan. She studied the only guard in the corridor as they arrived. He nodded at them as they passed him. "Good afternoon," Palesa said politely.

"Miss," he replied gruffly.

After they had changed a few of the rooms, the cart was full of dirty linen, and they had run out of fresh sheets. "Take the cart to the washroom, deliver the dirty ones, and fill it with clean sheets. Ask Thoro to bring the second cart of clean linen back with you. I'm going to check on some of the other girls in a minute so I might not be here when you get back. Just get on with what we have been doing," Kacia told her.

Palesa couldn't believe her luck as she hurried away. Once she came back, she and Thoro would be alone with the guard. She rushed into the washroom and went straight to Thoro. "Quick, we have to unload and load this trolley and Kacia wants you to bring another one back with me. She has gone off to see the other girls."

"Who is there, anyone?"

"Just one of Yaholo's loyal guards," she whispered.

Thoro's eyes lit up with excitement. "Let's go then. We want to be there before she comes back."

They quickly loaded the carts and charged out the door. In the corridor, they spotted the guard standing just before an open room and hurried to him.

"We have to get a message to Yaholo," Palesa said breathlessly.

"What could you possibly know that Yaholo would be interested in?" the guard asked gruffly.

Palesa glanced at Thoro. He nodded. "The whereabouts of Baldasarre's twins," she said, searching the corridor to make sure Kacia wasn't coming back.

The guard cocked his head to one side. "Is that so? And where would they be then?"

"We will only tell that to Yaholo," Thoro said putting his hand on Palesa's arm to quieten her.

"Fair enough. You had better come with me then. You can wait in this room for him to come back." He ushered them into the room beside him.

Waiting in the room was Faizar and Kacia. "Very interesting, Palesa. Now we know where your true loyalties lie. Where you're being taken, you're going to wish you were still washing dishes," Faizar said.

The guard took Thoro by the collar. "And you, young man, are going to wish you had never seen this young lady."

Palesa looked at Faizar, horror showing on her face. "I didn't mean it. I was... was... just trying to see if Thoro would do it. You know I'm loyal to the twins. They're my friends," she stuttered.

"We know that is not true now, so don't bother lying. You will be locked up until the king is back on the throne then be tried as a traitor. You too, Thoro," Faizar said. She looked sadly at the boy. "I trusted you, Thoro, and let you into my house. I would have sworn you were loyal to the king."

"I am. It was just the reward. I'm sick of working in the washroom and thought if I had some of the reward, I could be more respected."

Faizar shook her head sadly. "Money doesn't buy respect, Thoro. It can only be earned through good deeds."

"Get them out of here before the other guards get back from the court, Pahana," Faizar said to the guard.

Pahana went to the back wall of the opulent office and opened a hidden door to a secret passage. He bustled the traitors into the dark tunnel, followed them and closed the door.

Shaking their head sadly, the women went back to work. Faizar went to the washroom and told the supervisor that Thoro had injured himself and wouldn't be back for a few suns.

Kanda hurried over to Kacia and Faizar as they returned to the kitchen. Faizar just nodded sadly and Kacia patted her arm. Kanda went back to work not sure if she should be happy or sad. She was happy that the threat had been removed, but sad that one of their party had turned traitor.

The suntime progressed as if nothing had happened. When everyone had gone and only Faizar and the twins were in the kitchen, Kanda filled Rais in on what had happened.

Rais couldn't believe that she had done it. He remembered how much he had liked her when they met. But he now realised that he was just attracted to her beauty. He had learnt a lot since he left the farm. "Where are they being kept?' he asked.

"In the cavern in the secret tunnel," Faizar said.

Rais and Kanda raised an eyebrow. "Secret tunnel?" they chorused.

"The one where we will hold our meeting," Faizar said, grimly.

Kanda's eyes narrowed in anger. "Well, I hope I can control myself if I see her."

"They will still be there when we go in, but we will move them before the meeting. The tunnel has several small caverns. They will be put in one of those until after the meeting," the housekeeper said.

"Speaking of moving, we had better go," Faizar said heading for the door to the small room. She went to a painting of the palace and pushed a section of the decoration on the frame. A door opened and they hurried in and closed it again.

Faizar lit a candle that was on a shelf, and they went down a set of stairs and into a dark tunnel. Kanda was transported back to their journey through all the passages and shivered and glanced at the walls. This one had the same musty scent but was a lot drier and wider and she continued confidently. They passed the tunnel that led from the king's private office where Palesa and Thoro were captured and followed it until they came to a large cave.

Faizar entered first and as soon as she saw her, Palesa called, "Please let me out of here. You can't keep me here like this. I didn't mean it. If you let me go, I won't say anything, I promise."

Faizar looked at her without pity. "You will be let out, Palesa. To be tried by the king for treason."

Kanda stopped to look at the girl. Her anger diminished a little as she took in the sight of her chained by the ankle to a metal ring fixed to the wall. Beside her was a cot and a bucket. Thoro was chained not very far away, but out of reach.

"Rais, you can't leave me here like this. I'm sorry. I promise I won't do it again. Please help me. The place is full of rats," Palesa begged.

Rais glared at her. "To think I once thought you were special. I even saved your life – and Kanda did – and this is how you repay us. As far as I'm concerned you can rot in here… both of you."

"How are the people getting here without being seen?" Kanda asked peering down the two tunnels that led from the room. "Where does that passage go?" she asked pointing to the one opposite the way they had entered the cavern.

"To the city. It meets up with the passage you told me you came through. It's also the one you escaped through as a child."

Two guards came through the tunnel and took Palesa and Thoro away. The twins watched in amazement as people hurried into the cave from both directions. Soon the cavern was crowded with at least 50 people. The heat from their bodies warmed the space and filled it with the stink of sweat. Nose twitching, Kanda stood still in shock. *How are we going to read all these minds?* she thought in panic. She turned to Rais and could see he was feeling the same way.

She expressed her concern to Faizar. She smiled. "One at a time, child. No rush, we will be here for some time."

Kanda and Rais divided the room between them, deciding where they would start. Taking a deep breath, Kanda moved amongst the crowd, trying to stay inconspicuous and started her job. Rais did the same. All went well for a while. The people they read were all angry because Edalene had been imprisoned for helping the king, and because of the length of time the king and Baldasarre had been captive.

As Kanda approached the front of the crowd, she saw a familiar back. *Leopold is here!* Her heart raced with excitement. She was just about to call his name when she remembered she wasn't supposed to know him. Walking close, she pretended to accidentally bump his arm. He glanced down and his eyes lit up with pleasure.

"Oh sorry," she said breathlessly, "Err ... I'm Nadie." She stuck out her hand.

Realising what she was doing he took her hand and said, "I'm Leopold."

Her hand tingled from his touch and warmth swept through her body. She smiled happily and moved on. After they finished their sections, the twins both approached a group of men who were standing together in a corner listening to the speaker, as he expressed the urgency of the task to overthrow Yaholo and free the prisoners. Kanda started on one of them. She was glad he had his back to her as she was sure her face registered the shock she felt when she read his thoughts. *This lot of losers will end up in the dungeon once I find out their plan. Yaholo will reward me well for this.*

Kanda quickly read the thoughts of those around him and found all but one other was loyal. She sidled up to Rais and pointed to the men. Rais tuned in and nodded grimly. They moved away so they could get a look at their faces. Rais shook his head in amazement. "One of them is my boss, the head gardener," he whispered to Kanda. *Why would I be surprised? He is always going on about pleasing Yaholo*, he thought. They moved to the back of the room where Faizar was standing. They told her about the men and described them and what they were wearing.

Faizar made her way to Dagma and told him. He spoke to a few men, and they quietly and carefully moved to surround the traitors. He then shouted over the babble of the crowd. "We have traitors in our midst. How do you propose we deal with them?"

The two men gave themselves away immediately by turning for the tunnel to the city. The loyal men grabbed them and hauled them back to the centre of the room.

"String them up, I say," one of the crowd shouted.

"Chain them to the wall and leave them for the rats," another called.

The head gardener lifted his head to say, "Others knew where we were going and why. If we go missing, they will know where to come to start the search."

As he was speaking, Rais and Kanda entered his mind then the mind of the other man. They turned to Dagma and shook their heads.

"You're lying. You are too greedy to share the reward. You wouldn't have told anyone," Dagma said.

The tavern owner stepped up. "Take them to my basement. They can enjoy a sleep with the rats there while we decide what to do with them." The men were taken away to the end of the passage and bound and gagged. They would be dealt with after the meeting.

Dagma took the twins aside. "Did you read everyone's mind?"

"I think so. I don't think we missed anyone," Kanda said biting her lip anxiously. She searched the faces of those around her looking for people she hadn't read. Rais did the same.

They shook their heads. "No, I didn't miss anyone," they both said.

"Okay, now we can speak freely," Dagma said.

A few members of the teen army stood talking in a huddle near the entrance to the tunnel from the city. Kaden, Kacia, Telitha, and Enolie hurried over.

Kanda bit her lip in anxiety. She sent a message to Rais. *It all comes down to us. If we stuff up and miss someone the whole plan will fail, and we will all die.*

Rais replied, *Then, we had better be on our toes and not miss anyone, hadn't we? I think it would be best if we both read everyone's minds again. That way we are sure they are not hiding their real thoughts. I'll go to the ones you read, and you do mine.*

Kanda nodded her agreement and they wandered around the room, stopping to greet people, and reading their mind.

The twins were both amazed at the passion they had picked up from the group assembled in the room. The hatred for Yaholo was burning in all of them.

Dagma picked up a tin mug and a spoon and tapped them together to get the attention of the assembled crowd. "Thank you for coming. This will be the last time we need to take the risk of assembling like this. Time is running out. We have worked out a plan for the overthrow and your part in it is vital. We will all have a role to play, and it will only work if we act when needed."

The group cheered. "When do we strike?" one of the men asked.

"We will discuss that with you individually, shortly. But we will give you all a chance to alert your team to be in the right place."

Dagma and his closest allies walked around the room giving each team leader their instructions. He told them not to discuss their actions with any other team. They had decided that they wouldn't divulge the total plan to anyone. Each person would just be told his or her part in the plan, so if they were caught and tortured, they couldn't give the main part of the plan away.

Leopold had come to stand next to Kanda while Dagma was talking. She looked up and smiled as he took her hand. One of the men dressed as a soldier stood giving each one of his troops a small bundle. Kanda watched with interest. "What is he doing?" she asked.

"He is handing out armbands, so the loyal troops are sure who is on their side. All the troops in the palace will be wearing Yaholo's uniforms in the battle next sun. The loyal troops will don their crimson armbands as soon as they get the signal the battle has begun."

"That's clever. Now I will know who is on our side too. I'm glad you told me."

When Dagma had finished, Leopold leant down to whisper, "Did you read everyone's minds... even the teens?"

Kanda frowned. "No, not theirs, why?"

"We thought Thoro was loyal and look what happened there. I want you to do it now without letting them know."

The other teens were standing close so, one by one, she read their minds. She smiled as she picked up only positive thoughts about helping the cause. She told Leopold and he seemed satisfied.

When the attendees were clear with what they had to do, they started to drift towards one entrance or the other. Soon, only Dagma, Faizar, Leopold, and the twins remained.

"So, what is our part in the plan?" Rais asked.

"The head guard is on our side. He has been manipulating the roster to make sure that the majority of the troops on duty next sun are loyal to the king. Unfortunately, the Gantis soldiers who protect Yaholo are always with him, and his troops will be in the dungeon and the tower. And we need to deal with the giant sentries outside the gate too."

Faizar put her hand on Kanda's arm. "Child, we need you to do the most vital part of the plan. We need to poison Yaholo and the court. Your mother could have made the toxic potion for us but now we have to rely on you. It needs to have a delayed reaction so they can all get back to their rooms before it takes effect."

Kanda gasped. "What... me... how can I do that?"

"Your mother told me many times that she had a poison recipe. She dreamed of the time we could use it on Yaholo. I'm sure it is in your book too."

"My book and potions are in your basement in the cupboard in Briador's backpack."

Dagma reached down and held up the backpack. "Not anymore."

Kanda pulled out her book of spells and checked the potions section. She found the one they wanted. She showed it to Faizar. "Do you know where to get these ingredients? I don't have some of them. I will have to use my pendant and a spell to make sure the effect is delayed."

Faizar nodded. "Your mother had a secret stash of ingredients for her potions in a hidden cupboard in the pantry. I think we will find what we need there. Let's go to the kitchen. We can pretend we are doing advance preparation for breakfast if we are seen. We will be doing that anyway, just not something they would want to eat."

They hurried to the kitchen and Rais and Dagma stood guard while they went to the pantry and found what they needed. In the safety of the pantry, they mixed enough potion to be blended in the breakfast meals for Yaholo's court and advisers. Kanda took out her pendant and said the chant needed to make it work as they wanted.

Dagma filled Rais in on his part of the plan. Rais gulped as he realised that the success of the plan depended on him. "Wow! I hope I can live up to what you want from me."

Dagma patted him on the back. "My boy, I know you can do it, and once we free Baldasarre, he can help."

When they were finished, Kanda and Faizar joined them. Faizar yawned. "All right we must get some sleep so we are on our toes at dawning… if we can possibly sleep, of course."

"I won't be sleeping, I can tell you that," Rais said. They all nodded in agreement.

CHAPTER TWENTY-THREE

Restoring Destiny

The next dawning the twins rose early and headed for the kitchen. They hadn't slept at all but weren't concerned. The adrenaline that had kept them awake was pumping through their bodies.

Faizar and Enolie were already there, preparing the breakfast trays. They hurried to help. Telitha, Kacia and Leopold soon joined them.

Faizar took them aside and told them the plan. "The rest of the serving staff don't need to know. They may give it away." They stood wide-eyed staring in disbelief. She turned to Rais. "Are you sure your magic is strong enough to do what is required."

Numbly he nodded. "I hope so… no… I'm sure I can do it."

Telitha spluttered. "What do you mean magic?" She stared at Rais.

Faizar explained who he and Kanda were, and the girl's face lit up.

"Wow! We really do have a chance of pulling this off," she said.

Faizar smiled and nodded. "Are you girls sure you can do your part without giving anything away?"

Telitha bit her lip anxiously as she looked at the other girls. Fear showed on their faces as they nodded. The group hurried to their tasks.

Leopold took Kanda's hand and said, "I'll be right behind you." She nodded and he strode off to the cleaning room.

Rais, Kanda and Telitha picked up the prisoner's breakfast trays and headed for the basement.

Enolie and Kacia joined Faizar. The rest of the staff arrived as they were leaving the kitchen. Under Faizar's instruction, the girls lifted the trays and strode off to the Great Hall.

At the top of the basement stairs, the first group paused. Rais took his place last in the line and nodded to Leopold who had come up behind him with the cleaning trolley. They were grateful that there were no guards in this corridor while the court was at breakfast. They were all guarding the Great Hall.

The girls took a deep breath and walked slowly down the stairs. The smell of unwashed bodies rushed up to meet them. The prisoners came to the gates, eagerly waiting for their meagre rations and greeting the girls with wolf whistles and lurid remarks. The girls ignored them and set about their task. They nodded a greeting to the guards on duty and proceeded to the cells, handing the bowls through the slot in the doors.

Kanda stopped near Briador's cell. As she went to push the bowl through the slot one of the guards called out. "Hey, lovely, that old guy doesn't deserve any food. He is not cooperating."

Kanda glanced his way, bumped the bowl on the door, and it dropped to the floor. The other girls rushed to her side to help her clean up the mess.

The guards laughed. The one that spoke said, "What have we here? The lovely lady must have been blinded by my good looks."

While their attention was focused on the girls, Rais quietly placed his tray on the stairs and, raising shaking hands, he sent a blast of magic towards the guards. The force was so strong their bodies lifted into the air and dropped to the floor. Rais raced over to check on them as Leopold tore down the stairs with a bundle in his arms.

Finding the guards unconscious, Rais took the keys off their belts and gave them to Kanda and Telitha. They raced along the lines of cells and opened the doors. The prisoners stood stunned. Rais shouted, "We are taking back the castle and getting rid of Yaholo. Who is with us?"

Great cheers echoed around the basement as the prisoners rushed out of the cells. Leopold stood on the stairs and stopped them from leaving. Unwrapping his bundle, he handed them all a weapon. The loyal guards had been collecting them for many moons. After several trips to his cleaning cart almost every one of the 30 prisoners had some form of weapon.

Telitha raced into Briador's cell. "Are you okay?" she said hugging him. He stepped back. "Telitha?" When she nodded, he reached out and hugged her. "I'm fine, my girl," he replied.

Kanda stared. Briador held Telitha's arm and hobbled to the door of the cell. Kanda had been to collect her mother and as they hurried in to check on him, he said, "Not many know this, but Telitha is my daughter."

"So that's where you get your mind reading powers," Kanda replied.

Eyes wide with shock, Telitha nodded. "I didn't know that you knew. So, you have them too."

"Yes, I do. When I found out, we were worried that you were a spy from Gantis."

"I didn't know you had a daughter, Briador," Edalene said.

"I didn't know until a couple of years ago. Her mother and I had a relationship that didn't last, and she never told me she had Telitha. If her powers hadn't started to show, I probably wouldn't know now."

Telitha nodded. "Mother was shocked when I started reading her mind and finally told me who my father was. She said only he could help me learn how to control my developing powers."

Briador nodded. "She sent me word to come to the town when I could, to help Telitha, but the troops had started asking people in Adaya if they knew me. So, I left and went to the cave. I knew that if I went to Telitha I would put her and her mother in danger too. Come, we had better help Rais. We will hopefully have lots of time to catch up in the coming moons."

Briador hurried to Rais. "I have something that can help with the plan." He whispered to Rais, who nodded.

Rais gave his mother a quick hug then stepped up beside Leopold and addressed the crowd. He pointed to two of the men who were about the size of the guards. "You and you, undress the guards, don their uniforms, tie them up, gag them and lock them in different cells in case they come to." The two men rushed to follow his command.

"The rest of you will wait here until I come for you. I will need your help to overcome the remaining guards after the first assault. But first I need to free King Marbon and Baldasarre." The men in the guard's uniform stepped up in front of him. "We want to help with that."

"That's what you will be doing. We will take the food up to them as usual, but while we are there, we will free them. You and Leo are to accompany us halfway up the stairs to the tower and wait there in case we need help, or other guards come up the stairs. Briador, you are in charge of making sure these men stay here until I come for them. Mother, we will take you back to the kitchen with us and leave you with Faizar. Leo, see you on the stairs. Let's go."

Edalene shook her head. "No, son, I will be coming with you. King Marbon and your father might need my healing to be strong enough to escape."

Rais nodded. "Kanda can do that… but as you wish. But be careful not to be seen. Wait in the room by the stairs. Show her the room and go with her, Kanda."

"I have a better idea," Leopold said, "Edalene can hop in my cart under the linen, and I will take her there."

Their mother smiled. "A much better idea."

They hurried to the top of the stairs. After Leopold had checked the corridor, Edalene climbed into the trolley, and they covered her with sheets. Leopold set off down the corridor confidently.

Briador sat wearily on the stairs, blocking the way of anyone who got too anxious to leave. He patted Telitha's hand when she put it on his shoulder as she brushed past. "Stay safe, all of you," he said.

Leopold headed to the room by the stairs. Rais, Kanda and the girls headed back to the kitchen. There they found Faizar waiting impatiently by the door. She sighed with relief to see them return. Rais nodded towards the small room so they wouldn't be heard by the rest of the staff who were cleaning up. "What happened? Is everything okay?" Faizar asked when they entered and closed the door.

Rais nodded. "Leo and Mother are in the room by the stairs. She insists on going with us to the tower. Leo will bring her into the stairs when he sees us go up. How did it go in the Great Hall?"

"Okay, I think. I left Enolie and Kacia in charge and the other girls serving and came back to see if you were all okay," she said.

As she spoke, Enolie rushed into the room. "They made Kaden taste the food. Quick, where's the antidote?"

They all turned, a look of horror on their faces. Faizar grabbed the back of the nearest chair for support as her legs gave way. Kanda reached into her pocket and pulled out a small vial. "Have they finished eating?"

"Yes. Some of them are leaving the room now. Quick, I must get that to Kaden." Enolie grabbed the vial and headed for the Great Hall.

Faizar turned to the twins and said, "Okay, quickly, go free the king and your father. It is nearly time for the second part of the plan to go into action. All hell will break loose soon, and we must have Baldasarre's help. I have to go and make sure Kaden is okay."

Kanda and Rais rushed into the kitchen, picked up the trays and headed for the stairs to the tower. The two prisoners dressed as guards had waited outside the kitchen and followed Rais and Kanda. Leopold, who had been lurking at the entrance to the room, checked the passage was clear, and he and Edalene followed them up the stairs.

At the last bend before the top, Rais motioned the others to stop, and he and Kanda continued. Rais took the lead and when they reached the cells he nodded at the guards and walked to his father's cell. When he approached, Baldasarre connected with his mind and asked, *What is happening? Is your mother okay?*

Rais nodded and slipped the tray through the slot. *So far everything is going to plan. The prisoners are free and waiting to do their part. The poison is taking effect, but we are running out of time. Our troops will attack at any moment. We must get you out of here so we can go and help them.*

Kanda stopped at the king's door and handed him the tray. He exclaimed, "What is this swill? I fed better food to my animals."

The guards stood and looked over. "Be thankful you get anything at all, you old fool."

Without hesitation this time, Rais turned and threw a blast of magic their way. Just as he did, one of them stepped towards Kanda. The blast hit the other one and he flew into the wall behind him. The one who had moved was thrown off his feet and struggled to rise. Before Rais could react, a blast hit the man in the chest, and he flew backwards over the floor and slammed into the wall.

"I have wanted to do that for far too long," Baldasarre said from behind him.

Leopold, Edalene, and the guards bounded up the stairs when they heard the blasts. They stopped as they realised they were not needed. Edalene rushed over to Baldasarre's cell.

Kanda ran and got the keys. Racing over to the king's cell she unlocked the door then hurried to her father's cell. Turning the lock and pushing the door open, she sighed with relief. "At last!' she said. He walked out and folded her into his arms.

Tears sprang to her eyes as he said, "At last indeed, my lovely young lady. How I love you both. Now we can get our lives back." He turned and took Edalene in his arms. "You stay with the king. He needs your healing." Letting go of her and hugging Rais to him Baldasarre said, "Let's do this, son. We have a war to win. What is our first task?"

"We have to get rid of the giant guards, so our troops can get into the palace."

Baldasarre grinned. "With great pleasure. Come, we must get out of here now. It's time for the changing of our guard. We don't want to meet them on the stairs… or perhaps we do. That would get rid of another couple."

Baldasarre turned to Leopold and the prisoners. "Leopold, you and these two, stay here and guard the king and Edalene. They are not to be brought down until the fighting is over."

"With our lives," one of the men said and turned to bow to the king.

Rais turned to the prisoner guards and said, "And lock those two unconscious guards in the other cell." He walked to the back wall of the tower, searched for a moment then pulled two square stones from the wall. Reaching in, he drew out a sword and a crossbow and arrow. The rest of the group watched in amazement as he took the sword over to Leopold. "Here. This is Briador's sword. He told me where to find it and to give it to you." He turned to Kanda and held out the crossbow and arrow. "And this is for you."

Kanda took the bow and arrow and frowned. "Why me? I'm not sure I can use this."

Baldasarre stared at the weapons and shook his head. "I wondered where the old fool had hidden them. We could have used them during the battle, but he didn't have them with him. I don't have time to explain the use of the weapons to you both but I'm sure their uniqueness will reveal itself to you when needed."

Baldasarre and Rais headed down the stairs. Leopold stared at the sword for a moment. It was certainly an impressive looking weapon. The handle was gold and the blade gleamed silver with a gold edge. He balanced it in his hand and said, "Yes, this could come in handy." He put it down and headed into the king's cell.

Kanda shrugged and ran her hands over the large, wooden bow. She studied the unusual shiny arrow. It gleamed like glass but seemed to be as strong as metal.

Finally, she put the bow and arrow down and she and Edalene followed Leopold. He reached down to help the rightful ruler to his feet while the other two men dragged the still bodies of the guards into the other cell and locked them in. Kanda bent down to help. Edalene stood waiting.

The king started to rise and looked up at Leopold to thank him. He froze. Leopold stopped lifting and said, "Sorry, did I hurt you? Are you okay?" Kanda stepped back.

"Willem?" the king muttered.

"Sorry, I'm Leopold."

"Yes, you are, son, Prince Willem Leopold Marbon," the king said clutching his hand. "You look so like me when I was your age."

"What… you're saying I'm your son?"

"Yes, I'm sure you are. I heard your mother died a few years ago. Is that right?"

"Yes. I was raised by my nanny. Then when she and her husband died "

The king interrupted, "I sent Varn to look after you."

Leopold stood staring at him. "Yes… Varn… so it's true… I'm your son."

"Yes, you are Prince Willem. Welcome home, son."

His eyes misted as he pulled himself up and hugged Leopold. Still stunned by the news Leopold didn't know what to say. He stepped back and stared at the old man as Edalene moved forward. She bowed and hugged the king then helped him out of the cell and sat him down on one of the guard's chairs.

Kanda stood staring from one to the other. "Wow," she muttered flinging herself into Leo's arms. "Prince Willem, eh? How awesome." He wrapped his arms around her.

Holding hands, they walked out to Edalene and the king.

Kanda reached into her pocket and took out the stone Briador had given her.

Edalene noticed that Kanda was distracted by something in her hand and frowned. "What is that you have there?"

Kanda opened the wrapping and showed her the stone. "Do you know what this is?"

Her mother's eyes grew wide. "Where did you get that?" she asked, her voice barely a whisper.

"Briador gave it to me this dawning. Said it would help keep me safe. What is it?"

"The Blood Stone of Rodair," her mother said, her voice showing the awe she was feeling.

"What or where is Rodair?" Kanda asked.

Edalene didn't seem to hear her. She stared at the stone. "Kanda, have you touched the stone ... held it in your hand?"

Kanda looked at her searchingly. "No. Why?"

"Do it. Take it out of the cloth, place it on your palm and fold your hand around it," Edalene said breathlessly.

Kanda shrugged and took the stone out of the wrapping and placed it on her left palm. She felt a tingle as it touched her, then as she closed her hand around it, she felt a surge of energy pass through her body, just like she did when she held her healers' pendant. She lifted her eyes to her mother's, her heart racing.

"Did you feel anything," her mother asked urgently.

Kanda nodded. "It feels a bit like when I hold the healers' pendant but stronger. What is it?"

Tears running down her cheeks her mother said, "It is so much more than that. That stone belonged to my mother. It holds much more power than our healing pendants. It holds the power of life or death."

Kanda looked at the stone in awe. "Is it yours then? How does it work?"

"The stone was left to me, but it didn't work for me. It only works if you are the chosen one. It connects with them, as it did for you. Sadly, I wasn't one of the chosen. But you are. How wonderful." She took Kanda in her arms and held her tight.

"How ... how does it work?"

"As long as you have that stone on you, you can never die, and if you are injured, you can immediately heal yourself. And if someone else is fatally wounded, you can use it as you do your healing pendant, and it will stop their death and heal them. It has greater healing power than your pendant."

"You mean it will bring someone back from the dead?" Kanda asked.

"No. Once they are gone there is nothing you can do. But as long as there is still a little life force, you can bring them back. And healing done with the stone is complete and immediate. They will not even know they were injured."

Kanda remembered the healing she had done on Leopold and how long it took him to heal. She wished Briador had given it to her then. "Wow, that's awesome. How come Briador had it?"

"I gave it to him for safe keeping. He was to give it to you when he thought your healing powers were strong enough. When you didn't mention it, I assumed he had hidden it away somewhere."

Kanda continued to stare at it in awe. Her heart and mind were racing. She was trying to take in what she just heard.

"What or where is Rodair?" she asked again.

"It's our homeland. Where our ancestors came from. It's over the sea, many moons away." She gazed at the stone dreamily, tears in her eyes. "Maybe we will all get to go there some time."

Kanda finally got her voice back. "How will I conceal this? What if I get searched? Should I hide it somewhere?"

"No. You must keep it on you at all times. Besides, you don't need to hide it. No one will search you while you have that on you. Keep it in a concealed pocket so you don't lose it. Even when you are sleeping." She reached out and touched the stone lovingly. "Well, at least I know you are safe."

Kanda put it back in her pocket. "I have to go and help Rais and Father. Leo, you protect mother and the king... sorry... your father."

He hugged her tightly as if he would never let go. "Stay safe," he muttered in her ear.

"It appears that I am always safe now," she said clutching her stone. "See you soon." She kissed him and her mother and headed for the stairs.

"Kanda, don't forget the bow and arrow," her mother called urgently.

Kanda grimaced but turned back, collected the weapon, and hurried down the stairs. She balanced it in her hand. *Not sure this will be any use, but I better take it.*

She had reached the last bend when she heard footsteps ahead of her. She peeped around the corner and saw two guards heading up the stairs. She retreated to the top. "Guards," she hissed at Leopold. He grabbed his sword and moved down the stairs. The men moved behind him with their swords.

Kanda stood beside Leopold at the last bend. He hissed, "Get back with your mother." She shook her head and loaded the arrow into the bow. *I guess this is a good time to try this out with Leo and the guards to back me up.* As the first guard came around the corner, she lifted the bow and pulled back the string. Suddenly, the arrow lit up and a blast of power flew from the tip and hit the guard in the chest. He flew backward just missing his companion and tumbled down the stairs. The arrows glow faded. Kanda stared in amazement. "I didn't even fire the arrow. It must have sent a blast of power at him."

The other guard charged at Leopold; sword drawn. The prince raised his blade and lunged at the guard. Suddenly, his weapon glowed red. As it clashed with the guard's sword, the red glow transferred from Leopold's blade to the guard's. His opponent's sword melted where they touched. The man screamed in agony as his hand was severely burnt by the heat that was transferred. He dropped his weapon and Leopold plunged the heated sword into his chest. He tumbled down the stairs after his companion.

Leopold and Kanda stood staring at Briador's sword and her bow. "Wow! What happened there," Leopold said.

Edalene came down behind them. "Briador's weapons are magic. While you have them you can never be killed. Keep them in your hand until this is over. Well done, both of you."

Suddenly, Kanda remembered Briador's words when she showed she had no fighting power and questioned her ability to help in the battle. 'I have something to help you with that,' he had said. *Well, I guess this is what he had in mind.*

She smiled confidently and clutched the bow. Hugging Leopold and her mother, Kanda said, "Well I had better go and see what I can do to help. Kaden was made to taste the food and I gave them the antidote to give him. I must make sure he is okay. Time is running out for the antidote to work."

She hurried to the kitchen. Faizar was pacing the floor while Enolie, Kacia and Telitha scraped dishes. They rushed to her side.

"All safe. Rais and Father are heading to the wall," Kanda said giving them a hug. "What happened with Kaden, is he okay?"

Enolie nodded. "When I got back to the dining room Kaden was by the main table playing his sitar. I didn't know what to do. I couldn't go to him and hand him the antidote. Luckily, Varn was there. He saw me hovering and came to see what I wanted. I told him what was happening. His eyes widened and he shook his head and muttered, 'Thank God I haven't eaten yet. No wonder we didn't find the twins. They were here the whole time.' He agreed to go to Kaden and give him the antidote. He went over on the pretext of asking for a special tune and with his back to the crowd held the vial to his lips. Kaden didn't miss a beat of his music as he swallowed the mixture. Varn recapped the bottle and hid it in his pocket. He gave me a nod. As the crowd started back to their rooms, I went in to clear the tables and sent Kaden back. He is here in the small room."

Faizar nodded. "Thank the Gods Varn was there. The meal is over, and the royal court has dispersed to their rooms. They are not yet feeling the effects of the poison, but it will kick in soon and they will die rapidly."

"Varn came over to me to tell me he would go with Yaholo to his room. He said he wanted to make sure he was in there with him when it happened. He will let us know," Enolie said.

Above them they heard a loud blast and falling rock, followed by a huge roar of voices. Kanda hurried Faizar,

Kacia, Telitha and Enolie into the small room off the kitchen. "Stay there with Kaden until I come for you."

As she raced towards the stairs to the battlements, a group of three soldiers charged ahead of her. She checked for the crimson armband of the loyal troops. Finding none, she loaded the arrow in the bow and pointed it at the back of the rear soldier. The arrow glowed and a blast of power shot into his back. He toppled into the man in front of him, causing him to fall. The other one turned and charged at her; swords drawn. Kanda pointed the weapon at him, and the blast sent him flying. She quickly turned to the third soldier and fired a blast at him as he attempted to rise.

Racing forward she reached the bottom of the stairs and stood guard.

***

Rais and Baldasarre had charged up the stairs to the battlements. A group of guards stood at the top, protecting the stairs. The crimson armbands announced their loyalty. Behind them Rais could see bodies lying along the wall.

"All clear. So good to see you out of that cell, Baldasarre," one of them said shaking his hand.

The Oracle slapped the guard on the shoulder. "Great to be out," he said as he and Rais brushed past. They moved quietly to where two large square blocks of rock stood on the top of the wall, marking the entrance gates. Looking cautiously over, they located the two giant guards. Nodding at Rais, Baldasarre stood back and aimed his hand at the base of the rock. Rais mirrored his move.

"Now!" Baldasarre said. A blast from both of their hands hit the base of the rocks. They flew into the air. The pair finished with a pushing gesture in the direction of the giants as it toppled over the edge. The sound of the rocks hitting the ground echoed around them.

A resounding roar of, "Freedom for the king!" from the hidden loyal troops greeted their ears as Rais, Baldasarre and the guards rushed to the edge and looked over.

As the dust from the explosion and fallen rocks cleared a little, they saw the welcome sight of the crimson armbands of the king's troops and many townspeople rushing the gates. The loyal troops inside had donned their armbands and opened the gate as they heard the rocks fall.

Rais, Baldasarre and the loyal troops rushed down the stairs. Kanda turned as she heard their steps, bow and arrow raised. She quickly lowered it when she saw who it was.

Baldasarre looked at the fallen men on the path and grinned. "I see you have discovered how to use your weapon."

Kanda smiled. "Yes. It's amazing. I don't need your power, Rais, now that I have this."

Rais frowned. "So how does it work?"

"You're about to find out, Rais. Show him, Kanda."

The twins turned. Racing towards them was one of the large Gantis guards. Kanda lifted the bow and loaded the arrow. Rais watched in amazement as the arrow started to glow as Kanda pulled back the string. He staggered in shock when the power surge left the arrow and pierced the chest of the guard.

"Holy cow, that is amazing. How does it do that, Father?"

"It channels Kanda's power into the weapon. It only works for someone with powers. Come on let's go, the loyal troops will need our help."

Baldasarre and Kanda joined the crowd charging the palace steps. Rais went through the gates to check on the giants. Walking around the fallen rocks, he could see only a giant leg sticking out from one and a huge hand from the other. Satisfied that they would be no more trouble, he went back and joined the assault on the remaining guards loyal to Yaholo. Swords clashed and bodies fell as the shouts of battle echoed around him.

Rais joined Kanda as Baldasarre charged up the stairs, heading for the hallway that led to the tower.

As they advanced towards the royal court, the sight of four large guards from Gantis towering over the advancing loyal Nevaah guards was daunting. But it didn't stop the loyal men. They stormed up the stairs crying, "Freedom for the king."

Rais and Kanda charged towards the Gantis guards. As they took out the two in the front, the next in line attacked. Just as one reached Kanda, she raised her bow and sent a blast at him. He fell backwards, hit the man behind him and tumbled towards her. She stepped aside. But not far enough. The guard's shoulder hit her in the chest. She fell to the ground struggling for breath. Rais sent a blast at the second one and as he fell, he raced to her side.

Kanda took his hand and pulled herself to her feet. "Are you okay?" Rais asked.

Panting for breath she muttered. "I will be. I think my ribs are broken. Cover me." She leant against the wall, took out the Blood Stone of Rodair and pressed it against her chest.

Rais was joined by loyal troops as they battled the Gantis guards around them.

Kanda sighed as the stone worked its magic and her pain disappeared. She quickly raised her bow and moved to join Rais.

Baldasarre had moved forward and positioned himself where he could control the guards coming from the hallways. A blast of power soon stopped them.

The numbers were two to one in their favour, and it didn't take long for the loyal troops to take control. With Kanda and Rais blasting their way through the Gantis troops they soon cleared a path to the hallway to the dungeon.

Rais rushed to the stairs and shouted as he went down, "It is time. Go and help our troops clear the grounds and the barracks."

The prisoners leapt to their feet and surged up the stairs. Briador had just enough time to get out of the way before he was trampled. Their adrenaline fuelled by hatred for the evil ruler for their imprisonment and his treatment of the king, the prisoners rushed towards the fight shouting the war cry they had heard, "Freedom for the king."

Coming up behind Yaholo's troops charging into the corridor, they soon defeated them and raced for the barracks.

The last remaining guards were sighted in the passages that led to Yaholo's room. Kanda and Rais joined Baldasarre, and she told them about Varn being back and with Yaholo. They headed down the passage to his room, followed by a group of loyal guards.

Baldasarre took out the first guard with a blast that shook the walls and caused the ceiling surface to crumble. The guard slammed into the one behind him and they both fell into a heap in the middle of the hall.

Rais and Kanda stepped over them and took the lead, allowing their father time to recover. Rais sent a blast at the troops blocking their way. More fell. As Kanda stepped up with her bow and arrow extended, swords clattered to the floor and with hands high in the air, the remaining guards surrendered. They knew they had no hope once they saw the power of the three assailants coming towards them.

The loyal troops following behind the three, dragged them off to the dungeon with the others they had captured.

Rais, Kanda and Baldasarre started searching the rooms in the living quarters to see if any members of Yaholo's court had survived. All were lying peacefully on their bed, deceased. The trio reached Yaholo's bedchamber at the same time and Baldasarre charged in.

They looked for Varn, but he was not there. They were relieved to see a very still body on the bed, lying face down. As they approached to make sure Yaholo was dead, they realised that it wasn't the evil ruler.

Baldasarre's face crumbled in shock. "Pahana," he cried. He reached for his arm to check his pulse. "He is one of my best friends and always loyal to the king."

Kanda had moved forward to check on him. "He helped capture Palesa and Thoro when they tried to hand us in."

Baldasarre frowned and turned to Kanda. "Who tried to hand you in?"

Intent on her task, Kanda ignored his question. "He's still alive, but only just. Help me turn him over." Rais and

Baldasarre grabbed him and lifted his body gently. When he was facing her, Kanda put her hand on his head and sought his life force. They all groaned as they saw the large red glow of a sword wound and the blood over the front of his tunic.

"I've got to save him," she cried in despair.

Baldasarre laid a hand on her arm. "It's too late, Kanda. He has lost too much blood."

Kanda shook her head. "Maybe not." She took the Blood Stone out and placed it on his chest with her hand holding it down. She said her healing spell and held her breath. Suddenly the soldier's body moved. She sought his life force and they watched in amazement as the wound healed before their eyes. He came to life immediately and sat up.

"What happened here?" Baldasarre asked as his friend sat dazed.

"I'm not sure. I stepped into the room, and someone ran me through with a sword. I don't remember much after that." He rubbed his chest. "How did…" He opened his shirt and saw the healed flesh where the sword had plunged into his body. He looked at them speechless.

"Kanda is a healer. She managed to bring you back from certain death. I'm not sure how," Baldasarre said staring at her, his eyes glowing with pride.

Kanda held up the stone and his eyes lit up. "The Blood Stone of Rodair. You can use it? Your mother was so upset when she couldn't. Well done, my girl." He hugged her and turned to Rais. "Who tried to turn you in?"

Rais sighed. "It's a long story. So where are Yaholo and Varn? Do you think he took him somewhere else to die?"

"I guess we will find out in due time. We had better go and make sure your mother and King Marbon are okay."

They returned to the tower stairs. As they started up, they came across the two bodies of Yaholo's guards. Kanda told them about the attack before she left. As they rounded the next bend, they found more bodies. Stepping over them they rushed up the remaining steps fearing the worst.

At the top they stopped suddenly. Leopold, having heard their steps charged forward waving his sword, the other two men close behind.

"Woah! It's us, Leo," Rais called.

Leopold stopped his charge and slumped against a wall. "Boy, am I glad to see all of you," he muttered.

Kanda rushed over to him and threw her arms around him. "Are you okay?"

"I am now," he said holding her tightly.

Baldasarre hurried over to Edalene and taking her in his arms said, "What happened here? That is quite a body count on the stairs."

"As soon as we heard the explosion out the front the troops came charging up the stairs. I guess they wanted to be sure they still had the king to use to stop the attack."

"But Willem and his magic sword soon put a stop to that," King Marbon said smiling proudly.

Frowning, Rais turned to look at Leopold. "Willem?"

Kanda laughed. "I didn't have time to tell you. Leo is actually King Marbon's son."

Rais raised an eyebrow. "His son – really?"

"Yes," Baldasarre said. "And so much like you when you were his age," he said to King Marbon. "But where is your sister, Leo... sorry... Willem?"

"I don't know. Father asked me that too, but I was raised on my own. I didn't remember I had a sister. We have been too busy to discuss it further."

"She lived with a clothing merchant in Adaya. Her name was changed to Palesa," the king said.

Kanda, Leopold and Rais turned to him with open mouths. All three said at once, "Palesa?"

"Yes. Do you know her or where she is?" the king asked hopefully.

"Yes... she came with us to the palace..." Kanda looked at Rais uncertain if she should tell him the truth. Rais shrugged and said, "Ahh... she ... ahh... tried to turn us in to Yaholo for the reward and was captured and locked in the cave in the escape tunnel."

King Marbon rose to his feet. "That can't be true. Why would she do that? Willem, is that true?"

Leopold said, "Yes, I'm afraid so. Yaholo offered a reward for the capture of the twins, and she wanted it. She had been scheming right from the start of the trip. She tried to get me to help. But I told her I would die before I let anyone hurt Kanda. I thought she had changed her mind, but I was wrong." Kanda hugged his arm as he said that.

King Marbon turned to Baldasarre. "We must get her out of that place. Send someone to get her."

Leopold looked at Rais. "We'll go." Rais nodded.

"We'll all go," said Baldasarre. "Edalene, after we have checked that it is safe, can you and the men please help the king down to his drawing room. We will be back soon."

When they reached the bottom of the stairs, four of the loyal troops were standing guard. "All over, Sir. Is His Majesty all right?" one of them said, saluting.

Baldassare smiled. "Well done. The king is fine. Let him know he can safely come down, please."

The guard raced up the stairs and delivered the message. "I'll carry the king," he said. He bowed to the monarch and gently lifted him. Edalene and the other men followed them down the stairs.

Rais led the way to the secret passage in the stateroom and they followed it towards the cave. As they got closer, they heard a voice shouting, "Help! Someone, help."

They rushed into the cave and slid to a halt. Sitting on his cot was Thoro, but Palesa was nowhere to be seen. "Where is Palesa?" Baldasarre said.

"They took her. I've been shouting for help ever since, but no one came."

"Who took her?" Rais asked.

"Varn and Yaholo. They came through the tunnel and saw us here. She begged them to take her with them. And they did."

"Yaholo!" They all shouted at the same time.

"Yes. He didn't look too well but Varn was helping him along."

Kanda's face went red with rage. "Varn must have saved some of the antidote he gave to Kaden and given it to Yaholo. The rotten traitor!"

Thoro nodded. "When I said I didn't want to go, Varn wanted to kill me. Yaholo decided to let me live so I could give the king a message."

"What message," Baldasarre said.

"He said, 'Tell the king I will be back and this time he won't live through my attack'."

Rais shook his head in disgust. "So, Varn was a traitor after all."

"Why didn't he just turn us in?" Kanda asked.

"He probably tried. Maybe he was the reason the troops searched the city for us. When they didn't find us, he must have believed Briador's story that we had left and were hiding in the forest. He went with them to carry out his plan, but when they didn't find us, he returned."

Leopold frowned in confusion. "Then when he knew there was no way to stop the overthrow, he decided to save Yaholo. But why? Having been employed by the king… Father… to care for me, he could have lived in the palace for the rest of his life."

"Maybe he wants more. I hate to say this, Leo, but maybe he was planning to turn you in to Yaholo too. He knew who you were. Yaholo would have paid extra for you. He wants to be rich and believes Yaholo will reward him well for saving him. But why take Palesa?" Baldasarre said.

"Maybe he knows who Palesa is and is going to blackmail the king? Oh… how will we tell the king that she has gone? He will blame us for putting her here in the first place," Kanda said.

"I don't think he will blame us. She did betray us. And Thoro will tell him she went willingly. But he will certainly want us to get her back," Rais said.

They freed Thoro and headed back to give the king the bad news. The two prisoner guards were standing by the door of the room with several other guards patrolling the corridor. The king was sitting in an easy chair with a fire going and sipping on a hot drink. Lounging nearby was

Edalene, Briador, Faizar, Kaden and the girls. The twins sighed in relief to see them all safe.

The king looked up expectantly as they entered. Seeing only Thoro with them he exclaimed. "Where is Arbela... or Palesa to you?"

Baldasarre sat down beside him and told him what had happened. The king went white with shock. He looked at Thoro for confirmation and he nodded.

King Marbon put his head in his hands. "First my darling wife and now my precious daughter... that man has a lot to answer for. And Varn... how could he betray me like this?"

Leopold asked the question that was on all their minds. "Father... do you think Varn knows that Palesa is your daughter?"

"No. I had no reason to tell him where she was hidden. We separated you so at least one of you would survive if they found my wife. No one knew but me, her foster parents and your mother."

"Thank goodness for that," Baldasarre said.

King Marbon nodded. "Yes, at least he won't try to blackmail me and threaten her life."

Reluctantly Baldasarre delivered the message that Yaholo gave Thoro. "I hate to say this, Your Majesty, but maybe she will join forces with them against you. Yaholo will come back again as soon as he raises an army large enough."

King Marbon rubbed his weary eyes. "At least this time we will be prepared. But we must find them fast before they return to Gantis. Baldasarre, amass the troops and begin the search."

"As you wish, Your Majesty," Baldasarre said bowing. He walked to the door and called over the loyal troops patrolling the corridor. He explained what had happened. They were shocked that the evil ruler had escaped. He gave the instruction that they must at once head for the border crossings and try to intercept Yaholo, Varn and Palesa. "Make sure the girl is returned unhurt," he ordered.

Saluting him, one charged off to carry out his orders. As he walked back, he asked, "Your Majesty, what do you want to do with our young prisoner?" He indicated Thoro.

King Marbon sighed. "He will have to be tried for his crime, as soon as order is restored."

"But, Your Majesty, I have always been loyal. I won't do anything stupid again," Thoro said dropping to his knees.

The king shook his head. "I would like to believe that. But you only get one chance to prove your loyalty and you failed. We will deal with you soon. Take him to the cells." One of the guards took Thoro by the arm and marched him out the door.

Baldasarre said, "Your Majesty, we need to let your people know that you are safe and well. They are waiting out the front of the palace for news."

"Come then, we will go and let them know. You must come too Briador, Baldasarre, Edalene and your twins. They would want to know you are safe too. And Willem... you will be by my side, so they know you have returned. Edalene, please arrange decent garments for us to wear. And make sure you are dressed according to your station. We need to let them see all is well."

In a very short time, the group assembled at the entrance to the balcony. All were dressed in the finest clothes they could find. King Marbon smiled and nodded his approval of Leopold's garments. He now wore a suit of crimson, the colour of his station as prince of the kingdom, the same as his father. Briador, Baldasarre, Edalene and the twins wore the royal blue of their station as court officials.

As they stepped out onto the balcony, Leopold drew Kanda to his side. The king glanced over but smiled and didn't object. Rais stepped up beside Baldasarre and Edalene. The roar of the crowd was deafening as they saw the king and his entourage.

Edalene glanced to the courtyard on the right. The gallows stood prepared for her planned execution this evening. She shuddered and gave thanks that she had been saved.

The king bowed and held up his hand for silence. The guard standing in the wings handed him a megaphone. "My loyal followers – it is over. The long occupation of the evil Yaholo has come to an end. Thank you for your loyal support. We could not have achieved this without you. I am very grateful for your sacrifice. Know that you will all be rewarded. I know how you have struggled under Yaholo's rule. To begin our return to prosperity, I am going to forego all tax for three moons and then we will return to the fair tax system we had in place before. There will be plentiful food as it will not be going to Gantis. Go to your homes and sleep soundly knowing you are safe… we are all safe."

The crowd roared their approval and gradually dispersed. The joy in the air was palpable. Bowing one more time, the king turned and walked back inside the palace. He hugged Willem and turned to the others. "Let us all rest now. Next sun will soon be with us. The future starts at next sun."

Watching the troops assemble in the courtyard to the left, Rais shook his head. *The future may not be as safe as the king thinks. Can we ever be safe with Yaholo alive?*

www.ingramcontent.com/pod-product-compliance
Lightning Source LLC
Chambersburg PA
CBHW060950030726
47503CB00003B/806